THE LAKE VYRNWY KILLINGS

A DI Ruth Hunter Crime Thriller #11

SIMON MCCLEAVE

STAMFORD
PUBLISHING

THE LAKE VYRNWY KILLINGS

By Simon McCleave

A DI Ruth Hunter Crime Thriller
Book 11

First published by Stamford Publishing Ltd in 2022

❀ Created with Vellum

Also by Simon McCleave

THE DI RUTH HUNTER SERIES

THE DC RUTH HUNTER MURDER CASE SERIES

THE ANGLESEY SERIES - DI LAURA HART
(Harper Collins / AVON Publishing)

Your FREE book is waiting for you now!

Get your FREE copy of the prequel to
the DI Ruth Hunter Series NOW
http://www.simonmccleave.com/vip-email-club
and join my VIP Email Club

For Lee, Keilie, Lowri and Seren x

Chapter 1

L *ake Vyrnwy, Snowdonia*
  Sunday 24ᵗʰ January 2021

EVEN THOUGH IT WAS AN ICY WINTER'S MORNING, CATRIN and her older sister Beth were determined to go paddle-boarding. Despite the heaters going at full blast, the inside of the car was freezing, and Catrin could see her breath come out in swirling clouds. She remembered when she and Beth used to steal cigarettes from their father's study and stand smoking them at the far end of the garden. They would then go inside, search for mints and cover each other in deodorant or perfume. How her parents never discovered them was a total mystery. The irony now was that neither of them smoked or even vaped.

Catrin touched the car brakes and felt the tyres skid a little under them. The car wobbled on the icy road before she regained control.

'God, it's really slippery,' she said, now feeling a little

1

uneasy. It was the first time she had ever lost control of a car, and even though it had been only a second or two, it had spooked her.

'Don't worry,' Beth reassured her. 'Just take it nice and slowly. There's no one else on the road.'

'Levitating' by *Dua Lipa* came on the radio, and Catrin cranked it up, determined to change her mood. They sang along – *I got you, moonlight, starlight, I need you all night …* Laughing with joy, they sang together at the top of their voices, even though neither of them could hold a tune.

In the boot of the car, they had their 5 mm winter wetsuits, rubber boots and gloves. Their family lived only a ten-minute drive from the spectacular Lake Vyrnwy, at the heart of Snowdonia. Having just turned seventeen, Catrin was learning to drive, so it was an opportunity for her to get in some practise with her older sister in the passenger seat. In fact, Beth was the only person in her family that Catrin could bear to go driving with. Both her mother and father were so incredibly bossy and nervous that the journey always descended into a shouting match and even tears.

Pulling into a small car park on the northern edge of the lake, Catrin turned down the music and parked her pride and joy – a nine-year-old white Ford Focus – She turned off the ignition with a satisfied sigh.

'You see,' she said, raising a triumphant eyebrow at her older sister. 'I don't know why Mum and Dad wet their pants every time they come with me. You don't.'

Beth shrugged. 'I guess they learned to drive like a hundred years ago. I can remember what it was like to learn to drive. And Dad was a bloody nightmare with me too.'

Catrin gave a laugh of recognition. 'He actually put his hands over his eyes when I went round a roundabout.'

'Yeah, well, I do that.' Beth grinned. 'You are actually meant to stop when you get to a roundabout. Not cross your fingers and hope that no one else will get in your way.'

Catrin gave her the finger. 'You can walk home then, bitch,' she joked.

Getting out of the car, they went to the boot and pulled out all the equipment they needed. The ground underneath their feet was hard and frosty, and it crunched underneath their boots.

Beth pointed to the filthy paintwork that was splashed with mud. 'Hey, you know they do this car in a lovely white,' she joked sardonically.

Catrin rolled her eyes. 'Hilarious.' She then turned and took in the stunning view of the lake through the dark conifer trees that seemed to have weaved themselves together in a thick line along its bank.

Lake Vyrnwy wasn't technically a lake at all. It was a vast reservoir that had been created when the Vyrnwy valley and the village of Llanwddyn had been deliberately flooded to supply water for Merseyside in England. Catrin was all too aware that some of her family actually came from the idyllic Welsh village that had been drowned to supply water to an English city. Her taid, Welsh for grandfather, had been part of the protest movement that gathered momentum in the 1950s. He told them he had been a proud member of the MCA – the *Mudiad Amddiffyn Cymru* or Movement for the Defence of Wales. They had even set off a bomb at a nearby electrical installation in their campaign to stop the flooding of the valley.

However, their protests were in vain, and Harold Macmillan's Conservative government allowed Liverpool City Council to create a compulsory purchase of the land to build the reservoir. 800 acres, including the school, post office, chapel, and a dozen farms, were destroyed. It did little for Anglo-Welsh relations.

Bloody English! Stuck up public school knobheads sitting there in London thinking that Britannia still rules the bloody world, her taid used to groan.

Catrin looked over at her sister and asked the question that had been buzzing around her head ever since they got in the car. 'Are you seeing Jason tonight?' she asked, trying her best to sound nonchalant – but failing miserably.

Beth grinned and shrugged. 'Maybe.'

Beth had been going out with boyfriend Jason for over a year now. The relationship had continued even though Beth was at university. It also just happened that he had a very cute eighteen-year-old brother called James, who had recently become single.

'You going to The Railway then?' Catrin said, trying desperately not to show her eagerness.

Beth laughed. 'Just say it.'

'Say what?'

I can't believe she's making this so difficult for me!

'Can you meet Jason at The Railway and get him to bring James with him,' Beth chuckled.

'Well, can you?' Catrin asked, feeling excited at the prospect.

'What's it worth?'

'Worth? You're my bloody sister!' Catrin exclaimed.

'Yeah, but I feel like I'm pimping you out,' Beth joked.

Catrin gave her a playful hit on the arm. 'Just do it, will you?'

'Okay, okay,' Beth smirked. 'You're desperate. I get it.'

'I'm not talking to you,' Catrin said with mock indigna-tion. She was relieved to have asked the question and got a positive response.

Holding their paddles and boards, they navigated their

way through the steep incline that was covered in round-leaved Sundew and Hare's-tail Cotton-grass to a small beach area beside the water's edge.

Gazing across the vast expanse of the lake, Catrin took in the stunning panorama before her. The lake was nearly five miles long. Someone told her once that its surface was the same as 600 football pitches. At its centre, it was nearly 100 ft deep and supplied over 50 million gallons of water to England a day. Rivers, waterfalls, and brooks flowed into the lake from the surrounding hillsides and mountains.

Three curlews circled stridently above her head. God, she loved this place. She loved everything about coming down here to paddle when her head needed to be cleared. It gave her a sense of perspective. Her fears and anxiety seemed somehow irrelevant in the face of the utter vastness of the lake and sky around her. She loved the silence – the enormity of the sky and the stillness of the water. Mostly, she loved the fact that it made her feel alive in a way that nothing else could. She even loved the biting cold that ate through her skin to her bones.

As the wind picked up, she felt the sub-zero wind burn her cheeks. She pulled a face at her sister. They had checked the forecast before they left. Ideally, they wanted the wind speed to be below 14 knots. Anything higher and paddling became unpredictable. It also made the lake choppy.

Beth rolled her eyes at her as she waded into the ice-cold water with her bright blue *Aqua Spirit* board. 'Come on, you wimp!'

'Last time it was like this, I got blown towards the middle,' Catrin groaned.

Beth shrugged. 'Well, sit here and watch me then.'

Sod that!

Tucking her own dark red board under her arm,

Catrin waded into the freezing water. Her rubber boots and wetsuit protected her from low temperature, but it was still bitterly cold.

By the time the water had got to her waist, Beth was already up and away.

'Woo hoo!' Beth yelled as she zipped across the water's surface with the wind at her back.

Bloody hell! Why is she better at everything than me? Catrin thought to herself with a twinge of envy.

Beth was in her third year of studying to be a dentist at Sheffield University. She was uber-intelligent and sailed through her A-levels, gaining two A*s and an A. When they were teenagers, they had fought like cat and dog, but now they were close.

Pushing down on the board, Catrin got herself up and then stood gingerly.

Come on, Catrin, you got this!

Feeling her legs wobble a little, she pushed her toes and feet into the board's surface and got her balance.

She pushed the paddle into the clear water as it quietly whooshed beneath the board.

And away we go.

ST ASAPH POLICE STATION

'TELL ME WHAT HAPPENED,' DETECTIVE INSPECTOR RUTH Hunter said calmly across the table to the 'suspect' Oliver Thorne.

Thorne had a ruddy, worn face that was covered by a thick, greying beard. His blue eyes had faded with age and looked milky. He kicked angrily at the table as he grunted, 'No chance.'

Thorne was fuming, and Ruth knew she had him against the ropes now. Like an ageing boxer who knows he's lost, Thorne had backed himself into a corner.

'We've got enough evidence to take this to trial, Oliver,' Ruth explained, pointing down at the folders on the table in front of her. 'I'm just not sure you want your elderly mother listening to the graphic details of how you raped a woman twice your own age.'

Thorne sneered at her, and his eyes narrowed. 'It was consensual. She enjoyed it.' Even he didn't sound convinced about what he had said.

Ruth frowned and asked in a deliberately curious tone, 'She had a fractured wrist and cheekbone, Oliver. How is that consensual?'

Without warning, Thorne shot up from his chair in anger. 'Fuck you. She loved it rough. She was a little prick-tease. Just because you like it missionary with lights turned off, doesn't mean we all do', he thundered.

'Sit down please, Oliver,' Ruth said in a composed tone.

Thorne gritted his teeth which were covered in spittle. 'It turned her on. Don't you get it? She liked to be submissive. She got off on it.'

'Sit down please, Oliver,' Ruth repeated, like a schoolteacher with an icy stare.

Thorne huffed, rubbed his bearded chin, and sat slowly back down in his seat.

'No, I don't get it, Oliver. Wendy was a frightened woman in her 60s. But that's what turns you on, isn't it? Frightening women. She said no to you, so you attacked and raped her. That's not consent, is it, Oliver?'

'Ah, that's bollocks,' Thorne said with a shrug – he wasn't giving anything away.

'Why is that *bollocks*?' Ruth asked innocuously.

'She's putting words into my mouth,' Thorne replied. 'I know what she told me.'

'It's the other way around, Oliver. Wendy said 'no' and you raped her. There isn't a jury anywhere that won't convict you.'

'I'll take my chances,' Thorne sneered at her.

'Listen, if you take this to trial, Oliver,' Ruth said, 'you'll get 10–12 years. Plead guilty, you might get as little as six years.'

There were a few seconds of silence.

'Okay, that's great,' said a voice from the other side of the room. 'Let's stop that there.'

It was DCI Paul Kennedy who was running the final morning session of an interview technique seminar for senior ranking CID officers in the North Wales Police Force.

Are you kidding me? Ruth thought.

Ruth was miffed. She thought she had DI Oliver Thorne on the ropes in the mock interview, but he had swerved her best efforts. If she could have just another five minutes, she might just get him to confess.

'I haven't finished yet,' she groaned. 'I nearly had him there.'

Looking at his watch, DCI Kennedy smiled. 'I admire your confidence, Ruth. It was a fantastic interview. Come on, we need to feedback next door.'

As they got up and scuttled back towards the briefing room, Thorne came by her side.

'Hey, that was good in there,' he said encouragingly.

Ruth gave him a dry smile. 'I liked the whole kicking the table and standing up. Very authentic, Oliver.'

'No, I mean it. You were great in there, Ruth,' Thorne said.

'Yeah, well, I've had nearly thirty years' practise,' she joked.

'Thirty years?' he said with a frown. 'That can't be right. Not unless you joined when you were ten.'

Oh my God. Is he flirting with me?

She thought that most of the coppers in North Wales knew she was gay. But she was happy to take the compliment.

'No,' she admitted. 'It's going to be thirty years next May.'

'We should go out for a drink sometime,' Thorne suggested flirtatiously. 'Compare notes about the old days. You used to be in the Met, didn't you?'

'Yep. I did twenty-five years in South London.'

'I bet you've got some stories, eh?'

Ruth laughed. 'Oh yeah. Stuff that will make your hair curl.'

'So are we on then?' he asked, raising an eyebrow. 'For a drink?'

'I think you might be deeply disappointed,' she said as they sat down.

'Why's that then?'

'I don't think you're my type,' she said with a bemused smile.

'Really?' Thorne snorted. 'I'm sure I can persuade you otherwise.'

'I'm gay, Oliver.' She wished she had eked their conversation out a little longer to increase his embarrassment. 'So, I think you might find that quite difficult.'

Thorne tried to brush off his awkwardness with a nonchalant shrug. 'That's fine. We can still go for a drink, can't we?'

'Of course.' Ruth knew that would never happen.

. . .

GAZING AT THE UNDULATING HILLS, THICK WITH PINE AND other dark green conifer trees, Catrin skimmed gently across the lake's surface. Was there anywhere more beautiful in the world? Although she was in Snowdonia, she thought the landscape was similar to Scandinavia or even Canada she'd seen on a nature documentary.

As she skimmed across the water's surface, she felt so free. Suddenly filled with the energy of an excited child, she gave a piercing shriek of total abandonment.

'Woooo hooo!'

Over to the right, she spotted the old straining tower. It was an imposing Gothic castle-like structure that rose up over 120 ft from the lake's surface. Its purpose was to remove debris and other detritus from the water. However, with its pointed turrets, Catrin and Beth always referred to it as the witch's tower. Rumour had it the tower had been modelled on the medieval castle of Chillon, which stood on Lake Geneva. The circular parapet and balustrade gave way to a steep conical roof that was covered in copper sheeting, which gave it a turquoise hue. The tower was connected to the shore by a stone bridge with four arches which were closed off by enormous piers and a pair of wrought-iron gates.

When they were younger, Catrin and Beth made up stories about imprisoned princesses and evil witches who inhabited the tower. They would dare each other to go up to the iron gates and sometimes even shout, before they pedaled away on their bikes, laughing or screaming in fear and delight.

Using her paddle to turn, Catrin spotted her sister in the distance towards the centre of the lake. She preferred to stay closer to shore. The air above was shattered by the noise of two RAF jets flying south. It reminded her of her taid again, who used to tell them that the RAF had used

Lake Vyrnwy as a practice run for the bombing of the German Mohne and Eder dams in 1943. Her taid was only a boy, and he claimed to have watched Lancaster bombers of the 617 Squadron dropping dummy bouncing bombs for the operation that became commonly known as *'The Dambusters.'*

As the wind picked up, she shivered and headed back for shore. Half an hour out on the lake in January was more than enough for her. She was looking forward to the steaming hot tea they had brought with them in their mother's old tartan-patterned flask.

With a few hard sweeps of the paddle, she whooshed gently to the part of the shore where they had started.

Hitting some sort of debris, Catrin glanced back, expecting to see a lump of driftwood.

Except the large object didn't look like driftwood or the branch from a tree. It was grey-blue in colour.

And as she peered more carefully, she could see what it actually was.

Oh my God!

A human foot.

Chapter 2

Twenty detectives from the North Wales police sat in the meeting room at St Asaph Police Station. It might have been 2021, but there were still only four female detectives in the room.

Outnumbered again, Ruth thought dryly to herself.

She had to admit there had been some progress for female police officers. Thirty years ago, she was still being called a *Doris* or a *Plonk*, which actually stood for *Person of little or no knowledge.* Duties in the early 90s included getting tea and biscuits for any higher-ranking male officer in the station, photocopying and getting your arse groped, and having to laugh for fear of being called *a dyke.*

Those were the days, eh? she thought sarcastically to herself.

DCI Kennedy strode to the front of the room. Ruth had spent the previous day in lectures and groups discussing interview techniques. There had been model interviews conducted by DCI Kennedy and some other senior officers. Plus training videos, most of which covered the interviewing basics. The UK police used a PEACE framework that comprised five different phases. Planning and preparation. Engage and explain. Account clarification and challenge. Closure. Evaluation.

'Right guys,' Kennedy said as he perched on the table. 'I know you're all experienced detectives in here, but I do need to flag something up that I've seen this morning. Under PACE, we can make no attempt to bully or threaten a suspect.'

He was referring to the rules and regulations for dealing with detainees as laid down in the Police and Criminal Evidence Act of 1984.

'I know some of you were getting carried away because this morning's session wasn't a real-life situation. However, there are a few of you, and I'm mentioning no names …'

Kennedy deliberately made eye contact with two or three of the younger, male detectives who had too much testosterone and thought they were in an episode of *The Sweeney*. There were a few laughs and sniggers of recognition.

'You need to have another look at Code C 2019 of PACE. The questioning of suspects aren't suggestions. They are mandatory. And if you fuck it up, you can get a suspect's defence team claiming that your interview is inadmissible in court. And that is a disaster for everyone.'

Ruth's phone vibrated. It was the CID office at Llancastell. She knew it must be important, as they had been instructed to only call her if something serious came in.

She excused herself, left the briefing room, and answered it.

It was nearly two hours later by the time Ruth and Nick turned into the road that circumnavigated Lake Vyrnwy.

'How was the course?' Nick asked.

'The usual box-ticking waste of time,' Ruth said. 'Here's an egg, and here's how to suck it.' If she was honest, she had learned very little that she didn't already know. She wondered if that made her arrogant or just honest.

'That bad was it?' Nick enquired with a yawn.

'There's a new initiative – *Quality first detective work.* It seemed to imply that what we've been doing up until now hasn't been quality. As far as I can see, it's just another buzz phrase that's stating the bleedin' obvious.'

Nick laughed as they drove around the bend and saw that they had cordoned the road off with blue police tape.

A low mist hung motionless across the road at about waist height, adding to the sinister look of the scene before them.

'And cue the dry ice machines,' Nick joked as they slowed.

'Yeah,' Ruth nodded dryly. 'Like some terrible 80s pop video. I'm half expecting Bonnie Tyler to come prancing out, singing in leather trousers and a waistcoat.'

'Hey,' Nick protested. 'I won't have anyone criticise the Queen of Welsh Pop!'

Taking out a cigarette, Ruth smiled. "Total Eclipse of the Heart' is a classic.'

'I think that was number one around the time I was born,' Nick said with a grin.

Ruth narrowed her eyes. She knew he was just having a pop at her about her age. 'Piss off, Nick. We all know I'm as old as God's dog. There's no need to rub it in.'

There were two marked patrol cars parked sideways as uniformed officers directed traffic to turn around. The white SOCO van had backed itself into the wooded area that flanked the shore. SOCO officers were ferrying small sample bags from the area into sealed compartments inside the back of the van for analysis. Another SOCO was taking photographs, as everything they took back to the lab needed to be photographed in situ first.

Ruth lit her cigarette, took a deep drag, and buzzed down the window. The air was damp and baltic, and she could smell the spicy fragrance of the nearby conifers; the lodgepole pine, Douglas fir, and the Norway spruce.

'CSI Dolgellau got here fast,' Nick quipped, gesturing to the forensic officers as Ruth pulled over and parked. Even though SOCO – Scene of Crime Officers – was their official name, Nick liked to joke about their title, contrasting an obscure Welsh place name with the far more glamorous TV series of *CSI Miami* or *CSI New York*.

'What was that bloke's name in *CSI Miami*?' Ruth asked with a frown as she turned off the ignition and took another long drag of her cigarette. 'He was always saying something he thought was profound while he took off his sunglasses.'

'That's right.' Nick laughed. 'Horatio. He'd say something like, *The verdict might be in, Frank* ... And then he'd take off his sunglasses and look at the camera. ... *But the jury is still out.*'

'That's spot on!' Ruth snorted as she stubbed out her cigarette in the car's ashtray. 'David Caruso, I think the actor was. Good American accent, by the way.'

'Thanks,' Nick shrugged. 'Not bad for a Welshman.'

Getting out of the car, Ruth looked down through the wooded area towards the lake. The distant trees were veiled in mist, their trunks covered in dark, bottle green bark from the endless rash of lichen. At points, the bark was gnarled and cracked. The further she peered down the shoreline, the more the trees became silhouettes against the blanket of white.

As they walked over from the car, Ruth could see the ground was covered in spongy moss and decaying leaves from the withered, skeletal branches above. The static mist seemed to have weaved itself around the tree trunks like candyfloss.

A young female PC stood nearby with a clipboard which had the Scene Log.

Ruth and Nick took out their warrant cards and flashed them. 'Detective Inspector Hunter and Detective Sergeant Evans, Llancastell CID. What have we got, Constable?'

The PC was young, with a nervous, uncertain blink, a sprinkle of freckles across her nose and high cheekbones. 'Two women had just started to paddleboard on the lake down there about 8.20 am when they discovered a severed foot floating in the water.'

Ruth glanced over at the two young women, wrapped in beach towels, who were sitting on the boot drinking tea from a flask. They couldn't have been more than late teens or early 20s.

Ruth gestured. 'Is that them over there?'

'Yes, ma'am,' the PC nodded as she peered diligently down at her notes. 'Beth and Catrin Clarke. They live locally.'

'Thank you, Constable,' Ruth said with a kind smile as she indicated to Nick that they should probably have a word.

They went over and showed them their warrant cards.

'Hi there. We're police officers from Llancastell CID,' Ruth explained with a sympathetic look. 'It must have been quite a shock. Are you okay?'

The younger girl, who seemed to be quite shaky, nodded.

'Was it you that made the discovery?' Nick asked gently.

The younger girl nodded and whispered. 'Yeah.'

'Catrin, is it?' Nick said.

'Yeah,' she replied.

The older girl put down the flask by her side. 'I'm Beth, her sister.'

'If you're up to it,' Ruth said, 'we'd like to ask you a few questions.'

They both nodded.

Taking out his notebook, Nick looked at them. 'What time did you arrive this morning?'

'Just after eight,' Beth explained.

Looking around, Ruth pointed to the perimeter road. 'And which way did you arrive from?'

'We live up in Llangedwyn,' Beth stated and gestured. 'The road comes from the north straight into the car park.'

Nick nodded at Ruth. 'Yeah, I know the road, boss.'

'How far is that from here?' Ruth asked, aware that her knowledge of Snowdonia was still sketchy, even after five years.

'Seven or eight miles,' Beth replied with a shrug. 'It's about a fifteen-minute drive.'

'And you come here regularly?' Nick asked.

'We do in the summer,' Catrin explained. 'Not so much at the moment.'

'Yeah.' Nick raised an eyebrow. 'Bit cold for paddle-boarding, isn't it?'

Ruth looked at Catrin. 'So, can you tell us exactly what happened?'

'We parked the car, got our stuff, and went down to the lake just over there,' Catrin explained as she pointed to where the SOCO officers were now standing. 'I got onto my board. After about twenty minutes, I felt something bang against it. I looked around and ...' She stopped speaking as the colour drained from her face at remembering what she had seen.

'And then you got out of the water and called us?' Nick asked to clarify.

They both nodded.

'Yeah,' Beth said.

Nick turned the page of his notebook. 'And you didn't touch what you found in the water?'

Catrin pulled a face. 'No.'

'This is really important,' Ruth said as she glanced over at them with a meaningful expression. 'Did you see anyone around when you arrived?'

'No.' Beth shook her head. 'There was no one around. That's why we like to come so early.'

'No one walking by the lake or cycling?'

'No.'

'Do you remember passing any cars as you approached the lake?' Nick asked.

Catrin shook her head. 'Sorry. I can't remember seeing anyone.'

'Okay, thank you.' Ruth reached inside her coat pocket, took out her card, and handed it over. 'This is my card. If you do think of anything else, however small, please give me a ring.'

'Okay, thank you,' Catrin said, taking the card.

Ruth and Nick turned and headed back towards the crime scene. On the far side, uniformed officers were letting through a dark blue van that had *North Wales USMU* – which stood for Underwater Search and Marine Unit – printed on the side.

'Scuba Steve and his merry men are here,' Nick joked under his breath.

Ruth ducked under the line of evidence tape. 'I don't know how they do it, do you?'

'Yeah, searching for bodies in freezing water isn't my idea of fun,' Nick replied.

'Or in our case, it looks like we're looking for body parts,' Ruth added as they approached a nearby SOCO in her light blue Tyvek forensic suit. Even in the fresh air, she could smell the distinctive chemical smell of the SOCO's forensic clothing.

'Morning,' Nick said. 'Who's the lead SOCO on site at the moment?'

'Tony Amis,' the SOCO replied.

Ruth had worked with Amis many times since she'd arrived in North Wales. He was thorough, and even though he seemed jovial, she had seen that he didn't suffer fools at a crime scene.

'Good old Anthony,' Nick muttered as the SOCO handed them their own forensic suits to put on. 'Or Tone the Bone, as I once heard him called.'

Dark, gallows humour was part and parcel of surviving police work.

Pulling the elastic around her freezing ears to secure her surgical face mask, Ruth got a waft of rubber from the purple gloves she had just snapped on.

Just what I needed on a Sunday morning, she thought acerbically.

Nick gestured for her to go down the icy bank towards the water. 'After you, boss.'

'Thanks,' she replied sarcastically as a couple of SOCOs made their way from the bank carrying evidence bags back to the SOCO van.

The air was musty and damp as she placed her shoe, now enveloped in a forensic shoe cover, onto the earth and manoeuvred herself down.

'Come on, grandma,' Nick quipped. 'Do you want to take my hand?'

'No, piss off,' Ruth snapped as her foot suddenly slid a few inches on the frozen soil, and she nearly lost her footing. 'For fuck's sake!'

Above them, a cawing of two crows, who flapped their inky wings, broke the eerie silence. It was as if they were laughing at her struggling down the incline.

Ruth edged down the bank again and eventually got to some level ground.

'Good morning, DI Hunter,' boomed a distinctly public school voice. It was Amis. He gave them both a salute from the water.

Far too cheery for a freezing Sunday morning by a lake with a severed foot, she moaned to herself.

Amis was wearing black wellies over his forensic suit, and the water was up to his shins.

Ruth forced a smile. 'Is it, Tony?'

Amis laughed at her grumpiness a little too loudly. She could see his milky white skin and bushy ginger eyebrows from behind his mask.

'Morning, Anthony,' Nick said.

'DS Evans … You two look like you'd prefer to still be in bed, rather than out in this fresh, healthy Snowdonia air,' Amis chortled.

'I think I'd prefer to be anywhere else than freezing my tits off out here looking at dismembered body parts,' Ruth said sarcastically.

Amis gave another booming laugh. 'Well yes, when you put it like that …'

Ruth gave him a quizzical look. 'Where is it then?'

Getting out of the water, Amis went over to a small white forensic sheet and pulled it back. On the ground was a clear evidence bag containing a severed foot. The skin was a grey-blue colour except for some purple around the toes. There was some matted hair around the ankle bone.

'What can you tell us?' Ruth asked, crouching down to take a closer look. She was glad she had skipped breakfast.

'The foot belongs to a man,' Amis informed her.

'Average height and build, at a guess. I can tell you more when I get it back to the lab.'

Ruth's attention was drawn to the sound of water as a SOCO pulled something from under driftwood and looked over. 'Sir. We've found something else.'

He held up a green wellington boot.

Amis stepped into the water carefully to take it. He peered at it as it dripped water. He then gave Ruth a meaningful look. 'This is for a left foot. And what we've got over there is a left foot too.'

Chapter 3

I t was early evening, and Nick had just read Megan a bedtime story – *A Squash and a Squeeze* by Julia Donaldson. Megan could now join in with some of the lines, and she thought the whole concept of bringing a cow into a house was hilarious. *Bring in the cow, said the wise old man. Bring in the cow? What a curious plan!* she would recite in fits of innocent laughter.

Propped up on the pink pillows and white padded bedstead, Nick watched as Megan drifted to sleep. She had blonde curls just like her mum. The word *angelic* was probably overused, but at that moment, as she slept holding her toy rabbit, she was absolutely angelic. Like the cherubs he'd seen on the ceiling of the Sistine Chapel.

Michelangelo painted it, didn't he?

Closing his eyes for a moment, Nick took a long deep breath and let it out slowly. It was like this that he could get a true perspective on his life – and immense feeling of gratitude. In two months' time, Nick would be four years sober. And that was a bloody miracle. Five years ago, he couldn't go four hours without a drink. He put his continued recovery down to Alcoholics Anonymous, where he had met Amanda. They both still continued to go to meetings – at least once or twice a week. Not because they needed to, but because they wanted to.

As he drifted towards sleep, Nick forced himself to open his eyes. Amanda was making them tea, and there was a new series on Netflix they wanted to watch. It was a new police series. Amanda found it hilarious that Nick spent his whole day in a CID office or out investigating crime in North Wales. And his favourite way to unwind was to watch a police series. He would even make comments about a badly written briefing scene or a post-mortem's lack of authenticity until she told him to *shut up*.

He drifted towards sleep again. It wouldn't be the first time that Nick had fallen asleep next to Megan. In fact, it probably happened at least once a week.

Putting his feet down onto the thick carpet, Nick stood up, feeling the soft fibres between his toes on his bare feet. Amanda was continually nagging him to wear slippers, but Nick maintained that with slippers came a pipe, old age, dementia, and then death. *I only suggested you wear slippers, you morose twerp*, was her response.

Amused by this dark thought, he walked along the landing and headed down the stairs. Whatever Amanda was cooking, it had a serious amount of garlic – which was fine by him.

As he entered the hallway, he saw Amanda at the cooker. She saw him out of the corner of her eye but carried on stirring something on the hob. He knew that she had seen him.

There's definitely something off about her in recent days, he thought.

Standing in the doorway, he leant on the frame and

looked at her with an exaggerated, quizzical expression. 'Erm, are you okay?'

'Yes, of course,' she said abruptly, without looking up.

For a few seconds, she didn't look at him. Then, as she turned, he could see there were tears in her eyes. As she blinked, he could instantly tell there was something dreadfully wrong.

What the hell is going on?

'It's fine,' she said in a flustered tone.

He went to her and put his hand on her shoulder, but felt her recoil for a second. 'Hey, what's going on?'

Biting her lip, she took a deep breath. 'I need to talk to you about something.'

With a surge of panic, Nick felt his stomach lurch. What did she mean? His mind raced with a stream of terrifying thoughts. That was his motto. If in doubt, catastrophise.

'Okay,' he said, putting a reassuring hand on her arm. He was feeling physically sick. What the hell was she about to tell him?

Gesturing to the living room, he manoeuvred her out of the kitchen. 'Come on. Whatever it is, we can sort it out.'

They went in and sat down.

For a few seconds, Amanda said nothing. Her eyes roamed nervously around the room. She seemed broken.

'Mand, you're really scaring me here,' Nick gasped as he sat forward in the armchair. His stomach was in knots.

She gave an imperceptible nod and then met his eyes. 'It's just I'm going to tell you something, and I don't know how you're going to react.'

He frowned. 'Are you having an affair?'

She shook her head emphatically. 'God, no. No. Of course not!'

He was hugely relieved it wasn't that, but now his mind went to other dark possibilities.

Oh my God, is she dying?

'Please, Mand,' he begged her.

She nodded and took a deep breath. 'I had a letter a couple of days ago.'

'Okay.'

'There's no easy way of saying this,' she stammered. 'When I was fifteen, I had a daughter. She's now eighteen, and she's written me a letter.'

There were several seconds of silence as Nick let the enormity of what she had told him sink in. In fact, at first, he doubted he had actually heard her correctly. Then he studied her face for a moment and knew it was true.

Bloody hell, I did not see that coming!

'You have a daughter?' he mumbled, still trying to comprehend why she had never told him.

'I know I should have told you,' she wept, 'but the longer we were together, the more I panicked.'

Even though he was shocked, Nick also felt a sense of relief. He wasn't comfortable thinking about the fact that she'd had a child. However, she wasn't dying or having an affair, so anything else was manageable.

Getting up from the chair, he went over to the sofa and took her hands in his. 'Listen, I'm a bit surprised. And you should have told me. But I've got a fairly dark past. I'm an alcoholic. I'm not in the position to judge anyone.'

Amanda smiled and rubbed the tears from her face with her palm. 'I thought you were going to go mad.'

'Hey, I thought you had a terminal illness, or you were having an affair,' Nick admitted with an uneasy smile.

'Don't be bloody stupid,' Amanda snorted.

'What's her name?' Nick asked.

'Francesca Chapel,' she said. 'Fran.'

'Fran. Okay.' Nick nodded. 'Does she live near here?'

'Welshpool.'

'Not far then. And she's okay?'

'Yeah. She says her adopted parents are lovely. And she's got two younger brothers,' Amanda explained.

'Well, she's got a little sister now, too,' Nick pointed out.

Amanda nodded. 'Yeah. As far as I could tell, she was really happy growing up.'

'That's great.' Nick smiled. 'You must be really relieved?'

'I am. It's always there in the back of my mind. And there's the guilt of having given her away,' she said. 'And the worry of what might have happened to her. Sometimes I'd feel sick at the thought that she'd been adopted by horrible people who were making her life a complete misery.'

'Now you know that's not true,' Nick said comfortingly as he put an arm around her.

Amanda blew out her cheeks and shook her head. 'I thought you'd be really angry.'

'No,' Nick shrugged. 'I'm a bit miffed you didn't tell me. But if you were anything like me, life was a chaotic, alcoholic mess from the time I started drinking. I was completely reckless.'

'Me too,' she admitted.

'And the one thing I have learnt,' Nick admitted, 'is that not everything is about me. What about her father?'

She pulled a face. 'Yeah, that's a bit of a difficult one.'

'You don't know who her father is, do you?'

'No.' She shook her head. 'I was completely out of control as a teenager. I was excluded from three schools.'

Nick didn't want to delve into the question of who the father was in any more depth. 'Does she want to see you?'

Amanda nodded. 'Yes, she does.'

'How do you feel about that?'

She thought for a moment. 'Happy … And scared.'

Moving closer, she kissed him and gazed directly into his eyes. 'What on earth did I do to deserve you, Nicholas Evans?'

Nick grinned. 'Erm, last night you called me an *utter bell-end*.'

'Oh yeah,' she laughed. 'Well, I take that back.'

'What about an *infantile twat*?'

She gave him a playful push. 'No, I meant that. If you stomp upstairs when we've had a row, then I'm afraid you are an *infantile twat*.'

'Fair point,' he said. 'If you want Fran to come here, I can take Megan out somewhere so you can be on your own.'

'I've thought about that. Maybe you could give us a bit of time on our own and then come back to meet her.'

Nick smiled. 'Yeah, that sounds like an excellent plan.'

Chapter 4

Monday 25th January

IT WAS 7 AM AND RUTH WOKE PEACEFULLY IN BED. FOR THE first few seconds, she noticed a tiny bubble of joy inside her chest and a relaxed feeling all over. She was so used to waking from terrible nightmares, full of anxiety and fear, that the sensation felt unfamiliar. As she drifted in and out of sleep, she was curious why she felt this good.

And then she felt the soft breath of the woman sleeping next to her on her neck. She turned and opened her eyes to look at her.

Sarah Goddard.

Is this another cruel dream? she thought warily.

Sarah's blonde hair was tucked behind her ear, her curled eyelashes were still, and her full lips parted slightly as she breathed deeply. If there were more lines on her face compared to seven years ago, then they suited her.

Her complexion was clear, and she looked healthy. It had taken several weeks for her to look like that after they returned from Paris. Then again, they were lucky to have got back from Paris at all.

No, I'm pretty sure this is real.

As the winter sun poked through the gap in the curtains, it drew a faint line across Sarah's face.

She really is quite beautiful.

For a moment, Ruth got that buzz in her chest again, as if her heart was stirring.

Then a flash in her mind's eye of the incredible story that had preceded them being together in *this* very bed at *this* very moment in North Wales.

It was a bloody miracle.

And when she tried to describe to anyone who asked how Ruth and Sarah were together, she could see that it blew their minds.

Bloody hell! They should make a film about that! was the usual response.

In 2013, Ruth and Sarah had been living together as a couple in their flat in Crystal Palace, South-East London. Sarah boarded a train to London Victoria one morning and simply vanished. No contact, no note, no idea where she had gone. As a copper, Ruth had made sure the CCTV footage from that day had been scoured. Every station on that line had been searched. There had been television appeals and articles in the press. There had been sightings of Sarah from all around the world. Ruth had even followed women who she thought looked like Sarah, but she had simply disappeared.

Little did Ruth know Sarah had become secretly embroiled in the seedy world of elite sex parties in London through a man named Jamie Parsons. A few days before she had vanished, Sarah had witnessed Lord David Weaver raping and then 'accidentally' killing a teenage girl in a bedroom at one of these *Secret Garden* sex parties. Lord Weaver was a life peer who had served as both Foreign Secretary and Chief Whip in the late 1980s. He was a very visible member of the House of Lords, often photographed with the great and the good, the rich and the famous. His wife Olivia moved in social circles with lesser members of the royal family.

To make matters worse, Sarah's presence in the room had been spotted by Jamie Parsons and three others. Jurgen Kessler, a German banker and close friend of Parsons, who was wanted by Berlin Police for questioning in connection to the murder of two young women. Patrice Le Bon, a multimillionaire owner of several Paris model agencies, who was under investigation for human trafficking. And Sergei Saratov, a Russian billionaire, who had gone underground when police investigated his extensive use of escorts and sex workers in hotels that he owned in an exclusive European ski resort. These men were very rich, very powerful – and therefore very dangerous. And Sarah was an eyewitness. She was taken away to France and was forced to move around Europe working as a high-class escort.

Ruth's first major breakthrough in her quest to find Sarah had occurred when she found CCTV, which showed Sarah entering The Dorchester Hotel in London in 2015 with Sergei Saratov. It proved, for the first time, that Sarah hadn't been attacked or murdered on the train from Crystal Palace in November 2013. However, it posed a whole new set of questions. Saratov had been implicated in various trafficking crimes, as well as allegations of sexual assault. Ruth had no idea what Sarah's relationship to Saratov was. With the help of Met Missing Persons Officer Stephen Flaherty, Ruth eventually tracked Sarah down to an elite escort agency, Global Escorts, in Paris. And that was where Ruth had her first glimpse of Sarah in over seven years during a FaceTime call. Before Sarah responded, the screen had gone blank, Ruth heard Sarah scream, and the call ended. Despite endless tracking by Ruth and then the Met Police Missing Persons Unit, the number couldn't be traced, and the Global Escorts website had been closed down.

It had now been just over three months since Ruth had flown to Paris and rescued Sarah from the clutches of Global Escorts. Nick, Sarah and she had nearly lost their lives.

'Are you watching me sleep?' Sarah mumbled wearily, without opening her eyes.

'Obviously not.'

'That's not true, is it?'

'No,' Ruth laughed gently. 'I spent so many mornings waking up hoping to see your face.'

'Yeah. I know. So did I.' Sarah slowly opened her eyes and gave her a quizzical smile. 'You weren't always on your own, though, were you?'

Ruth looked at her for a few seconds. 'You mean Sian?'

'Of course,' Sarah said, now squinting at her as the pale blue light of the winter sun spilled in through the curtains. 'You told me you lived together?'

Oh, are we having this conversation right now? Ruth wondered uneasily.

'We did,' Ruth replied. 'On and off. We could never seem to make it work.' It felt so incredibly awkward talking to Sarah about Sian. Since Sarah arrived in Wales, they had never really discussed the thorny issue of Ruth trying to get on with her life and even moving in with another woman. There had been fleeting comments within conversations, but nothing with any depth.

'Why was that?' Sarah asked in a tone that implied she was genuinely interested.

'That's a tricky one.' Ruth propped herself up on her elbow. 'Actually, it was because of you.'

Sarah frowned. 'Explain.'

'I could never stop hoping that you were alive. That one day I would find you,' Ruth admitted with the kind of honesty that she had often lacked in the past. 'Even though I knew the odds of that actually happening were very slim.'

'You thought I was dead?' Sarah asked with no hint of judgement.

'No. I don't know.' Ruth scrambled around for the right thing to say and then realised that she just needed to be totally honest. 'I'm an experienced copper. My head told me that the chances of a woman disappearing from a train, then vanishing without a trace, and then turning up alive years later were a million to one. My heart told me that while there was a chance, I had to keep hoping that you were alive.'

Sarah blinked as she took in what Ruth had told her. 'And I guess that made you impossible to live with?'

'Yeah, I was,' Ruth said in a whisper. 'I really was.'

'Do you mind me asking what happened to her?' Sarah asked gently.

'No, of course not.' Ruth thought of Sian, and all that had happened to her suddenly weighed heavily on her. 'It was a couple of years ago. Ironically, Sian had just moved out, and we had sort of split up. We were investigating a religious cult out close to Ffestiniog. They had this charismatic leader called Rachel, who we suspected of being involved in several disappearances and possibly even murder. In the surveillance operation, Sian was kidnapped. Armed officers were sent in to rescue her, and this Rachel shot her. We got Sian to hospital, but she didn't make it.'

For a moment, Ruth felt like she was recounting a dream. And then the emotion of what had happened hit her. A tear welled in her eye, and she wiped it away.

'Sorry …'

'Don't apologise.' Sarah reached up and put her hand to her face. 'That sounds horrible.'

'It was,' Ruth admitted, taking in a deep breath and trying to hold back the tears. 'It feels weird talking to you about her.'

Sarah gave her a kind smile. 'I think after everything we've been through, we just have to be totally honest about everything.'

'Yeah, that's very true.'

Sarah gave her a meaningful look. 'And if you ever want to talk about Sian, you can talk to me about her. Seriously.'

Ruth smiled and hugged her. 'Thank you. You two would have got along famously.'

Sarah nodded. 'I bet we would.'

Chapter 5

Sipping her coffee as she strode down the corridor, Ruth turned and came through the double doors into the CID office. The discovery of the severed foot in Lake Vyrnwy was a new one, even for her. She had worked a couple of cases in the Met where body parts had been discovered. However, she had never worked a case where just one body part had been found.

She was taken back to a case that she worked on in the Met in 2001, when she was a DS, on secondment to Tower Hill Police station. The dismembered torso of a young Afro-Caribbean boy had been found floating in the Thames by Tower Bridge. The post-mortem put the boy's age at between four and eight-years-old. Police officers gave him the name '*Adam*' to humanise what had happened to him. The investigation found no match for Adam in the databases of missing children in Britain and Europe. The case remained a complete mystery until 2003, when Ruth had returned to Peckham nick. Officers from the Met travelled to South Africa and made a startling discovery. They suspected Adam had been trafficked to

Britain from a region of southern Nigeria called Benin City, known as the birthplace of voodoo. Adam had been taken to London specifically for a Muti killing, which was a ritual sacrifice performed by a witch doctor. The other parts of Adam were used to create *muti*, a medicinal potion with magical properties. To this day, no one had ever been convicted of Adam's murder, and so the case remained unsolved.

'Right guys,' Ruth said, bringing her mind back to the job in hand as she arrived at the far end of the office. 'If we can settle down, please.' She went over to a case board which had virtually nothing on it except for a map showing Lake Vyrnwy and a photograph of the severed foot. 'As some of you already know, a foot was discovered floating in Lake Vyrnwy yesterday morning. We know very little at the moment, except that it is a left foot, and it belongs to an adult male of average height and build.'

'And we're looking for anyone who fits that description and has been spotted hopping around in the area,' Nick joked darkly.

Detective Sergeant Daniel French rolled his eyes. There were a few groans from some of the other detectives.

'Thank you, Nick,' Ruth said sarcastically.

Nick shrugged. 'Hey, it's a Monday morning. It's the best I've got.'

Ruth went back to the board and pointed to another photo. 'We also found a green wellington boot floating nearby. It's also a left foot and looks to be similar in size. They might be linked, but forensics will be able to tell us more … What else have we got, Nick?'

Nick glanced up from where he was sitting and rubbed his beard. 'Uniform are taking statements from a couple of houses that overlook the lake. We also have the hotel here. Some rooms have balconies that overlook the area. The dining area where breakfast is served also has a view. Reception are getting us a list of all the guests that would have been in the hotel so we can see if anyone saw anything suspicious that morning.'

French frowned. 'Any idea how long the foot had been in the water, boss?'

Ruth shook her head. 'Not yet. But the narrower a time frame we can get, the better. But I would suggest we ask the residents of the hotel and houses nearby if they had seen anything suspicious in the last week. My feeling is that the foot wasn't dropped into the lake yesterday morning.'

'POLSA is doing a fingertip search of the banks of the lake this morning, and the dog unit is going to be there too,' Nick explained.

'Okay.' Ruth processed the information for a moment. 'There doesn't seem to be much more we can do until we get forensics and the PM back. Dan, can you check to see if there are traffic cameras close to that spot? It might be worth having a look to see if anyone is acting suspiciously or looking like they're going to dump anything in the lake.' Ruth then looked over at Detective Constable Jim Garrow and Detective Constable Georgina Wild – known as Georgie – the two most junior members of CID.

'Jim and Georgie,' she said. 'On a separate matter, I have a 'special request'. I need you to talk to a Bella Freudmann. Her husband has been missing for a couple of days.'

Georgie frowned. 'No offence, boss, but isn't that a job for uniform?'

'Yeah, normally it would be,' Ruth agreed. 'However, her husband is a Mark Freudmann. And so her mother-in-law is Deputy Chief Constable Susanna Freudmann. She seems worried enough to call us.'

DCC Susanna Freudmann was the second highest

ranking police officer in the North Wales Police. And when she asked for a favour, Ruth knew you didn't hesitate. Susanna was also one of the founding members of the BAWP – the British Association of Women in Policing – which had started in the late 80s, so Ruth felt a certain obligation to help her out with anything she needed.

Georgie gave her a knowing expression. 'Ah, okay,'

'What do we know?' Garrow asked.

'Not a lot,' Ruth said. 'I've done some digging, and Mark Freudmann has a habit of disappearing from the family home, usually when he's lost a lot of money gambling. Just go and show your faces, ask a few questions and that should keep the DCC off our backs for a bit.'

Chapter 6

An hour later, Georgie and Garrow made their way from Llancastell out towards the small village of Llwydiarth where Mark and Bella Freudmann lived. Spotting a sign to Porthmadog, Georgie remembered a family holiday when she was very young. They had rented a small cottage close to the sea. It was a blissful time. Even though she could never remember the actual moment her parents had told her she was adopted, they had never made a secret of the fact. If anyone actually thought about it, her mum had ginger hair and burned to a freckle as soon as she looked at the sun. And her dad still had that blonde hair and blue eyes thing going on well into his 50s. In contrast, Georgie had heavily lashed deep brown eyes, coal-black hair, and dark olive skin. In fact, some kids at school made racist comments. And in terms of genetics, it really wouldn't have made any sense to an outsider looking on at them as a family. But no one ever mentioned it, and they didn't care.

Being adopted had never been any kind of issue for Georgie. She heard of other adopted kids being angry or confused, but she just counted herself as lucky. She had everything she could have ever wanted. A stable, loving home and a happy childhood. But she noticed in recent years, a gnawing feeling of uneasiness about her adoption had festered. Why wasn't she loveable enough for her mother to keep her? Why hadn't she had any contact from her birth parents now she was in her 20s? Did she have any siblings? What were they like? It was questions like these that kept her awake at night.

At the risk of indulging in a bit of cold self-analysis, she wondered if those feelings of not being enough were driving her naked ambition. She was going to make something of her life. She would show the parents that had so brutally abandoned her. She would rise the ranks of the police force and then hunt them down to prove her self-worth. *Hey, thanks for ditching me. By the way, I'm now the youngest ever female DCI in the Welsh Police Force, so fuck you!*

With her stomach now twisting with these uncomfortable thoughts, Georgie took an audible breath.

'You okay?' Garrow asked, as if he could sense her anguish.

'Yeah, fine,' Georgie said dismissively as they drew up outside a large, detached house on the outskirts of Llwydiarth, a small village about five miles to the south of Lake Vyrnwy. The house was large and modern, with clean lines and lots of glass. It was definitely a statement of wealth and style. A brand new, white Porsche Cayenne Turbo GT sat on the sweeping gravel drive.

'Nice place,' Georgie said with a touch of envy as they got out of the car. There weren't many houses in North Wales like this.

Garrow nodded as he peered around. 'There aren't many places you can get away with a French Riviera-style fountain on the front drive. If that's your kind of thing.'

A French what?

She'd forgotten that Jim was a bit of a brainbox. That's what a university education gave you, she thought sarcastically. A head full of useless facts, such as what a French Riviera fountain looked like.

'You sound like you disapprove, Jim?' Georgie asked with a knowing smirk.

'It's a clash of styles,' Garrow said. 'But each to their own, I guess.'

Walking up to the sizeable front door, Georgie pressed the intercom buzzer and waited. What she would give for a house like this, she thought. It was the sort of place people bought when they won the lottery.

From behind the door came the loud barking of dogs.

Georgie was startled at the sudden noise and glanced at Garrow – *they sound big and scary.*

'Hello?' came a flustered female voice on the intercom.

'Hi, there. It's North Wales Police. We're looking for a Bella Freudmann,' Georgie replied.

'Jesus! Hang on a second, will you?' the female voice said impatiently.

Garrow gave Georgie a sardonic look. 'She sounds pleased we're here.'

A few seconds later, the tall front door opened and a glamorous-looking woman peered out at them. She was holding the collar of a large, black dog – maybe a Rottweiler – which snarled at them.

I hope she doesn't let go of that bloody collar, Georgie thought to herself.

Bella was in her 40s, blonde hair, slim, possibly too much make-up for that time in the morning. Georgie could see that *she'd had some work done.* Fillers, lips, and Botox. Too much time on the tennis court, sunbeds, and by the pool had left her skin unnaturally tanned. Or maybe it was just out of a bottle. It was hard to tell these days. She wore white designer jogging bottoms and a grey Burberry hoodie.

From her expression, Georgie could see that she really wasn't pleased to see them. In fact, she looked like she had just tasted something horrible in her mouth.

'Yes?' she said.

Georgie clocked the well-manicured nails and designer jewellery.

They flashed their warrant cards.

'Hi there. DC Wild and DC Garrow, Llancastell CID,' she explained with a forced smile.

'What do you want?' Bella snapped as she struggled to hold the dog.

'We understand your husband has gone missing?' Garrow explained.

'Jesus Christ!' Bella snapped angrily. 'Wait there while I put the dogs away, will you?'

It was now that Georgie could clearly hear that Bella had a thick Mancunian accent.

The front door slammed loudly in their faces.

'Well, they do say that money can't buy you class,' Georgie joked under her breath.

Before Garrow could respond, the door opened again, and Bella beckoned them inside. 'I suppose Susanna put you up to this, did she?' she growled.

They followed her through the impressive hallway, which was fashionably decorated with modern art and two pieces of sculpture. The walls were painted with a dark olive green.

'Deputy Chief Constable Freudmann asked us to come over,' Georgie explained. 'She explained that your husband Mark has gone missing?'

Bella led them into an enormous glass kitchen and

dining area. It was immaculate with bespoke cabinets, marble tops, and designer furniture.

Jesus, this is incredible, Georgie thought.

Bella pointed to a breakfast bar where there was a line of aluminium stools. 'Sit down there, if you want.'

'Thank you,' Garrow said uncertainly.

Bella let out a sigh. 'Sorry. Crazy morning, that's all.'

Georgie wasn't sure if that was an apology for her initial rudeness and gave her a polite smile. 'It's just a couple of routine questions, and then we'll be out of your hair.'

'Kettle's boiled,' Bella said, mellowing. 'Do you want tea or coffee?'

Georgie smiled, slightly confused by Bella's switch from anger to gentle politeness in the space of a few minutes. 'We're fine, thanks.'

Bella took a deep breath and leaned against one of the worktops. She seemed frustrated. 'Look, this isn't the first time this has happened.'

Georgie frowned as she took out her notebook. 'You mean your husband has disappeared before?'

Bella snorted with a wry smile. 'Yeah, you could say that.'

Garrow looked over at her. 'And your husband's name is Mark, is that right?'

'Yeah,' Bella said with a withering expression. '*Mark.*'

'When you say that Mark has disappeared before, can you tell us what you mean?' Georgie asked.

'Mark is essentially a fucking child,' Bella explained. 'He's a gambling addict. And every few months, he goes on a spree, loses lots of money, drinks too much, and goes missing for a couple of days. He then goes crawling back to his mother. Then she brings him here with his tail between his legs, with both of them promising that it will never happen again. But it always does.'

'Any idea where he might have gone?' Garrow said.

Bella shrugged. 'He normally goes up to Liverpool and hides out there. He's got a mate who owns a nightclub. God knows what they get up to, but frankly, I'm beyond caring.'

'Could you give us this man's name?' Georgie asked.

'Terry Fowles.'

'And the name of the nightclub?'

'The Attic. It's on the Albert Docks, near the Cream bar,' Bella explained.

Garrow shifted on his stool. 'Can you tell us the last time you saw Mark?'

'End of last week.' Bella paused for thought. 'Thursday possibly.'

'And how did Mark seem?' Georgie asked.

'Seem?' Bella said. 'He seemed his usual cocky, annoying self. I'm not going to pretend that our marriage is perfect.'

Spotting a couple of photographs over on the windowsill, Georgie asked, 'Do you have children?'

'No, we don't,' Bella explained. 'Listen, if I'm honest, this is a total waste of your time. Mark has gone on some bender, and no doubt he'll be back tomorrow or the day after. Mark was an only child, and his father died when he was very young. Susanna has always spoiled Mark and bailed him out when he was in trouble. He's just a big mummy's boy. I'm sorry that Susanna has wasted your time like this.'

Georgie looked at Garrow. It didn't sound like there was anything remotely suspicious about what Bella had told them.

Chapter 7

Ruth and Nick got into the lift on the ground floor of Llancastell's University Hospital. The silver steel doors clunked together, and the lift pitched as it descended towards the basement. There was a metallic whine from above.

Christ, that doesn't sound good. I do not want to get stuck in this bloody thing, she thought. She got claustrophobia in lifts at the best of times.

Nick had been unusually quiet and distracted since they left CID half an hour earlier.

For a few seconds, they stood together in silence as the lift went down slowly towards the basement where the hospital's mortuary was situated.

'Penny for them,' Ruth said, eventually breaking silence.

'Sorry?' Nick had been totally lost in his thoughts.

'Everything all right?'

It clearly wasn't, as he was rarely this distracted at work.

He looked at her for a moment. 'Yeah. Slightly unusual turn of events at home last night.'

'Okay,' Ruth shrugged. 'It's not the first time you and Amanda have had a row or fallen out. Mainly because you've been an immature knob, might I add.'

Nick gave a dry smile. 'Yeah, that's the thing. We didn't have a row. She told me she had a child when she was fifteen that she gave up for adoption.'

Wow. I didn't see that coming.

'Bloody hell. Right.' Ruth raised an eyebrow. 'And I take it you didn't know this?'

'Nope,' Nick replied. 'Bit of a shock, if I'm honest.'

'I can imagine … Did she explain why she had never told you?'

'At first, she said she was too scared to tell me. She thought I might not want to be with her if she told me. Then it went past the point at which she felt she could tell me.'

Ruth frowned. 'So, why bring it up now?'

'Her daughter, Fran, is now eighteen,' he replied. 'She went through the Adoption Contact Register, got our address, and wrote Amanda a letter.'

'Blimey,' Ruth said as the lift stopped and the doors opened with a metallic clunk. 'That must have been a bolt from the blue for her?'

'I think it was,' Nick said as they walked out of the lift, turned left, and headed down the windowless corridor. It reeked of disinfectant and cleaning fluids.

'How do you feel about it?'

'I would never have judged her for having a child adopted when she was fifteen. My past is littered with terrible choices and mistakes.' Nick shrugged. 'But I am a bit annoyed she didn't tell me. And it is weird to think that Megan now has a sister.'

The black double doors to the mortuary loomed ahead.

'Are they planning to meet up?' Ruth asked.

'Yeah,' Nick said. 'Amanda is going to see if Fran wants to come round tonight.'

'You know what?' Ruth said. 'In the long run, Amanda is going to feel a lot better she doesn't have this big secret she's keeping from you.'

'Yeah. I could tell she was relieved even this morning. We'll get through it. And I think I have to see it as a positive thing going forward,' Nick said quietly.

Ruth gave him a quizzical look.

'What?' Nick smiled. 'Bogey hanging off my nose? Food stuck in my beard?'

Ruth shrugged. 'You're being very thoughtful and grown up about it, that's all.'

'Erm, when am I ever not thoughtful and grown up?' he asked with mock indignation.

Ruth raised an eyebrow. 'You really want me to answer that?'

'No,' Nick laughed. 'I really don't.'

Ruth reluctantly pushed the double doors open and walked into the mortuary where Professor Tony Amis was just starting his preliminary examination of the severed foot. Her shoes squeaked on the white-tiled floor – the noise grated on her teeth. She was already feeling uncomfortable.

'This place gives me the willies,' Ruth admitted in a virtual whisper.

'Willies?' Nick snorted. 'God, you sound like my nain.'

'Oh, thanks. I'm paranoid enough about my age as it is, without you comparing me to your grandmother.'

Nick shrugged with a grin. 'Sorry, boss. I didn't mean to get off on the wrong *foot* with you this morning.'

'Really?' Ruth groaned sarcastically. 'Maybe you should do stand-up, Nicholas?'

Dark humour was part of the coping mechanism of all experienced detectives.

Ruth often got spooked by mortuaries, which she knew was silly. She had been to dozens during her time as a police officer, but they were too quiet, too sterile, and too lifeless. The lighting was cold and stark, and the steel scales used to weigh internal organs were unsettlingly shiny and clean. The underlying hum of fans and the air conditioning added to the eerie atmosphere.

Ruth glanced up and saw that Nick was now staring at the foot, which lay like a large chunk of meat on the gurney. Maybe he was now regretting his infantile joke. After all, the foot belonged to someone who might well have been murdered. She couldn't ever remember hearing about a body part being discarded by someone who was still alive.

'What can you tell us, Tony?' Ruth asked. She was hoping for some clues as to the origin of the foot.

Dressed in pastel green surgical scrubs, Amis came over. He adjusted his black rubber apron and turned off the microphone. He had been making a digital recording of his findings.

'As I said yesterday, the foot belongs to an adult male Caucasian. From the thickness and fat content around the ankle joint, I'm guessing average build,' Amis then pointed to the sole of the foot. 'Some corns and calluses here on the pads on the balls of the foot. There's some significant build-up of skin.'

'What does that tell us?' Nick asked as he wrote in his notepad.

'Repetitive exercise,' Amis explained. 'My guess would be that your victim is a runner.'

Ruth peered closely at the foot and the toes.

Amis continued. 'I'm no expert, but this person seemed to have taken care of his nails. In fact, I might even go as far as to suggest that he's had a pedicure. I think that's the right word, isn't it?'

Ruth nodded. 'Yes.'

Nick snorted. 'There aren't many men in North Wales who get pedicures.'

'No.' Amis gave an ironic chortle. 'All far too metrosexual for my liking.'

Ruth peered at where the foot had been cut from the leg. 'What about the actual incision?'

Amis frowned. 'How do you mean?'

'Anything you can tell us about who did it? Surgeon, butcher, chef?'

Amis gave a wry smile. 'No, I'm afraid not. From the serrations on the skin and bone, whoever chopped off the foot was by no means an expert. It's a botched job, if you know what I mean.'

'Yes.' Ruth asked. 'What about some kind of timescale?'

'The top of the foot has been slightly gnawed.' Amis pointed to some frayed bit of skin. 'Could be rats or crabs.'

Nick pulled a face. 'Nice.'

'Does that help us calculate how long the foot had been in the water?' Ruth asked.

'Possibly. It's unlikely the foot had been in the water for less than twenty-four hours,' Amis said. 'The problem we have is that the water in the lake is freezing. Effectively, it refrigerates the flesh and stops it from rotting.'

Ruth was irritated. Amis was going off on one of his usual tangents, and she didn't have time for it. 'Ballpark, Tony. Had that foot been in the water for a year, a few months or weeks?'

'Right, yes.' Amis scratched his chin through his mask for a moment. 'Given the condition of the foot, I'd say only a few days, maybe a week at the most.'

That's more like it, Ruth thought. *We can work with that.*

HAVING FINISHED TALKING TO BELLA FREUDMANN, Georgie and Garrow headed back to the car.

'What did you think?' Georgie asked.

Garrow shrugged casually. 'What she told us sounds plausible. Mark Freudmann has got previous for going off radar, so I don't think there's anything suspicious.'

'I wouldn't want to get on the wrong side of her, though, would you?' Georgie said with a wry smile.

'No,' Garrow grinned. 'Definitely not. A *formidable woman,* as my dad used to say when what he meant was *scary bitch.*'

Out of the corner of her eye, Georgie spotted someone looking out of the first-floor window of the smaller house that was next door.

'Interesting,' she said.

'What's that?'

Georgie furtively indicated the house. 'Our presence has been spotted by a neighbour.'

'Shall we have a quick word?' Garrow suggested.

'Just to be on the safe side,' Georgie said in agreement as they turned and walked down the garden path towards the neighbour's front door.

The house was in stark contrast to the ultra-modern design of the Freudmann's glass mansion. With dark red brick walls and a grey slate roof, its appearance was far more in keeping with a small North Wales village.

Garrow knocked, then stood back as they pulled out their warrant cards.

A few seconds later, a woman in her late 60s opened the door and gave them a quizzical look. 'Yes?'

'We're police officers from Llancastell CID,' Garrow explained. 'I wonder if we could come in for a minute? It's just a couple of routine questions, so it's nothing to worry about.'

'Erm, yes, of course,' the woman said as she opened the door.

Georgie gave her a kind smile and asked, 'It's Mrs …?'

'Oh, it's Val,' she said with a nervous laugh.

They followed her through to a small, dark kitchen that was a little cluttered with wooden furniture, a Welsh dresser, and shelves piled high with books and magazines.

Garrow took out his notebook and gestured to the Freudmann's house next door. 'We're just making some enquiries about Mark Freudmann?'

'Yes.' Val pointed to the table. 'Do you want to sit down?'

Georgie pulled out a chair. 'Thanks.'

'I've just made a pot of tea if you fancy a brew?' Val said, gesturing to the dark green teapot.

Georgie smiled at her. 'You know what, Val, that would be lovely. We both take it milk, no sugar.'

Garrow clicked his pen and looked over at Val as she pottered around, getting out cups from a cupboard. 'How well do you know your neighbours?'

'Oh, you know,' Val said with a shrug. 'We wave hello. Take deliveries for each other. That sort of thing.'

'But you're not friends?' Georgie asked.

'No, no,' Val chuckled.

Georgie gave her a quizzical look. 'Why did you say it like that?' she asked gently.

'They're a bit, you know,' Val said as she tucked a strand of hair behind her ear. 'I think they think I'm an old fuddy-duddy. They have parties there. Lots of younger people, music until all hours.'

'Can you remember the last time you saw Mark Freudmann?' Garrow asked.

Val approached the table and put down two patterned cups of tea on saucers in front of them.

'Thanks,' Georgie said with a smile.

'Mark?' Val asked, thinking out loud. 'Come to think of it, haven't seen him for a few days.'

Georgie looked at her. 'Is that unusual?'

'He's at the house most days,' Val explained. 'But I haven't seen him since the end of the last week.'

'Can you try to remember when that was?' Garrow asked as he sipped his tea.

'Last Thursday. In the evening, and ...' Val said, but something bothered her as she said it – as if she was hiding something.

'Where was that?' Georgie asked.

'I was upstairs,' Val explained. 'And Mark and Bella were out on their patio. I remembering thinking it was weird because it was so cold. And then I saw they had one of those fire pits.'

'And that's the last time you saw him?' Garrow asked.

'Yes, that's right,' Val said.

Georgie suspected she was holding something back.

'How did they seem?' Georgie asked.

'How do you mean?'

'Did Mark and Bella seem to be getting on and having a nice time sitting by their fire pit?'

'No, definitely not,' Val snorted.

Garrow glanced up from his notepad. 'Why do you say that?'

'They were having another one of their terrible rows,'

Val explained. 'Bella was screaming at him. That's why I looked out of the window.'

'What was Mark doing when Bella was screaming at him?' Garrow asked.

'He looked a bit scared. Bella threw a glass at him. I've seen her do that before,' Val admitted. 'And then Frank came out to calm them down.'

'Frank?' Georgie said.

'Bella's brother,' Val said. 'He's been staying with them for a few weeks. I heard that he'd been through a nasty divorce.'

Georgie and Garrow exchanged a look.

'And you haven't seen Mark since then?' Garrow asked.

'No,' Val said. 'And I'm not one for prying, but I know that Mark has gone away for few days at a time in the past, if, you know what I mean?'

Chapter 8

I t was early afternoon, and Sarah had driven over to Chester Police Station to meet officers from the London Met who were compiling evidence based on her allegations of what she had witnessed on Friday 1st November 2013.

The meeting room was on the ground floor of Chester Police Station. It was modern, light, and furnished with dark green padded chairs and matching carpet. There were several police information posters on the wall. One of them featured the word IMPACT in red lettering and advertised a helpline for those who wanted to give information about organised crime in the area.

Sitting opposite Sarah on the table were Detective Chief Inspector Kevin Orchard and Chief Superintendent Michael Niven, from the Homicide and Serious Crime Command (SCD1), working in conjunction with the MIT, the Met's Murder Investigation Team. Sarah knew that what she had witnessed was possibly more shocking and explosive than the recent Weinstein or Epstein cases.

Orchard was a severe-looking man in his 50s with a

pointed nose, sallow complexion, and glasses. He was taking detailed notes on Sarah's testimony. They needed every detail of both the lead up to and the events of early November 2013.

A small video camera on a tripod sat on the carpet to her right, its red recording light flashing ominously.

Orchard stopped writing and looked up at her. 'You went to several of these Secret Garden parties with Jamie Parsons?'

Sarah nodded. 'Yes.'

'And what did you do there?' Niven asked. He was thickset, with a decent head of greying hair, bulbous nose, and a gravelly Yorkshire accent.

Sarah shrugged. 'You know. I met some of Jamie's friends. Had a few drinks.'

'Drugs?' Orchard asked with no particular tone of judgement.

'Sometimes,' she replied. She didn't want to admit that she had taken cocaine every time she attended. They were police officers, after all.

Orchard stopped writing again, blinked as if he was trying to remember something, and then peered at her. 'It's my understanding that these were sex parties? Is that correct?'

Sarah frowned. 'I suppose they were. Yes.'

'Orgies?'

'I don't know. Possibly,' Sarah said.

'Can you run me through what actually happens at these parties?' Niven said.

She felt a little awkward as she cleared her throat. It was embarrassing to admit to two middle-aged, high-ranking police officers what happened at a Secret Garden party. 'Erm, well, at first, it's just like a normal party.

People drinking, chatting, dancing. It's mainly couples who go.'

'Is there some kind of vetting process?' Orchard asked.

'Yes,' Sarah explained. 'If you want to go, you have to send in photographs of yourself and your partner. If you're attractive enough, then you can attend.'

God, that sounds so horribly shallow!

Niven sat forward in his chair. 'I'm guessing there are other ways that you can attend too?'

Sarah nodded. 'Of course. If you're incredibly rich, famous, or powerful, then Jamie would make an exception.'

'So, Jamie Parsons made the final decision on who *did* and *didn't* attend the parties?' Niven asked.

'Yes.'

Orchard looked down at his notes. 'You say that these parties would start like any other party. Can you explain when and how they would change?'

Sarah paused for a moment to think. 'I suppose when it got towards midnight, things started to happen. The venue always had a lot of side rooms. They were furnished with enormous beds and sofas. And couples used to go off to these rooms and … start to have sex.'

'With each other?' Niven asked to clarify.

'Sometimes,' Sarah said. 'But sometimes with other couples.'

'So, what you might call *swinging*?' Orchard said.

Sarah nodded. 'Yes.'

Niven sniffed, rubbed his nose, and then glanced over at her. 'But if you were very rich, famous or powerful, and you had come alone, how might that work?'

'Jamie always invited a selection of single women, along with high-end escorts, to the parties. If you were on

Jamie's VIP list, then you could be matched up with one of these women or an escort.'

'Now you say that there were *single women*. However, it is my understanding that some of them were actually teenagers?' Orchard asked, looking for confirmation.

Sarah hesitated and then said, 'Yes.'

Orchard shifted in his seat. 'Would you say that the majority of the women, or girls, that Jamie Parsons invited to these parties were teenagers?'

'They were young,' Sarah admitted. 'But I know some of them were in their early 20s too.'

'When you say *young*, how young do you think some of the girls at these parties might have been?'

'It's hard to say. And Jamie never checked anyone's age. But I suppose some of them might have been sixteen or seventeen.' Sarah was feeling quite uncomfortable about what she had allowed herself to become involved with. 'They always looked older, so it was hard to tell.'

'And Jamie would set up introductions between these girls, or young women, and those that were on his VIP list?'

'Yes.'

Orchard peered over at Niven and then asked, 'And you saw this happen?'

'Yes. Lots of times,' Sarah said.

'What type of people would be on this VIP list?'

'Actors, musicians, politicians, footballers. You name it.'

Niven glanced up. 'And what would you be doing while all this was happening?'

'I was with Jamie.'

'Do you mean you were having sex in one of these rooms with Jamie Parsons?'

'No, no.' Sarah shook her head. 'Jamie was the host of

the party. He circulated and made sure that everyone was having a great time and had everything they needed.'

'Drugs?'

'Yes.'

'How would that work?' Orchard asked.

'Jamie had a drug dealer, Theo, whose function at these parties was to sell drugs to anyone who wanted them. Mainly cocaine.'

'And you saw these actors, musicians, politicians, sportsmen buying drugs and having sex with teenage girls?' Niven asked.

Sarah paused for a moment, taking in what Niven had just said.

'Not all of them,' she explained. 'But there were some who liked that kind of thing.'

Niven nodded.

WHILE THE CID TEAM GOT ON WITH VARIOUS LEADS FOR the investigation, Ruth and Nick went down two flights to the Forensic Science labs that were now in an annexe at the rear of the station. Two white-coated technicians were scooping mud from the plastic containers, mixing it with water, and then sieving it. Any resulting fragments, even the tiniest specks, were being examined.

On one side, the green wellington boot that had been discovered in the lake was under a bright spotlight.

Ruth and Nick put on forensic masks and gloves that were located beside the door and approached to see what had been found.

The older technician had separated various forensic items and lined them up in shallow trays on the bench.

'What have we got?' Ruth asked.

'Some good news,' the technician explained. 'This wellington boot is made by a company called *Le Chameau*.'

Ruth shrugged. 'Is that good?'

'The best,' the technician replied, sounding surprised that she didn't know. 'In fact, the Queen only wears *Le Chameau* wellies. It's the Royals' wellington of choice.'

'Is it indeed?' Nick said dryly.

'Are they easy to get?' Ruth asked, wondering if this might narrow down the identity of their victim.

The technician pulled a face. 'I've checked. The bad news is that you can get them online.'

Well, that doesn't narrow it down at all.

Ruth raised an eyebrow. 'And the good news?'

'The boot is leather lined, which makes it far more difficult to find online,' he said. 'And it means that the pair would have set someone back over £350.'

'So, we're looking for someone with a considerable income if they're willing to spend that on a pair of wellies,' Nick observed.

'And if you're going to spend £350, wouldn't you want to try them on first? I know I would,' Ruth said. 'Let's see how many places in North Wales actually stock *Le Chameau* wellington boots.'

Another technician came over. He had some woven material held in stainless steel tweezers. 'Ma'am, this was stuffed into the end of the boot.'

'What is it?' she asked.

'It's a sock. Size 10, so the same as the foot and the boot,' he explained.

'Anything else?' Nick said.

'Yes. It's made from cashmere,' the technician replied.

Ruth looked at Nick – they were definitely searching for someone who liked the luxurious things in life.

Chapter 9

Taking a sip of water, Sarah sat back in her chair. Recounting the events of November 2013 was more difficult than she had imagined it was going to be. Maybe she had just locked away what she had witnessed that night for so long that dredging it all up was making her very uneasy and emotional.

Niven gave her a sympathetic smile. 'Do you want to take a break? We've been doing this for over an hour now?'

'I'm fine, really.' Sarah shook her head. 'I sort of want to get it over with and get it all off my chest.'

Niven nodded. 'Of course.'

Orchard, who seemed less sympathetic, turned the page of the pad on which he was taking notes. She wondered why he wasn't using a laptop – maybe he was just old-school.

'Can you expand on what you were doing in the minutes leading up to you seeing Lord Weaver in the bedroom on the night of the 1st November 2013?'

'Erm … I was in one of the en suites at the Secret Garden,' she explained.

'And where was this party being held?'

'The Grosvenor Hotel in Kensington.'

'Were you on your own?'

'Yes.'

'What were you doing?'

'Taking cocaine.'

'And then what happened?'

'Before I could get out of the bathroom, I heard some kind of argument in the bedroom. Then there was a scream and some shouting. I opened the door slightly to have a look. A man was on top of a girl on the bed. She couldn't have been more than seventeen …' Sarah's voice broke a little with the emotion of recounting what she had seen.

'And you got a very clear look at this girl?' Niven asked.

'Yes,' Sarah replied. 'I'd seen her several times that night. She was very pretty, but I noticed how young she looked. It made me feel worried.'

Orchard fished a photograph from the folder in front of him. He showed it to her. 'Is this the girl you saw in the room that night?'

Sarah studied it. For a second, she relived the moment she had seen the girl being attacked. The sounds of her screams and the physical struggle echoed in her head. Sarah took a deep breath – she was feeling shaky.

'Sorry, I …'

Niven glanced at her and said gently, 'It's all right. Take your time.'

Peering at the photo again, she looked at the beautiful olive skin and deep brown eyes of the girl she knew was called Gabriella Cardoso. The girl she had seen being raped and murdered.

Ruth had filled her in with what the Met suspected when they got back from Paris. Gabriella was seventeen at the time. She had come to London to work as an au pair for a family in Holland Park. The father was some kind of city hedge funder. She told the family that she was going out with friends in Notting Hill on Friday November 1st 2013, and never came home. There was a police investigation, but there was a suggestion that she might have travelled to Australia to meet up with backpacker friends from Portugal out there. There was no record of her travelling out of the country in the days after her disappearance.

Sarah nodded. 'Yes, that's definitely her.'

'And you saw she was being attacked by a man, is that right?' Niven asked.

'Yes,' Sarah replied. 'I … I thought he was raping her. I was about to go and stop him … but then I realised she had stopped making any sound and wasn't moving. The man had his right hand around her throat … and …'

There were several seconds of silence. She didn't really know what to say next.

'And at this point, you hadn't seen the man who was with this girl?' Orchard asked.

'No.'

'And what did you do then?'

'Nothing. I just froze.' Sarah looked at them as her eyes filled with tears. 'I knew she was dead … I knew he must have strangled her.'

Silence.

'I didn't know what to do,' Sarah whispered, fighting the tremor in her voice. 'And then the room door opened, and four men came in.'

'Did you know them?'

'Yes.' Sarah blinked away the tears. 'It was Jamie Parsons, his friend Jurgen Kessler, Patrice Le Bon, and Sergei Saratov. He's a Russian billionaire who …'

Orchard interrupted her. 'It's all right. I know who all of them are.'

Sarah's eyes widened. 'Even Jurgen Kessler?'

'Yes. What happened next?'

'When they realised the girl was dead, they panicked and argued about what they were going to do about it. Then I saw the man on the bed. I knew it was Lord Weaver because I'd seen him in the papers and on the television. He kept saying it was an accident. He said that he'd had sex with Gabriella before, that she enjoyed being choked during it, and something had gone wrong.'

At the time, she had assumed that Lord Weaver was talking about sexual asphyxiation.

'When you saw them, did it look like a sex game that had gone wrong?'

'No,' Sarah said. 'I definitely heard her scream. She sounded like she was struggling and trying to fight him off.'

'So, your first impression was that Lord Weaver was attacking Gabriella Cordosa, not having consensual sex?' Orchard asked.

'Yes,' Sarah replied. 'I didn't see her for more than a few seconds, but whatever was happening to her, she was distressed and scared. She looked like she was being strangled, and she couldn't breathe.'

For a second, Gabriella's wide frightened eyes and twisted mouth came into Sarah's mind's eye. Taking a deep breath, Sarah tried to stop herself from crying again.

'Sorry … I …' she whispered.

'It's fine, Sarah,' Niven said gently. 'You're doing a brilliant job. What you went through that night and in the years after that has been incredibly traumatic. And what you're telling us today will help us put these men in prison for a very long time.'

That was what she was worried about. What she had witnessed put her in a great deal of danger.

She sipped her water and composed herself.

'Can you tell us what happened next?'

'They agreed it had to be covered up, and they needed to get rid of the girl's body. Lord Weaver was crying and kept repeating that it was a terrible accident …'

'At what point did they realise you were watching what was happening?' Niven said.

'A few minutes later. I was waiting for them all to go, but I knew they weren't going to leave that poor girl there. I must have knocked the lock with my hand or something because Jamie heard a noise and came over. He opened the door fully and saw me standing there in the bathroom. Then all hell broke loose. They talked about what to do with me. Jamie ushered me away to another room. I thought they were going to kill me too.' Sarah's eyes filled with tears again. 'He told me the only way for me to stay alive was to disappear. He would arrange for it to happen, but I couldn't tell anyone. Saratov wanted me to be killed and got rid of, so this was my only option.'

'And what happened after that?'

'Jamie took me to his apartment and told me to wait for him there,' she said. 'Eventually, he came back and explained what he agreed I would do. He told me I had to do exactly what he told me to do, or they would kill me.'

'And what was that?'

Sarah looked over at them. 'I was to go home and pretend that nothing had happened. And then, three days later, I got on a train to Victoria and met Jurgen Kessler. We got off at Vauxhall. A car took me over to the heliport at Battersea, and a helicopter took us across the channel to some place in France.'

'And after that?' Niven asked.

'After that?' Sarah said with a dark expression, 'After that, I was sex trafficked around Europe for the next seven years.'

Chapter 10

I t was late afternoon, and Ruth returned to the CID office with a mug of decent coffee instead of the pigswill from the machine. She had called an impromptu briefing for all CID officers that were in the building to catch up on the day's developments.

'Right, listen up, everyone,' Ruth said as she took a swig of her coffee, realising that it was actually too hot. 'I just want to get everyone up to speed. It might be a bit of a stretch, but I'm wondering if our two cases are now connected.'

'Thought had crossed my mind too, boss.' Georgie nodded as she sat forward in her seat. Ruth liked Georgie's unashamed ambition, and she was a very good copper. However, she was a flirt, which made some of the male officers uncomfortable. She and Nick still had a flirtatious relationship, which she hoped was still only harmless fun.

'You think the foot found in Lake Vyrnwy might be Mark Freudmann?' French asked as he shifted forward in his seat.

'It's a possibility.' Ruth went over to the scene board.

'It's likely that we have a middle-aged white man murdered somewhere around Lake Vyrnwy. And we have someone missing that fits that description.'

Garrow frowned. 'Bella Freudmann claimed her husband had disappeared on several occasions before. He has a gambling problem. She said that he goes on these gambling and drinking benders for a few days and then returns home. I didn't think there was anything suspicious about him disappearing for a few days.'

'Unless she was lying to you,' Ruth said.

'Does she know where he goes on these sprees?' Nick asked.

Garrow nodded. 'Yeah. He's a got a mate who owns a club in Liverpool.'

Nick sat forward in his chair. 'Did you get a name?'

Garrow flicked over a page of his notebook. 'Terry Fowles. Attic nightclub on the Albert Docks.'

Ruth saw Nick visibly bristle at the name. 'Jesus Christ,' he sighed.

'Take it you know Fowles, or you've heard of him?' Ruth asked.

'Oh yeah,' Nick said knowingly. 'He's an associate of Curtis Blake.'

There were a few murmurs of recognition from some of the older detectives.

Curtis Blake was a powerful Liverpudlian drug dealer who Nick had encountered frequently. They had a dark history going back to when Nick was a PC on the beat. A few years earlier, Blake had bribed a detective sergeant in Llancastell CID to provide information – it had resulted in that officer's death. There was little love lost between Blake and the North Wales Police force.

'Is Blake still in Rhoswen?' Ruth asked.

HMP Rhoswen was a new 'super prison' in North

Wales and the last she knew, Blake was in there serving time for drug offences.

'As far as I know,' Nick replied. 'But if Mark Freudmann is a friend or associate of Fowles, then that makes his disappearance a little more suspicious.'

Ruth caught Garrow's eye. 'Jim, can you and Georgie go up to Liverpool first thing tomorrow, track down Fowles and see if he's seen Mark recently? It's probably worth talking to the Merseyside OCP. See if Mark Freudmann is on their radar at all.'

The Merseyside Organised Crime Partnership was a specialist team set up by the National Crime Agency and Merseyside Police to tackle organised crime groups. Their principal objective was to stop drugs and firearms being bought and sold, as well as the growing problem of County Lines networks.

'Yes, guv,' Garrow said as he scribbled in his notebook. Even though he had a slight nerdiness about him, Ruth was very fond of Jim and his sharp, methodical approach to detective work.

Nick, who had been tapping at a computer, turned the screen for everyone to see. It was a photo of a thickset, tough looking man in his 50s. 'This is Terry Fowles.'

Georgie went over, took out her phone, and photographed the image. 'Thanks, Sarge.'

Ruth pointed to the photo of the wellington boot. 'They found this boot close to where we found the severed foot. It's a *Le Chameau*.'

French pulled a face. 'A Le what?'

'*Le Chameau*. Apparently, it's the Rolls Royce of wellies,' Nick joked.

'It's what the royal family wears,' Ruth explained. 'It's the same size as the foot and leather lined. And it will set you back over £350 for a pair.'

'Bloody hell,' Georgie muttered.

'From the looks of it, you can only buy them in a couple of shops in the area. And we've got a serial number. Let's see if we can track it down,' Ruth suggested. 'We also found a cashmere sock that had been shoved down the end of the boot. It's also a size 10. So, we're looking for someone who has a lot of money and likes the best that money can buy.'

'You should see the Freudmann's house, boss,' Georgie said. 'It's an incredible place. And Bella Freudmann was wearing a Burberry hoodie. I've just checked online, and they're £850. She and Mark have very expensive tastes.'

'And we've got the next-door neighbour, Valerie Simpson, who claims she saw Mark and Bella rowing a few days before he disappeared,' Garrow added.

Ruth raised an eyebrow and then took a board pen. 'Do we have the exact time and day of this row?'

Garrow flicked the pages back in his notebook. 'Last Thursday. The 21st. Mark and Bella were sitting by the fire pit outside. Bella threw a glass at Mark. And then Bella's brother, Frank, came out to try and calm things down.'

'And that was the last time she saw Mark Freudmann?' Nick asked.

Georgie nodded. 'Yeah. I get the feeling that Valerie Simpson is a bit of a curtain-twitcher, if you know what I mean? She spotted us pretty sharpish when we left the Freudmanns' house.'

'What's the deal with the brother?' Ruth said.

'Apparently, he's been through a nasty divorce, and he's staying with Bella,' Garrow explained.

Ruth rubbed her chin. 'Have we done any background or PNC checks on them yet?'

Georgie shook her head. 'Not yet, boss. But I did Google them to see what came up.'

'Anything interesting?' Nick asked.

'All their money comes from her side of the family,' Georgie explained. 'Her dad, Charlie Collard, owns four of the largest pig farms across North and West Wales. He's a multimillionaire.'

Nick raised an eyebrow. 'Pig farms?'

'Hey, there's a lot of money in bacon and sausages, Nick,' Georgie said. 'Especially if you own 18,000 pigs.'

Nick gave a sarcastic smile. 'And that might explain why they can afford Le Chameau wellies.'

French came marching into CID. 'Phone call from the Marine Unit, boss. They've found something else in the lake.'

Chapter 11

Having sent the whole CID team home, Ruth had made her way out to Lake Vyrnwy on her own in the darkness of early evening. As she turned the corner to the lake, she had to apply the brakes as she was met with an impenetrable blanket of fog.

Jesus. I can't see a bloody thing, she thought.

Now crawling at around 5 mph, she drove along the road that surrounded the lake, heading for where she knew there was a car park. She became aware of bright lights coming from down by the shore, close to where Amis had shown her the foot and the wellington boot. It must be where the Marine Unit and the SOCOs were based. She turned left into the tourist car park, saw the dark outline of a police van, and parked carefully beside it.

How the hell am I going to find my way down to the water? she wondered.

She got out of the car, locked the door, and the orange flash of the indicators coloured the thick mist for a second.

It was so quiet that all she could hear was the sound of her own breathing. She walked carefully out of the car park towards where the arc lighting was coming from. The sound of her own footsteps on the gravel seemed loud in the silence. Then suddenly, a grating, piercing noise. It sounded like a woman screaming.

What the bloody hell is that? she thought, now a little startled.

Glancing up to the sky, she squinted and realised it was the squawk of an enormous bird flying above her towards the fog-strewn treetops.

Now feeling decidedly unsettled, Ruth crossed the road and found herself on the edge of the wooded area that led down to the water's edge. The damp mist had enveloped everything. She heard a shout and then the sound of someone wading through the water.

'Hello?' she shouted as she carefully took a few steps down the muddy bank.

She was getting closer to the water, and the fog had become damp and musty. It hung around the trees like thick cobwebs and had a distinct, watery smell.

'We're down this way!' came the shout of a voice.

Yeah, that doesn't bloody help me! she thought, getting frustrated.

She was now unnerved and disorientated – *if I'm not careful, I'm going to walk straight into that sodding lake.*

'DI Hunter, is that you?' called a voice she recognised. It was Tony Amis.

'Tony?' she growled. 'I can't see a fucking thing!'

'All part of the fun,' Amis joked.

Suddenly, one of the enormous halogen lights arced around and lit up the bank she was walking down.

Out of the swirling mist came a figure.

'And tonight, Matthew, I'm going to be Midge Ure,' Amis said, mimicking a British TV show where contestants appeared out of thick, dry ice as their favourite pop stars.

And, if memory served Ruth correctly, bore no resemblance to them.

'Bloody hell! Don't you ever get down, depressed or
even scared, Tony?' Ruth laughed as Amis drew closer,
taking off his mask to reveal his customary smirk.

'Only if England loses the Ashes, I'm afraid,' he said
with a shrug. 'My wife says my cheerfulness is churlish and
infantile.'

Ruth thought she was probably right, but she wanted
to get on with the investigation. 'What have the Marine
Unit found?'

'A section of leg from the knee joint to the groin,' Amis
explained.

'Same victim?' she asked.

Amis shrugged. 'Hard to tell until I get it back to the
lab. But it looks like it's going to be the same. Male,
Caucasian, and middle-aged.'

Ruth took a few seconds and then said, 'What the hell
is going on, Tony? Why has it taken us several days to find
another body part?'

'Could be the undercurrents,' Amis suggested.
'Although, if these body parts had all been thrown in
together, they would all be floating on the surface now. And
the Marine Unit has been across the lake dozens of times.'

'You think this section of the leg could have been
thrown into the lake at a different time?' Ruth was
bewildered.

'That would be one explanation.'

'But that means someone has been to the lake since
we've been searching it and thrown this body part in with
no one noticing.'

'Think about how long and wide this lake is, detective,'
Amis pointed out. 'It's not beyond the realm of possibility.'

'No, I suppose not … Maybe this is someone's idea of

a sick joke,' Ruth said, thinking aloud. 'Cut up the victim and then throw a part of the body into the lake every few days?'

Amis gave her a dark look. 'I've got a horrible feeling that might explain why we've only found it tonight.'

Ruth got an uneasy feeling – were they now dealing with some unhinged killer who was playing games with the police by spacing out dumping the remains of his victim like some horrendous jigsaw puzzle.

`

Chapter 12

It was dark and raining as Nick parked outside his house. He got out of the car and opened the back door. Megan, who was strapped into the car seat, grinned up at him.

'Daddy!' she cried with a grin as if she hadn't seen him in days.

They had been to the supermarket while Amanda went and picked up Fran and brought her back for them to spend time together. Nick felt a little nervous as he wondered how it was going. He hoped they were getting on.

Taking Megan in his arms, Nick grabbed a shopping bag from the back seat, went to the front door, and let himself into the house.

'Hello?' he called in a cheerful voice.

Putting Megan down on the floor, he watched as she toddled down the hallway and into the living room. He could hear the sound of talking, laughter, and music playing.

Sounds like it's going well.

He went into the kitchen and spent five minutes putting away the shopping. It would allow Amanda to introduce Megan to Fran.

With the fridge neatly stacked, Nick made his way back into the hallway and slowly pushed open the door to the living room.

A young, willowy girl with dyed black and blue hair sat on the sofa with Amanda. She had dark eye make-up, which made her eyes seem large.

'Hey, we were wondering where you had got to,' Amanda said with a smile.

'Dutifully putting away the shopping, darling,' he laughed.

'I've got him well-trained,' Amanda said to the girl. 'This is my better half, Nick … This is Fran.'

Nick smiled. 'Nice to meet you.'

'Yeah,' Fran said with a confident smile. 'You too. Amanda's been telling me all about you.'

'Oh God,' Nick groaned as he sat down in the armchair. 'It's all lies.'

'Don't worry. It was all very nice,' Fran laughed. 'I love your house. It's so cosy.'

Wow, she is very self-assured for an eighteen-year-old.

Amanda looked at Nick. 'Fran has been telling me all about her mum and dad. Paul and Caroline. They're both teachers.'

'Secondary or Primary?' Nick asked.

'They both teach in the local comprehensive,' Fran explained.

Amanda pulled a face. 'I don't envy them that job.'

'It's a pretty decent school,' Fran said. 'The head doesn't tolerate the knobheads.'

Nick laughed as he studied Fran's face. He was beginning to recognise her from somewhere. The hair was different, but he was sure he'd met her before somewhere. Given his job, the thought was making him feel uneasy.

'Rather than get the last train,' Amanda said. 'I told Fran that she's more than welcome to stay on the sofa, and I'll drop her home in the morning.'

'Sounds good,' Nick said, but he was racking his brains about where he had encountered Fran before.

SARAH ENTERED HER LIVING ROOM WITH A TRAY. ON IT were two mugs of steaming tea and a plate of expensive biscuits for her guest. She could still smell where she had cleaned the house from top to bottom, scrubbing every surface with disinfectant. Now, with the ceiling lights burning bright, and the chipped paint and time-worn tiles noticeably visible, it seemed her work had counted for very little. It was frustrating. She was aware that cleaning and tidying had become a coping mechanism to the point of obsession. But having everything neat, ordered, and clean made her feel calm, so she didn't care. It was better than using heroin, which had been her previous coping mechanism, she thought.

The house provided by the UK Protected Person's Scheme – the UKPPS – was close to the tiny village of Hanmer, but it was actually in the middle of nowhere. It was small and tidy. The rooms were dated, antiquated, and from another age, probably the 70s, she thought. It even had an archetypal avocado bathroom suite. The walls were marked with scuffs and flaking paintwork. The roller blinds looked like they had been stained with cigarette smoke. She had resolved to replace them as soon as she could afford to. The doors creaked onerously as they were opened, which spooked her late at night.

Sarah couldn't complain. After some of the more soulless, characterless apartments she had experienced while being held by Le Bon and Saratov, a small, cosy Welsh cottage was a dream come true. Ruth had helped her make the place homely, even though she spent nearly every night at Ruth's home with her. They had lost too much time already. However, part of the stipulation of being in the UKPPS was that she had a designated UK residence.

Sitting on the sofa was Maggie Pryce, who worked for the Protected Person Service. She was late 40s, smartly dressed with brown wavy hair and fashionable glasses. She spoke with the hint of a Scottish accent – maybe Glaswegian, Sarah thought.

Maggie had made her way over from Manchester, where she was based. Until now, Sarah had been passed from pillar to post by the police, MI5, and PPS. However, Maggie had reassured her on the phone that she was now her permanent point of contact.

The UKPPS had recently become more centralised under the leadership of the NCA – the National Crime Agency. However, Sarah had been told she was a unique case given both the nature of the crime she had witnessed and the status of the man she had seen commit the crime – i.e. a peer of the realm. And the international nature of the other men she had seen trying to cover up the murder.

'Here you go,' Sarah said, putting the tea down on the wobbly table beside the patterned armchair in which Maggie was sitting.

Sarah went over and sat down on the sofa and gave an awkward smile.

'So, are you technically my *handler*?' she asked as she took a sip of her tea.

Maggie smiled back. 'I wouldn't say handler. That's a term someone might use when dealing with an informant.'

'Oh, okay,' Sarah said with a self-effacing laugh. 'I must have seen it on a TV programme.'

'I'm your point of contact while you are within the PPS,' Maggie explained. 'Anything you need, any concerns, anything at all, you just pick up the phone. Seriously. I had a woman ring me because she had a flat tyre and didn't know how to fix it or who to call.'

'Thanks,' Sarah said. 'That's really good to know. Although I should let you know, I can actually change a tyre.'

'That's impressive because I can't,' Maggie chortled before reaching down into her briefcase and taking out a notebook. 'While I'm here, I need to clarify a few things for our records.' She turned over a few pages and glanced over at Sarah. 'Your family is from Doncaster, is that right?'

For a split second, Sarah saw the market town close to where she had grown up. It was famous for its coal and horse racing, which is why Sarah had headed south to London as soon as she could. It occurred to her she hadn't thought of South Yorkshire for a long time.

'Yes. Well, actually a little village called Hickleton, which is in the West Riding part of South Yorkshire and everyone says *'Ow do?'* she joked, in a thick Yorkshire accent. 'But Doncaster is the nearest place anyone has ever heard of.'

Maggie smiled and then pushed her glasses up the bridge of her nose. 'And I have down here that you were an only child? Is that correct?'

'Yes,' Sarah replied with a grin. 'I'm a classic *only child*. Spoiled, selfish, maladjusted. And those are my good qualities.'

I really do make a lot of jokes when I'm nervous, don't I?

'I'm an only child, so I know how that goes.' Maggie laughed. 'And it's just your mum, is it? Doreen?'

'Yeah,' Sarah said. The emotion of thinking about her mother hit her like a train. Her poor mum, who still thought she was missing. She couldn't imagine how she must be feeling.

Even though Sarah had been adamant when she returned to the UK that they needed to let her mother know she was alive and well, Special Branch, MI5, and the PPS had insisted that while Sarah was giving her evidence, her existence as an eyewitness needed to be kept a secret. If the men involved in covering up Gabriella Cardoso's murder knew Sarah was in the UK and giving her testimony to the police, then anyone close to her was at risk. They could threaten her loved ones in order to force her to keep her mouth shut. It was safer for her mum that she still believed Sarah was missing, however hard that was to deal with.

The PPS had also promised that if the Crown Prosecution Service agreed that there was enough evidence to charge Lord Weaver with killing Gabriella Cardoso, and charge the other men with conspiracy to pervert the course of justice, then Sarah could contact Doreen and she would also be afforded Witness Protection under the PPS.

'And you understand that while you are giving evidence prior to any charges being brought, you must not contact your mother?' Maggie said with a serious expression.

Sarah nodded sadly. 'Yes.'

Maggie gave her a sympathetic look. 'And I know that's difficult in your case because your mum still believes that you went missing seven years ago.'

'Yeah,' Sarah said with a sigh. 'I just don't want her to suffer any more. If she knew I was alive and well, that would give her a huge amount of relief.'

Maggie narrowed her eyes. 'But it would also put her in

danger. And we can't promise to protect her until we know we can press charges and go to trial.'

'It doesn't really make any sense to me,' Sarah admitted. 'I could tell her I'm okay and to promise not to tell anyone else.'

Maggie shook her head. 'It only takes her to tell one person, a friend or a relative. I've seen it before. Everyone tells someone else and tells them to keep it quiet. It pops up on social media, and then the press and the entire world knows. And then your mum, and anyone you're close to, is in danger. The last anyone knows is that you boarded a Eurostar train. And then you vanished. And we want to keep it that way.'

Sarah nodded. She understood, but it had been something she was struggling with on a daily basis. 'Yes. Sorry. I'm just finding it difficult.'

'Of course, you are,' Maggie said. 'But this is for the best. And when the men are charged, you can contact her.' Maggie sipped her tea and then looked down at her notebook. 'We have allowed you to maintain contact with a Detective Inspector Ruth Hunter?'

'Yes.'

'And she understands the constraints of your contact with each other?'

'Yes,' Sarah replied.

'How are your neighbours?'

There was a bungalow, about 500 yards down the track where she lived where a lovely, retired couple lived.

'Fine,' Sarah replied. 'Keep themselves to themselves. We say hello, but that's about it.'

'And so far, you've not seen anyone or anything that has aroused your suspicion that your true identity has been compromised?'

'No. Nothing.'

'And you understand how to use the panic buttons?' Maggie asked.

The PPS had installed three panic buttons in the house – hallway, kitchen, and bedroom – so that if Sarah was scared for her safety, she could just hit the alarm, and the police would be alerted.

'Yes,' Sarah said.

After a few seconds, Maggie gave her a benign smile. 'We're going to get you through all this, Sarah. And there will be times when you'll think that all this is horribly unfair. And it is horribly unfair. But by being so brave and giving us your testimony, you are putting a stop to a handful of very powerful, rich, and abusive men who have destroyed hundreds of women and girls' lives. And you're getting justice for them. You need to remember that.'

Sarah nodded, feeling the weight and gravity of what she was doing.

Chapter 13

Tuesday 26th January

IT WAS GONE TEN BY THE TIME GARROW PULLED THE CAR into a car park at Albert Dock in Liverpool. Georgie glanced around. She loved Liverpool – especially since all the regeneration and gentrification had smoothed some of the rougher edges of the city.

Over to the left, she spotted the large bronze statues of The Beatles over by the Pierhead. Her taid, Alwyn Wild, used to bring her to Liverpool on her birthday every year when she was a child. Her nain – Welsh for grandmother – took her shopping while Alwyn met up with some old pals for a pint and to talk about the old days. He had worked as a plasterer on the development and regeneration of the Royal Albert Dock in the 70s and 80s.

Alwyn also claimed that he and his best friend Eryl had attended the last concert The Beatles ever played in

Liverpool. It was the 5th December 1965 at the Empire Theatre. They had only been in their 20s and had spent the whole day hitching lifts over to Liverpool from Llancastell. Alwyn told her that The Beatles had played tracks from the greatest album ever recorded – *Rubber Soul*. Georgie had been more into bands like the *Sugababes* and *McFly*. In more recent years, she had listened to The Beatles, agreeing with her taid that they were an incredible band.

Opening the car door, Georgie was immediately hit by the icy wind that blew in from the Mersey. There was a slightly unpleasant smell of the river in the air as gulls swooped and cawed noisily overhead.

Garrow had called the Attic nightclub trying to track down Terry Fowles. The person answering the phone had been very cagey but confirmed that someone would be there that morning and that they would contact Fowles to tell him that detectives from North Wales police wished to speak to him.

'This has changed so much since I was a kid,' Garrow said, indicating the Albert Docks as they made their way across the car park and towards the club.

Georgie pulled up her collar against the wind. 'Yeah. I was just thinking the same. My nain and taid used to bring me up here on my birthday every year. He once showed me a photograph he took of this place when he worked here in the 70s. There was nothing here. All these warehouses were empty and derelict.'

Garrow raised an eyebrow. 'And now you can get a skinny macchiato, a designer handbag, and stay at a Malmaison hotel.'

'Malmaison? Get you,' Georgie joked as she teased him.

'You need to remember that I'm very middle class,'

Garrow said with an exaggerated posh accent. 'I don't *do* Premier Inns.'

Georgie laughed as they moved past a series of bars and restaurants that were now closed.

Arriving at the door to The Attic nightclub, she pressed the intercom buzzer.

'Can I help?' came a friendly woman's voice with a thick Scouse accent.

'North Wales Police,' Georgie said. 'We spoke to someone earlier.'

'Oh yeah, that was me,' chirped the voice.

A few seconds later, the black door opened and a woman in her late 30s looked at them. She had bleached blonde hair extensions, lots of make-up, trout pout – the lot.

She has Scouse Wag written all over her, Georgie thought.

The woman gave them a cheery grin. 'Hiya.' It wasn't often they were greeted like that.

Garrow flashed his warrant card. 'We're from Llan-castell CID. I spoke to someone earlier.'

'That was me, chuck,' she said in a tone that was verging on flirty. 'I'm Debs … You're not how I imagined you on the phone. Much younger and much better looking.'

Bloody hell, she's pretty full on!

Garrow seemed awkward as Georgie gave him a smirk.

'We're hoping that we can have a word with Terry Fowles,' Georgie explained, moving the subject along.

Debs raised one of her thick eyebrows. 'I'm not sure if Terry's in yet. D'you wanna come in and get out of the cold? It's bleedin' freezin' out there.'

They followed her inside, down a dark corridor, and then up a flight of stairs. The décor was dark, and the warm air smelt of stale alcohol and cheap perfume.

'Come and park yourselves in here,' Debs said as she indicated a small, cluttered office with a low black sofa and some assorted chairs. 'If it's something to do with the club, I'm the manager, so I might be able to help.'

Georgie and Garrow exchanged a look. In Georgie's books, the more people they spoke to, the more likely it was that they would get to the truth. A lot of police work relied on the concept of *provable lies*. Concentrate on probing one suspect's account – and then compare with another's.

A quick look from Garrow confirmed he was happy for them to divulge the nature of their visit.

'We're actually looking for a man called Mark Freudmann,' Georgie explained.

'Mark?' Debs asked and immediately reacted with a smile. She clearly knew him.

'I take it you know Mark Freudmann?' Garrow asked, reaching for his notebook and pen.

'I've known Mark for years. Right little scallywag,' Debs said with a knowing smile. 'That man could charm the birds from the trees. And the pants off half the women in Liverpool.' She gave a throaty cackle. 'But I didn't tell you that, eh? I know he's married.'

'Can you remember the last time you saw him?' Georgie asked.

Debs frowned for a few seconds. 'At least two months ago, if not three.'

Garrow looked at her. 'Are you sure he wasn't at the club last week at any point?'

'No. I would have seen him.' Debs shook her head as she reached for her pink vape pen and took a drag. 'And Terry would have told me Mark was in.'

Blowing the vape smoke, Georgie got a waft of its pungent strawberry smell.

Debs gestured to the corridor outside. 'Let me check if Terry's in yet.'

A few seconds after Debs had disappeared, Georgie got up from her seat. 'What do you think?'

'Doesn't sound like he's been up here, does it?' Garrow said. 'But it sounds like Mark is a bit of ladies' man.'

'Maybe that's what he and Bella were rowing about. Maybe she found out that he'd been playing away in Liverpool,' Georgie suggested.

Garrow frowned. 'So she chopped him up into pieces and chucked him into Lake Vyrnwy?'

Georgie shrugged as she wandered over to a window on the far side of the office. 'You never know. If he was gambling away their money *and* cheating on her, that's a decent motive for murder.'

From the window, Georgie peered across the car park towards the Liverpool One shopping centre. A group of 20-something women, laden down with shopping bags, came out of the shopping centre. She didn't understand the whole concept of *going shopping*. In fact, she couldn't think of a worse use of her spare time.

Out of the corner of her eye, she spotted a figure marching away across the car park towards Strand Street. She recognised him from somewhere. Then it came to her.

Terry Fowles.

She had seen him on Nick's computer screen in the CID office.

'Shit!' she snapped as she raced for the door.

'What's going on?' Garrow asked with a perplexed expression.

'I've just spotted Terry Fowles doing a bloody runner across the car park,' Georgie yelled as she sprinted from the office and down the stairs.

Opening the door, she ran towards the car park. She

was trying to work out where Fowles was going and why he had decided to run. Debs must have tipped him off – *what a bitch!*

Now running flat out, Fowles must have sensed her presence because he spun around and saw her running after him.

There was the sound of an irate driver pumping their horn as Fowles darted through the traffic. Up ahead was a three storey, glass-fronted gym, fitness suite, and café .

Oh, bollocks, he's going in there.

She watched as Fowles ran into the building and disappeared.

Thirty seconds later, Georgie arrived at the gym and fitness centre reception. Sucking in a breath, she stopped running and looked around. Her chest was burning, and her shoes were now rubbing the back of her feet. The building smelled of deodorant and herbal tea.

The irony of being this out of breath in a fitness centre wasn't lost on her.

Jesus, I'm unfit!

Glancing around, she spotted several people dressed in sports gear waiting for the lift. To the left of that were glass double doors to a staircase. It was a fair bet he had taken the stairs.

Going through the doors to the stairwell, Georgie stopped, listened, and heard movement from higher up – it was the sound of someone running.

Where the hell is he going?

Picking up the pace, Georgie reached out and held onto the black handrail to keep her balance. Her head was swimming from the effort of chasing him.

The sound of movement and of doors opening came echoing from above.

Georgie yelled – her voice reverberating around the

stairwell. 'Terry! Just stop. We want to ask you a couple of questions, that's all.'

She took the steps two at a time, gasping for breath again as she went. The muscles in her thighs began to burn. She wasn't about to let him disappear.

The staircase ended.

There was a door out to the gym and leisure complex's car park, which was open air and on the roof. As she opened the door, a swirling gust of wind blew against her.

'What the fuck do you want?' growled a voice.

A figure appeared from behind a nearby wall.

It was Terry Fowles.

For a second, Georgie wasn't sure whether she should be scared. Fowles didn't look like he was about to attack her. In fact, he seemed very relaxed.

'What are you running for?' Georgie asked as she took out her warrant card and showed him.

Fowles shrugged. 'I don't like bizzies.'

Georgie fixed him with a stare. 'Yeah, well, I've got a few questions for you, so I'd like you to come with me.'

Fowles raised an eyebrow. 'I take it that's not a friendly request?'

Georgie shook her head. 'Not now you've made me chase you. You're lucky I don't put you in cuffs.'

Chapter 14

Ruth and Nick strode purposefully along the main street in Betwys-y-Coed, a town that many saw as the gateway to Snowdonia. With its alpine atmosphere, it stood in a valley where the River Llugwy and the River Lledr joined the River Conwy. It was also the only place they could find in North Wales that stocked the exclusive *Le Chameau* wellington boots they had found in Lake Vyrnwy.

'Did you meet Amanda's daughter last night?' Ruth asked as they scanned the high street for *The Outdoor Warehouse*.

'Yeah, Fran,' he said.

'How was that?' she asked.

'She seems really nice,' Nick replied. 'Very confident.'

Ruth looked at him – there was something he wasn't telling her. 'But?'

'I'm convinced I know her from somewhere,' Nick said. 'I just can't place her face. But my instinct is that she was involved in something dodgy.'

'Did you tell Amanda?'

Nick shook his head. 'No. I can't tell her anything until I actually remember where it is I know her from.'

They stopped outside *The Outdoor Warehouse*. The window was full of expensive, colourful walking jackets and other clothing equipment.

They went in and approached the counter where a man with a ponytail was thumbing through a catalogue.

Ruth flashed her warrant card. 'DI Hunter and DS Evans from Llancastell CID.'

'Oh, right.' The man nodded seriously as he looked up at them. 'Erm, how can I help?'

Taking out his phone, Nick opened up a photograph of the *Le Chameau* wellington boot they had found in the lake. 'Can you tell us if you stock this type of boot?'

The man peered at the image for a second and then nodded. 'Yes. It's a leather lined, men's Saint-Hubert, Heritage wellington boot.'

Christ, that's a bloody mouthful! I got my wellies from George at Asda, she thought dryly.

Nick frowned. 'And you can tell all that from this photo?'

'They're a very distinctive type of boot,' the man said, getting a little haughty. 'And very expensive.'

'Do you sell very many?' Ruth asked.

'No, not a lot,' the man said.

Nick looked at him. 'And we understand that this shop is one of the few stockists in North Wales?'

'That's right.' He was clearly proud of that fact.

Nick flicked to another photo. 'If I show you the serial number on the sole of the boot, can you look at your records and tell me if you sold this actual boot?'

The man nodded. 'Yes. We have a record of all our Le Chameau purchases. They have a two-year warranty.'

'And you would have the name of the person who

purchased the boots, then?' Ruth asked, hoping that this might give them a decent lead.

'Yes.' The man went to the computer at the other end of the counter and tapped away. 'If you can show me the serial number again, please?'

Nick went over and said, 'It's 7536-2930221.'

After a few seconds, the man nodded. 'Yes, we sold those boots to a customer last year.'

'Can we have their name?' Ruth asked.

The man looked at them. 'Mark Freudmann.'

Georgie and Garrow had taken Terry Fowles to St Anne Street Police Station in Liverpool. Even though he wasn't under arrest, they had made it very clear that he needed to give them an interview under caution.

The interview room was chilly and in need of a fresh coat of paint. The dark green carpet was stained by what Georgie hoped was tea or coffee – and not blood.

With his legs crossed, Fowles gave an audible sigh as Georgie pulled in her chair as they prepared to start the interview.

'Boring you, are we Terry?' Georgie asked.

'Would have been a lot easier if we could have done this at your club, rather than you doing a runner,' Garrow said.

Garrow waited for a few seconds and then asked, 'What did you run for Terry?'

Fowles shrugged. 'I've told her already. I don't like bizzies.'

Georgie snorted. 'What? So, every time you see a police officer, you leg it? You run a nightclub, Terry. You must have contact with the police all the time?'

'I know all the bizzies round here, don't I?' Fowles rolled his eyes. 'I don't recognise you two.'

Garrow frowned. 'If you've got nothing to hide, why does that make you nervous?'

Fowles narrowed his eyes aggressively. 'I don't know where you grew up, but round here, bizzies were the enemy, you know what I mean? I was taught, if in doubt you get away on your toes, and answer questions later.'

'Okay,' Georgie said. 'Now's your chance. We're trying to find a man called Mark Freudmann. We understand that he's a friend of yours?'

'Yeah, he is. So what?' Fowles growled. 'Is that it?'

'He's been missing since last Thursday,' Garrow explained. 'And his wife seems to think that he has a habit of disappearing up here and staying with you.'

'Is that Bella? Christ! Don't believe a word that bitch tells you,' Fowles snapped. 'She's not right. She's a fucking psycho.'

Garrow shifted forward in his seat. 'Have you seen Mark in the last few days?'

'No,' Fowles replied. 'Not a peep.'

'Can you tell us the last time you did see Mark?' Garrow asked.

'Couple of months. I've had a few texts about the footie and that. But he's not been up here for a while. How long did you say he'd been missing?'

'Since last Thursday,' Georgie said.

Fowles appeared to be a little uneasy as he took in what they had told him.

Garrow looked up from writing in his notepad. 'Can you tell us where you were last Thursday evening?'

'In my club,' Fowles replied with a withering look. 'Thursday is student night, so it's always packed.'

'And you have people who will verify that?' Garrow asked.

Fowles nodded. 'Of course. Security staff, bar staff, take your pick.'

Something that Fowles had said a minute earlier bothered Georgie.

'I take it you don't like Bella Freudmann?' Georgie asked.

'No. I don't,' Fowles snorted.

'You said she was *a psycho*. What do you mean by that?'

'She's not right in the head,' Fowles replied. 'She has these temper tantrums and goes crazy.'

Garrow glanced over. 'Has she ever been violent towards Mark?'

Fowles gave an expression as though this was a stupid question. 'Loads of times. Don't you know?'

Georgie shrugged. 'Know what?'

'Last year, she took a baseball bat to him,' he said. 'Broke his jaw and put him in hospital for a week.'

Georgie exchanged a look with Garrow.

Looks like we need to have another word with Bella Freudmann.

Chapter 15

The CID office at Llancastell was busy with officers at computers or using phones. As Ruth wandered through, heading for her corner office, she remembered how tedious and time-consuming police work had been in the 90s when she was just a detective constable. You would get a tip-off of a suspect with a surname *Harvey*. Then you would have to plough through the London phone directory, ringing everyone in the area with that surname. If the line was busy, you sat and waited before redialling. When you eventually got through, the routine was always the same. *Mr Harvey. I'm a detective constable based at Peckham Police Station, and I'm carrying out some routine inquiries. I wonder if you can help me. Did you ever live at number seventy-five Garland Avenue, Catford? … No? Okay, thanks for your help today.* Tick the name off the list and start again. What they would have given for the wonders of the internet and the ability to access addresses, records, and hidden information within seconds.

'Boss,' said a voice. It was Nick. He was carrying some printouts with him.

'Come and sit down.' Ruth wandered into her office. She sat down in her swivel chair and tilted her head to look at him. 'What have we got?'

'Mobile phone records for Mark Freudmann,' he said, gesturing to the papers he was holding.

'Anything interesting?' she asked.

'Last activity on his mobile number was a text on Thursday afternoon.'

Ruth raised an eyebrow. 'And nothing since that?'

'No, nothing.' Nick shook his head. 'And looking back at his records, he was using his phone for calls or texts at least ten to fifteen times a day prior to last Thursday.'

Ruth pulled a face. 'Yeah, that doesn't sound good, does it?'

'No, boss,' he replied. 'His bank records came over this morning, and they show the same.'

'No activity?'

'Last withdrawal was the cashpoint at the HSBC in Dolgellau last Wednesday night. He withdrew two hundred pounds.'

Ruth crossed her legs and frowned. 'We need to do a DNA match between the foot we've got and Mark Freudmann's DNA. I hope we can get something from the house as I don't want to be the one to ask the Deputy Chief Constable for a familial DNA swab.'

'No,' Nick agreed. 'We don't believe in coincidences, do we? So, if it's his boot in the water, then it's his foot too. If we combine that with his phone and bank activity, then there's only one thing we can conclude.'

Ruth gave him a dark look. 'Mark Freudmann is dead, and someone dumped him in Lake Vyrnwy. Now we just have to work out who put him there.'

. . .

Having released Fowles, Georgie and Garrow were now sitting in a side office upstairs at St Ann Street Police Station with DCI Kevin Finnan, who was heading up the Merseyside Organised Crime Partnership.

Finnan was blond, with milky skin and quick, intelligent eyes. Georgie immediately fancied him and looked for a wedding ring. There wasn't one.

Mmm, interesting.

'What's the interest in Terry Fowles?' Finnan asked as he sat back in his chair. He had an air of quiet authority that Georgie found very attractive.

I wonder what he's like in bed, she thought.

'It's not really Fowles we're looking at,' Georgie explained.

Garrow took out a phone, found a photo of Mark Freudmann, and showed him. 'We're looking for this man. Mark Freudmann. He went missing at the end of last week, and no one's seen him since.'

Finnan frowned. 'He's been missing for four or five days, and you're already up here snooping around. Bit premature, isn't it?'

Georgie looked at him. 'You've heard of Deputy Chief Constable Susanna Freudmann?'

'Only by reputation.' Finnan pulled a face. 'I think the polite way it was put to me was that she doesn't suffer fools.' And then the penny dropped. 'Ah, and this is her son, is it?'

'Got it in one,' Georgie said with her best sexy smile.

'And she's leaning on you to find him?' Finnan chortled darkly.

Garrow leaned forward in his seat. 'Exactly.'

'Sounds like she's worried,' Finnan said.

'I'm not sure,' Georgie said. 'I get the feeling she's overprotective.'

Finnan frowned. 'And you think he's connected with Fowles?'

'Apparently, they're old mates,' Georgie replied.

'Bloody hell!' Finnan laughed. 'I bet his mum loves that. Although in my experience, if you grow up around coppers, you either become one, or you decide to piss everyone off by fraternising with scumbags.'

'Sounds about right. According to his wife, Mark goes on gambling and alcohol benders and ends up spending a few days hiding out with Fowles up here.'

'We've had Fowles under surveillance for 18 months.' Finnan nodded as he peered again at the photo. 'Yeah, I do recognise him. He was wearing a baseball cap. He was up here a few weeks ago. Knocking about with Fowles.' Finnan looked at them after a few seconds. 'That might explain him going missing.'

'Why do you say that?' Garrow asked.

'Fowles has got himself in a very dangerous situation in recent weeks. And if he's not careful, he's going to get himself killed.'

Garrow raised an eyebrow. 'How do you mean?'

'Between the four walls of this office, Fowles owns the Attic club on Albert Dock. He has employed the same security firm to run the door for the past decade. And that security firm is basically run by the Croxteth Crew, who are one of the biggest OCGs in the Merseyside area. If you control the door, you control the drugs,' Finnan explained. 'Four weeks ago, Fowles decided to change security firms, round about the time your mate here turned up in Liverpool. It looks like Fowles decided he would run the door, control the drugs inside, and keep all the money. I don't know if this Mark Freudmann had anything to do with it, but it's a big coincidence if not.'

'I take it this decision didn't go down very well with the Croxteth Crew?' Georgie said.

'No, it didn't,' Finnan said darkly. 'We've got a CHIS on the periphery of the gang.'

CHIS stood for Covert Human Intelligence Source and was police speak for an informant or a grass.

Finnan continued. 'He reckons Terry Fowles is now a dead man walking. And if this Mark Freudmann was somehow involved, then I would suggest his disappearance is suspicious.'

Chapter 16

Sarah walked into her living room with a cup of tea and sat down on the sofa. Even though living in North Wales was beginning to feel normal, she still had moments where she had to pinch herself that it was real. The psychological damage of the last eight years had taken their toll. She had been diagnosed with PTSD; put on the appropriate medication, and Ruth had organised for her to see a trauma counsellor. She had also just stopped taking a low dose of methadone, which she had used to recover from her addiction to heroin. Ruth had suggested that she attend some Narcotics Anonymous meetings – she'd seen how much AA meetings had helped Nick with his addiction to alcohol. Sarah wasn't so keen. Maybe in the future. If she was honest, she was scared to go to a meeting full of strangers and talk about her past. It would make her feel vulnerable. It also occurred to her she wouldn't be able to be completely honest about who she was and what she had been through.

Taking a sip of her tea, Sarah gave a satisfied sigh. There was a wonderful feeling of silence and stillness in the house. As she peered out of the patio doors, she could see a blue tit, with blue cap, white cheeks, black eye stripes, and blue tail and wings. It was pecking at the lawn, looking for food.

Suddenly, there was a noise from the front of the house.

What the hell was that?

Her heart pounded. It sounded like someone was trying to get in through the front door.

What the hell is going on?

Getting up from the sofa, she could feel her breathing getting faster and more shallow.

Another metallic clunk.

Oh my God! Someone's trying to get in!

Running from the living room, she dashed into the kitchen. She frantically opened the cutlery drawers and grabbed a large carving knife.

Treading carefully into the hall, she listened again. The metal of the knife handle was cold in her palm.

Silence.

All she could hear was the throbbing of her pulse in her ear.

Was I imagining things?

PING.

The sound of something metallic landing on the stone floor in the tiny atrium by the front door.

She was feeling physically sick.

Had Le Bon or Saratov found out where she was living? Were there hired assassins trying to break into her home and kill her?

Jesus, what the hell am I going to do?

Grabbing the phone from her pocket, she dialled 999 and waited.

CRASH!

Someone kicked open the front door.

A figure appeared and came into the hallway.

They were wearing a black balaclava and black clothing.

In his right gloved hand was a gun with a silencer attached.

This is it. I'm going to die.

Without thinking, she charged at her would be killer with the carving knife raised above her head.

CRACK!

The sound of a gunshot.

Then blackness.

Sarah woke with a start on the sofa and glanced around.

Her mouth was dry, and her heart racing.

Jesus!

Sitting up on the sofa, she realised she was alive, and the house was silent.

Thank God!

Taking a deep breath, Sarah could feel her pulse slowing. At the moment, she was plagued by nightmares. Her counsellor had told her it was to be expected after all she'd been through. Her subconscious was trying to make sense of the trauma.

Leaning forward, she took her mug from the table and sipped from it.

That's better.

There was a knock at the front door.

She frowned, as she wasn't expecting anyone.

Getting up from the sofa, she went into the hallway, still in a daze from her nap.

From a tiny window in the hallway, she could see a figure standing back from the front door.

It was a man.

He was wearing a black motorbike helmet and black leathers.

Her pulse started to race again.

Are you kidding me?

The man moved forward and knocked on the door again.

Sarah couldn't get her breath – she was having some kind of panic attack.

A few seconds later, she heard the metallic clang of the letterbox.

The man had posted something through it.

Waiting a few more seconds, she went gingerly into the cold atrium beside the front door.

A small calling card with some handwriting on it lay on the doormat.

The man had been a delivery driver.

With an enormous sense of relief, she read the note, which informed her that her packages had been left behind the large flower pot beside the front door.

Bloody hell!

She retrieved the cardboard packages, returned to the living room, and rang Ruth.

'Hey, you,' Ruth said as she answered the phone. 'Everything okay?'

'Sort of,' Sarah replied unconvincingly.

'Why *sort of?*'

'I had another nightmare,' she explained. 'And then I thought the delivery man was an assassin.'

'Okay.' Ruth laughed. 'I assume he wasn't.'

'No,' she chortled. 'To be fair, he was wearing a black motorbike helmet and black leathers.'

'Yeah, well, that is your classic assassin outfit.'

Sarah snorted. 'It is, isnt' it? I knew I wasn't being paranoid.'

Talking to Ruth for just thirty seconds had dissipated all her anxiety.

'What was the delivery?'

'Just some books from Amazon.'

'Yeah, I think hitmen are the only thing you can't order from Amazon.' Ruth quipped.

'I just wanted to talk to someone for a minute.'

'Of course,' Ruth said gently. 'Why don't I get us fish and chips on the way home from that place we love in Overton?'

'Bottle of white wine?'

'Obviously.'

'Sounds perfect.'

Do you know how much I love you?' Sarah asked.

'I'm guessing *a lot*,' Ruth replied. 'And I would say the same back, but I've got a couple of hairy-arsed detective constables within earshot. I'll see you later.'

'Yeah, see you later.'

Chapter 17

The CID team was assembled for a four o'clock briefing. There was an odd atmosphere, which Ruth assumed was to do with the fact that Mark Freudmann's disappearance was throwing up a series of conflicting leads. She did, however, believe that he was dead – she just didn't know who had killed him or why.

Ruth stood in front of the board, her eyes raking over her team. It had been a while since she had taken stock of her time in the North Wales Police force. Five years. She couldn't believe it. It was a weird paradox of still feeling like she had only just arrived and that she was still a stranger to the area, with a comforting feeling that this was her home. She and the CID team had been through so much in that time. They had lost three officers – and she had lost Sian.

As she surveyed them, she couldn't have asked for a better team of detectives. Their honesty, dedication, and tireless pursuit of getting to the truth of the crimes they investigated was incredible.

'Right, guys,' she said, aware that she had a tiny glow

of pride. Turning to the scene board, she saw it was now full of photos, maps, and other evidence relating to Mark Freudmann's disappearance. As a team, they couldn't officially move into Incident Room 1 until she could confirm that this was a major crime. 'Let's get on with this. For those of you who aren't up to speed yet, the Marine Unit discovered a severed part of a leg in Lake Vyrnwy. Until forensics have a look, we can't confirm that it comes from the same victim as the severed foot. We also have a strange anomaly, as it seems unlikely that the leg was dumped into the lake at the same time as the foot.'

French frowned. 'I don't understand, boss. Why would someone take separate trips to dispose of body parts? It makes it far more likely they'll be caught.'

'We don't know that yet,' Ruth explained. 'I'll press on with what we do know. Nick and I visited a shop in Betwys-y-Coed this morning. It's the only place in North Wales that stocks *Le Chameau* wellington boots. The owner checked the serial number on the boot, and Mark Freudmann bought them last year. Although we don't have the forensic evidence back yet, I think it's a fair assumption that the severed foot and leg we found also belongs to Mark … Nick?'

'I've checked Mark Freudmann's bank account and the log for his mobile phone,' Nick explained. 'Neither have been used since last Thursday.'

Garrow frowned. 'Are we now treating this as a murder case?'

'Yes.' Ruth nodded. 'I think we have to.'

There were a few murmurs from the assembled detectives.

She looked over at Georgie. 'Can you get us up to speed with what you and Jim found in Liverpool, Georgie?'

Georgie got up and went over to the board. 'According

to Bella Freudmann, Mark spends some time in Liverpool with an old friend of his, Terry Fowles. As Nick said yesterday, Fowles owns the Attic nightclub on the Albert Docks and has a lot of very dodgy friends. He's also been under surveillance by MOCP for over eighteen months. The security firm who run the door at Attic are part of the Croxteth Crew. Which means they sell the drugs in the club. And anyone else trying to sell drugs in there gets thrown out or worse.'

'How does Mark Freudmann fit into any of this?' Ruth asked.

'DCI Finnan recognised Mark and remembers seeing him and Fowles together a few weeks ago,' Garrow explained. 'Which was exactly the same time that Fowles decided he was going to sack the security firm who ran the door at Attic and employ his own security guys.'

Nick's eyes widened. 'Christ, that's a ballsy move.'

'Ballsy or suicidal?' Ruth said, shaking her head.

Georgie looked at them. 'If Mark had anything to do with Fowles' decision to run the door himself, that could explain why someone would want him dead.'

'The Croxteth Crew,' Nick said. 'They wouldn't think twice about killing someone who was stopping them selling drugs in a club.'

Garrow frowned. 'But we found him 80 miles away in Lake Vyrnwy?'

Nick shrugged. 'Maybe they sent someone down to kill him?'

'We interviewed Fowles after he'd done a runner,' Georgie explained. 'At the time, we didn't have the intel about the security firm at Attic. However, Fowles described Bella Freudmann as a psychopath. He claims she attacked Mark with a baseball bat, broke his jaw, and put him in hospital for a couple of weeks.'

'When was this?' Ruth asked.

'Last year,' Garrow replied. 'He seemed to think Bella was a nasty piece of work.'

'Ironic when you think of the people Fowles likes to do business with,' Nick joked.

Ruth was thinking out loud. 'And the neighbour saw Bella and Mark arguing on Thursday night?'

Georgie nodded. 'That's what she told us, boss.'

Nick looked at her. 'You think Bella might have killed him?'

Ruth shrugged. 'Mark was gambling away her family's money.'

'Boss,' Georgie said, interrupting her. 'Fowles reckons Mark was a proper charmer. He also reckoned that he'd slept with half the women in Liverpool.'

'If Bella found out that Mark was cheating on her,' Ruth said, '…maybe she lost her temper and killed him?'

Garrow glanced over. 'Except her brother Frank was in the house last Thursday night.'

'Maybe he didn't see anything?' Nick said.

'Or maybe he's covering for his sister?' Georgie suggested.

'Sounds like we need to interview the brother, for starters,' Ruth said. 'And Mark Freudmann's DNA isn't on our database. We need to find something we can use or get a familial DNA from someone. I want to match his DNA to that foot and leg as soon as we can.'

At that moment, a tall, wiry PC walked in and looked around. 'Looking for DC Wild?'

Georgie approached. 'Yes, Constable? How can I help?'

'We've got a woman downstairs,' the PC explained and then read from his notebook. 'A Valerie Simpson.'

Georgie nodded. 'Yes, I know her.'

'She claims she just saw Mark Freudmann at a cash-point in Llancastell,' the PC said. 'She thought you would want to know?'

How is that possible?

Ruth looked over at Georgie with a confused expression.

FIFTEEN MINUTES LATER, RUTH AND GEORGIE WERE sitting opposite Val Simpson in Interview Room 2. Taking out her notepad, Georgie could see that Val was nervous. This was the first time that she had been asked by Ruth to help in an interview with her – and she was keen to impress.

Ruth had commented a few times in recent months on Georgie's police work and the improvements she was making as a detective. Georgie was clear in her own mind about how ambitious she was. In fact, she wanted to be running her own CID team before she was forty, if not sooner. Ruth was her role model, although she thought Ruth veered on the touchy-feely sometimes.

'Thank you so much for coming to see us, Val.' Georgie moved the chair a little closer to the desk and clicked her pen. 'Now, can you tell us exactly what you saw?'

'I'd just done my weekly shop at Tescos,' she said. 'I pulled out of the car park, and I saw Mark over by the cash machines that are down the right side of the supermarket. Do you know where I mean?'

'Yeah, I do,' Georgie replied. 'Are you sure it was Mark?'

'Definitely,' Val said with no hesitation.

Ruth gave her a quizzical look. 'How can you be sure?'

Val pulled a face as if this was a ridiculous thing to say. 'He's my neighbour. I've seen him loads of times before.'

Georgie nodded. 'It is quite a distance from the road to those cash machines. And you were driving.'

'It was definitely him.' Val seemed irritated. 'I thought you'd be pleased. From the way you spoke to me the other day, I assumed he was missing or something. And now I've seen him.'

Ruth gave her a kind smile. 'We're very grateful that you've come in. We just want to make sure that it was definitely Mark.'

'It was him. I could tell by the way he was standing,' Val said. 'And he had a white baseball cap on which he always wears. And then, when he turned, I saw his face. It was Mark Freudmann.'

Georgie exchanged a look with Ruth – if it was Mark Freudmann, then who did the severed foot and leg belong to, and why had Mark vanished off the face of the earth for the past five days?

Chapter 18

N ick sat staring at his computer screen and wracking his brains. He had just called Amanda to tell her he was going to stay at work for another hour before returning home. What he didn't tell her was that he now had an inkling where he might know Fran from. He just needed to do some digging around. He was sure she had been involved in an arson attack with a lad called Wayne Summers. If he remembered correctly, it had been about two years ago. There had been a dispute between two small-time drug dealers. Wayne Summers was one of them. He had resorted to firebombing the rival drug dealer's house with two young children inside. There had been some heroic rescue, and Nick distinctly remembered the newspaper article the following day. Not only did he remember the name Francesca Chapel from the article, he also remembered her photo being beside the article. Why was that? He searched his memory again and wondered if she had been Summers' girlfriend at the time.

That was it, wasn't it? She was his girlfriend.

Nick also remembered that Summers had resisted

arrest when uniform and CID officers had arrived at his flat to arrest him for attempted murder. Nick had spotted Summers down in the custody suite – bloodied nose, twisted sneer – and thought what a low life scumbag he was. He'd nearly murdered two innocent children over a few poxy bags of weed. Nick wondered if he had also seen Fran down in the custody suite too – is that why he recognised her? That must be it.

Jumping on the PNC, Nick tapped noisily on the keys and soon found Wayne Summers' criminal record – petty theft, assault, GBH, and then an eight-year sentence in April 2018 for attempted murder and arson. Summers' photo showed he was a disappointingly predictable neanderthal – shaved head, squashed, puggy nose, and an expression that made him look constipated. The small gene pool of Rhyl had done him no favours.

However, a quick search for Francesca Chapel revealed she didn't have any kind of criminal record. Not even a speeding ticket, as the saying goes.

Shutting down his computer for the night, Nick grabbed his jacket, went to his car, and headed home. Had he been mistaken? His instinct still told him she was somehow involved with Summers, and that made him feel uneasy. If she had knocked about with that scumbag, who else did she know? He wasn't comfortable knowing that she had contacted Amanda. As a copper, he was naturally suspicious by nature. So, what did Fran want? Was it simply to make contact with her birth mother, or was there a darker purpose to her letter? Was there an ulterior motive? Was she going to ask for guilt money?

Opening the front door, Nick came in, but he was still preoccupied with these thoughts. He didn't even notice the smell of the home-made curry Amanda had been preparing. Then he got the a distracting scent of spices and knew that she was cooking her *world-famous* jalfrezi.

'Megan's in our bed,' Amanda explained as she approached and gave him a kiss on the mouth. 'She's got a bit of a temperature, so I thought she could go in there?'

'Erm, okay. Of course,' Nick said distractedly as they went into the living room where the television was on. 'Is she okay?' he asked as his thoughts switched to his daughter.

'Yeah, you know. Temperature, snotty nose, bit of cough,' Amanda replied. 'Probably just a bug she's picked up from nursery. You okay?'

'Yeah,' Nick replied, but he wasn't feeling okay. He hoped it wasn't obvious.

'Oh yeah.' Amanda lay back on the sofa and plonked her legs and feet on his lap. 'You owe me a foot massage.'

'Do I?'

'Yes,' she said. 'Don't try to get out of it.'

'I know it's reciprocal, but your foot massages are pretty brutal. The kind of thing the Vietcong did to American soldiers to get them to talk,' Nick joked. 'In fact, I think you've cracked a metatarsal in my right foot.'

Amanda rolled her eyes and gave him a playful hit. 'You loved it, really.'

Nick raised an eyebrow. 'I think the howling and tears in my eyes were a clue that I really didn't.'

'Oh shut up,' she groaned. 'Oh, while I remember, Fran has got a job interview tomorrow afternoon in Llancastell, so I suggested she pop round for tea.'

Nick frowned. 'She was only here on Monday, wasn't she?'

Amanda bristled.

As soon as he said it, he regretted it.

Oh shit! What did you say that for?

Lifting her feet from his lap, Amanda glared at him. 'We haven't had contact for 18 years. What the hell are you talking about? Is there now some limit on the amount of times I can see my own daughter every week?'

Amanda sat upright on the sofa – she was fuming.

I think I may have touched a nerve here.

'Sorry,' Nick winced. 'That's not what I meant.'

'What did you mean, then?'

'It's all very new … and raw,' Nick said calmly. 'I just don't want you to rush into anything and get hurt. Or for anything to go wrong.'

'I abandoned Fran eighteen years ago! I'm hardly rushing into anything.'

Nick nodded. 'I know that. I'm sorry. She's welcome here anytime. Of course, she is.'

Amanda wasn't buying it – she had an acute radar for Nick's bullshit and when he wasn't telling her something.

She narrowed her eyes and fixed him with a stare. 'What is it?'

'What's what?'

'There's something you're not telling me,' she thundered. 'What is it, Nick?'

'It's nothing.'

'So there is something.'

Bloody hell, this is like being in a verbal boxing match.

Nick looked at her and pulled a face. 'I just thought I recognised Fran from somewhere.'

'From where?' Amanda snapped. 'From work?'

'Yes,' Nick said, taking a deep breath.

'You think you've arrested her?'

'No.' Nick shook his head. 'I'd remember that. I just thought I remembered her being mixed up with some toerag called Wayne Summers.'

'And what did this toerag do?'

'He firebombed a rival drug dealer's house and nearly killed his two kids,' Nick explained.

'Oh, so you think she was mixed up with a drug dealing arsonist?' Amanda asked.

'I don't know.'

'You don't know!'

Nick shrugged. 'I'm not sure. It's just my instinct.'

'What? So now I can't see Fran because your instinct thinks you *might* have come across her before. And she *might* have been mixed up with some drug dealer?'

'No, I didn't mean that,' Nick protested. 'I just wanted to flag up a concern, that's all.'

Amanda stood up. 'That's okay. When I see her tomorrow, I'll ask her if she's ever been in trouble with the police or if she has a police record, shall I?'

Nick winced.

'You've looked her up, haven't you?' Amanda thundered.

Nick didn't answer – there was no point lying.

'You know what, you're a fucking dickhead, Nick!' Amanda yelled. 'I'm assuming that she doesn't have a criminal record, otherwise you would have mentioned it.'

Nick didn't say anything and just squirmed.

'Prick,' Amanda snorted angrily as she left the room.

SIPPING FROM HER WINE, RUTH KICKED OFF HER SHOES AND stretched out her toes. The muscles in her calves felt tight, and she leant down and massaged them for a few seconds.

God, that feels better.

Sarah came in from the kitchen where she had been cooking. Holding a bottle of white wine in her hand, she came over and filled Ruth's glass.

'Hey,' Ruth frowned. 'Are you trying to get me drunk?'

'Yes,' Sarah laughed with a twinkle in her eye.

Ruth had noticed that Sarah had a growing ease and joy about her in recent weeks. The bouts of anxiety and dark depression were getting less and less. The combination of therapy and medication was really working. Thank God.

'Ooh, what are we having?' Ruth asked in anticipation.

'Salmon with a beurre blanc sauce and a potato, red onion, and garlic dauphinoise,' Sarah replied in a jokey French accent.

'Crikey. I mean *zut alors!*' Ruth snorted. 'That definitely beats a *Bombay Bad Boy Pot Noodle* in my book.'

Sarah laughed and took the Chirk Castle tea towel that she was holding, casually draping it over her shoulder. 'Yeah, well, one of the few benefits of being taken all over the world is that I learned to cook very well.'

Ruth raised her glass. 'Cheers to that.' She knew that part of her mind was still trying to process what Valerie Simpson had told them. Just as they were convinced that they were dealing with a murder case, she had come and thrown a spanner in the works.

'Anyway, never mind what I'm cooking.' Sarah slumped down in the armchair and took a mouthful of wine. 'What's happening about the foot and leg in the lake?'

Ruth rolled her eyes. 'You say it like it's the latest episode of a Miss Marple TV series. These are parts of someone's actual body, and that means they are probably dead.'

'Sorry.'

Ruth laughed. 'No, you're not.'

'Oh, stop being so boring and tell me,' Sarah groaned.

'I'm not really meant to discuss it with you.'

'Piss off. It's never stopped you before, and I've had a bloody tedious day.'

'I'd give anything for a *tedious* day,' Ruth sighed.

Sarah ignored her, grabbed a laptop from the coffee table, opened it up, and turned it on.

Ruth frowned. 'What are you doing?'

'Nothing really,' Sarah replied with a shrug. 'Just looking at boring social media crap … So, back to the body in a lake.'

'Okay, the boot we found in the lake belongs to Mark Freudmann. It's a *Le Chameau*,' Ruth explained.

Sarah raised an eyebrow, 'Oh a *Le Chameau, oui, oui.* Very nice.'

'You know what that is?' she asked.

'Yes, thank you very much,' Sarah said in mock indignation. 'I might have been brought up in deepest Yorkshire, but I know all about decent but overpriced wellies.'

'Do you now?' Ruth laughed. That was what Ruth loved about Sarah. Her dry sense of humour. 'Mark Freudmann hasn't used his phone or his bank account since last Thursday.'

'So, you assume the foot and leg in the lake are his? And if he's vanished, then he's probably dead?'

'Yes.' Ruth nodded. 'And he's been knocking around with some very unsavoury types in Liverpool.'

'Well, that doesn't narrow it down much,' Sarah joked as she tapped and read something on the laptop.

'Yeah, we're talking gangs and drugs.'

'Oh, right.' Sarah glanced up from the laptop and frowned. 'And you think one of them came down here, shot him, cut him up, and chucked him in the lake? That's a bit scary.'

'It's a possible line of enquiry,' Ruth replied with a shrug. 'He was also seen having a blazing row with his wife on Thursday night. She threw a glass at him. She also has previous.'

'How do you mean?'

'She attacked him last year, broke his jaw, and put him in hospital.'

'Why would she want to kill him?' Sarah asked.

'Mark Freudmann is a degenerate gambler. Bella Freudmann comes from a very rich family. Don't laugh, but they own most of the pigs in Snowdonia.'

'Pigs?'

'I know. Who knew?' Ruth said. 'It sounds ridiculous, but the Collard family are worth millions. And Mark is doing a good job of gambling a lot of it away. Plus, by all accounts, he's shagging everything in sight when he's up in Liverpool.'

'Christ, if he was my husband, I'd chop him up and chuck him in a bloody lake.' Sarah exclaimed. 'What a tosser.'

'Sarah!' Ruth said.

'Come on,' Sarah grinned. 'That's one of the major benefits of being gay. You don't have be in a relationship with men, most of whom are immature, selfish, woman-ising pricks.'

'Not that you're generalising or anything?'

'What about the DNA from the foot or the leg?' Sarah asked. 'Can't you get some DNA from Mark Freudmann and then make a match?'

Ruth smirked. 'I really think you spend too much time watching *Silent Witness* repeats.'

'Funny ... Did you get a match or not?'

'The lab tried it earlier today,' Ruth explained. 'The flesh on the foot has deteriorated too much, so now they're having to extract DNA from the bones in the foot.'

'Ewww. Which is good to know just before we eat,' Sarah joked.

'Hey, you asked, missy,' Ruth said with a smile. 'And as

of about three hours ago, we have a major spanner in the works.'

'Which is?'

'Mark Freudmann's neighbour walked into Llancastell nick and said she'd just seen him getting cash from a cash-point at Tescos in town,' Ruth explained.

Sarah snorted. 'What? How can he do that if he's chopped up and in a lake?'

'No idea. Either she's got it wrong, or we're back to square one with our victim.'

Sarah didn't respond for a few seconds. It didn't look like she had heard what Ruth had just said. Instead, she was looking something up on the laptop.

'You okay?' Ruth asked, wondering what she was staring at ashen-faced.

'Sorry, I …?' Sarah was completely distracted.

'Are you okay?'

'Not really.'

'What are you looking at?' Ruth asked.

'My mum's got cancer,' Sarah said in a whisper as she peered at the screen.

'What?'

Sarah took a breath and looked over at her. 'My mum's got lung cancer.'

'How do you know that?' Ruth asked.

'I'm on Facebook,' Sarah explained, pointing at the laptop and sounding choked. 'I was just looking at the Facebook pages of some of my cousins who still live near mum. One of them, Pete, who's my age, is doing the London Marathon to raise money for Cancer Research. He wrote about my mum being ill with lung cancer and that they were all thinking of her.'

Noticing that Sarah had a tear in her eye, Ruth went over to her. 'I'm so sorry.'

'What am I going to do?' Sarah asked.

'How do you mean?' Ruth asked.

'The PPS have told me I can't have any contact with her,' Sarah said. 'But she's got cancer. And I don't know how serious it is, but lung cancer isn't good, is it?'

'No, it's not,' Ruth agreed as she put a sympathetic hand on her shoulder. 'But you know why the PPS has told you not to contact her.'

'Well, they can fuck off,' Sarah shrugged angrily. 'I'm not waiting for months or even years to see her if she's got cancer. She might be dying.'

Ruth nodded. 'Okay, let's take this one step at a time. We can talk to Maggie at the PPS and see what they can do.'

Ruth put her arms around Sarah and gave her a hug.

'I'm going to see her,' Sarah insisted under her breath. 'I don't care what anyone says.'

Chapter 19

Wednesday 27th January

HAVING CONDUCTED THE MORNING BRIEFING, RUTH AND Nick headed to Lake Vyrnwy to check on the continuing operation to search the lake for any more body parts. They were then due to visit Bella Freudmann at her home to gather Mark's DNA to check against the DNA of the severed foot and leg. Ruth was also keen to talk to Bella's brother, Frank.

The fact that Valerie Simpson had seen Mark Freudmann the day before at a cashpoint clearly changed the focus of the investigation. They were now waiting for the supermarket CCTV to be sent over so they could check to see if it really was Mark Freudmann or if Valerie had been somehow mistaken – or she was lying for some reason.

Ruth gazed out over the immense expanse of Lake Vyrnwy as Nick pulled into the car park at the south end of the lake. The sky was a metallic grey, and the jagged, mountainous landscape in the distance was covered with a thin veil of fog. At its highest ridges, the Berwyn mountains were dark and hazy, ominous shapes. The main summits were Cadair Berwyn, Moel Sych, and Cadair Bronwen, all of which were over 2,500 ft high. To the south, the Milltir Cerrig mountain pass crossed the range and was 1,500 ft high.

Getting out of the car, Ruth felt the piercing iciness of the wind that blew across from the lake. Across the perimeter road, she could see the dark blue van of the North Wales Underwater Search and Marine Unit parked close to where the foot and leg had been discovered. Further out on the water was a black police RIB – rigid inflatable boat. Several police divers in black drysuits, masks, and breathing apparatus were bobbing around in the water. Others were sitting in the boat, using the two-way radios and maintaining the orange-coloured safety lines.

'There isn't enough money in the world that would persuade me to do that,' Nick said as he wrapped his navy scarf around his neck.

'Nope,' Ruth agreed. 'I get claustrophobic at the best of times.'

They crossed the road, ducked under the police tape, and made their way down the slippery, muddy bank towards the dark water.

A male DS, in a black drysuit, was standing at the water's edge as he took off his gloves. Ruth assumed he was the senior officer for the USMU.

Getting out her warrant card, Ruth cleared her throat to get his attention. 'Morning, Sergeant.'

The sergeant turned around. His balding scalp was wet and his face ruddy.

'DI Ruth Hunter and DS Nick Evans, Llancastell CID,' she explained.

'You the SIO on this case?' he asked in a grumpy tone. SIO stood for Senior Investigating Officer.

'Yes,' she replied, wondering why he sounded so fed up. She guessed searching for body parts in the dirty, icy water wasn't something that would fill anyone with joy. 'How are we doing?'

'Nothing so far, I'm afraid.' The sergeant gave a loud sniff, shook his head, and gestured out to the water. 'It might look calm and steady out there. But it's a reservoir. So, it's incredibly deep, and the currents underneath are very strong.'

Nick pulled a face. 'Does that mean you can't narrow down your search area?'

'Not really,' the sergeant replied. 'If I'm honest, after a couple of days, any objects of a decent size, like a body part, could be anywhere out there. And we're talking four and a half square kilometres of water, which is the same as 600 football pitches. And it's nearly a 100 ft deep out in the middle.'

'Effectively, we're looking for a needle in a haystack,' Ruth said.

Nick's mobile phone rang, and he walked up the bank to answer it.

'Yes.' The sergeant nodded. 'The only genuine hope we've got is that something gets caught in the dam or the straining towers.'

Ruth knew how much it cost to keep a full police diving team on site at a place like Lake Vyrnwy.

'I'll talk to my DCI,' Ruth said. 'But from what you're telling me, we're throwing good money after bad.'

'I'm afraid so.' The sergeant still sounded grumpy. 'We could be out here for months and still not find a thing.'

'Okay. Thanks,' Ruth said, spotting Nick coming her way.

'Duty Sergeant at Llancastell,' he said, gesturing to his phone. 'Bella Freudmann is there and wants to speak to whoever is in charge. Apparently, Mark has cleared out their bank account.'

FORTY MINUTES LATER, RUTH AND NICK WERE SITTING opposite Bella Freudmann in Interview Room 1. She was wearing a designer coat and sheepskin, trapper's style hat with long ear flaps.

Nick, who was scribbling in his notebook, looked over at her. 'Can you tell us how much your husband has withdrawn?'

Bella was clearly furious. 'He's taken £500 out in cash. And then he transferred £17,000 from the joint account to his own account, which has cleared us out. He's such a tosser.'

'Do you have a savings account?' Nick asked.

'Yes. But that needs two signatures for a withdrawal. Thank God.'

'And these other transactions definitely happened yesterday,' Ruth asked. It was sounding as if Valerie Simpson wasn't mistaken when she claimed she had seen Mark Freudmann at a cashpoint. And that made things very confusing.

'Yes, yesterday,' Bella said with an audible huff. 'I need to take an injunction out against him. He's taken it too far this time. I don't want him coming to the house again.'

Ruth gave her an understanding look. 'You'll have to talk to a solicitor about that.'

'And we will have to actually see your husband to confirm that he is no longer missing,' Nick explained.

'Who the hell do you think took out the money and transferred it to his account?' Bella snorted angrily. 'His bloody ghost?' She sat back, and her eyes welled up with tears. It was clearly all too much for her. 'He's gone off with someone. I've always suspected that he was having affairs, but he always came back to me. I can't believe he's done this to me.'

Ruth took a tissue from her pocket and handed it to Bella, 'Here you go.'

'Thanks,' she said with a sniff. 'Now all my bloody make-up has run too. Jesus.'

'While this is still a missing persons case,' Ruth said gently, 'I would like to come and speak to your brother. Frank is it?'

Bella frowned. 'Why?'

'Frank is living with you, isn't he?' Ruth asked.

'Yes,' Bella replied defensively. 'What's he got to do with anything?'

'As I explained, until we actually see Mark and formally identify him, we still have to treat this as a missing persons case. I'd like to talk to Frank about the days leading up to Mark's disappearance.'

'Really?' Bella was baffled. 'I don't understand why, but I'm sure he'll talk to you. It's not like he's got anything to hide, is it?'

'I also need to come and collect a DNA sample for Mark. A toothbrush, hairbrush, even a razor,' Ruth said.

Bella shrugged, but she was clearly annoyed. 'Fine. I can't see the point, but I'll be in all afternoon.'

'One more thing.' Nick looked up from his notepad. 'We understand Mark was taken to hospital last year with a broken jaw. Our records show officers were called to a disturbance that night, but no charges were pressed. Is there anything you can tell us about that?'

Bella shrugged. 'I hit him with a baseball bat.'

'You attacked him?' Ruth asked.

'No.' Bella shook her head. 'Mark was drunk and waving around a shotgun. He threatened to shoot me, so I hit him with a bat.'

Chapter 20

As Ruth and Nick whizzed along the road out of Llancastell, Nick reached over to the stereo and pressed play. He clearly had loaded whatever his latest CD was into their car.

Oh God, what is it going to be this time? she thought.

She and Nick often disagreed in their musical tastes. However, it was the agreement that whoever was driving could choose the soundtrack for the day. And that was usually Nick.

A male voice with a guitar played.

'Is this Ed Sheeran?' she asked.

'What?' Nick asked in utter disbelief. 'This is *Post Malone's* new album.'

'Post who?'

'*Post Malone!*'

'Sounds like Ed Sheeran to me,' Ruth grumbled.

'No, it doesn't.'

'Or that other bloke. The Scottish one.' Ruth searched her memory for his name. Why was it she could name every track and artist on *Now That's What I Call Music Vol 1*, in the right order, but these days she couldn't remember a thing?

'Lewis Capaldi?'

'That's the fella,' Ruth said triumphantly.

'I give up,' Nick laughed as they continued.

'They all sound the same to me.'

Ruth took in the surrounding countryside. Usually, she was way too busy with whatever case they were working on to notice. In fact, she had become accustomed to the stunning landscapes of Snowdonia, which she felt was a shame. But something inside her today made her look and take in the view. The rolling fields that were peppered with sheep. The dark mountains that were dusted with snow this time of year.

What an incredible place to call home, she thought.

If she really wanted to get some perspective and gratitude, she just needed to remember some of the bloodshed she had witnessed in Peckham, SE15. She remembered the last operation that she ever worked on before leaving the Met. She had raided a flat in Crane House, on Peckham's notorious Pelican Estate. Ruth was looking for Kossi Asumana, aka Taz, who was a drug dealer and a member of a violent gang, The Peckham Boys. They had been linked to serious crime, drug dealing, and murder for decades.

As she and the unit of AFOs – Authorised Firearms Officers – crashed through the front door with their arrest and search warrants, Ruth was confronted with a horrendous sight. Asumana was lying dead on his sofa, covered in blood from the gunshot wound to his chest. His wife, Zaria, was holding a handgun, shaking and in utter shock. Meanwhile, their two young daughters were hiding, trembling, and crying in terror in a bedroom wardrobe. Ruth took it all in her stride. She had become immune to the violence and horror of the street crime in South London. And that was why she had to leave.

Thank God I don't have to deal with that every day, she thought gratefully.

'You were miles away, boss,' Nick said with a friendly smile.

'Just remembering the last operation I ever worked in Peckham,' she replied. 'It made me glad I'm sitting here with you.'

'That's not what you normally say,' Nick joked.

'That's because you drive like an acne-ridden, seventeen-year-old boy racer,' she joked.

The car's TETRA radio crackled, and a voice said, 'Control to three-six, are you receiving, over?'

Ruth grabbed the handset and pressed the grey speak button. 'Control from three-six, we are receiving, go ahead, over.'

'We have a report of a disturbance at a residence in Llwydiarth,' the dispatch controller said. 'The residence is registered to a Mark and Bella Freudmann, over.'

Ruth looked over at Nick. 'Three-six, received. We are on our way, out.'

'Hey, time to test out your theory, boss,' Nick said with a grin as he dropped the car down into third gear and gunned the engine.

'Oh, great.' Ruth reached up to hold on to the plastic grab handle in preparation to steady herself.

Nick gestured excitedly to the dashboard. 'Blues and twos, boss?'

'It really is like being with a toddler,' Ruth groaned as Nick switched on their two-tone siren and blue lights which lit up their radiator grill.

'Don't worry, boss. I'll have us there in a flash.'

'Oh good,' she said sarcastically.

. . .

By the time Ruth and Nick arrived at the Freudmanns' home in Llwydiarth, there was a police patrol car outside.

'What's going on here?' Ruth asked as Nick pulled the car over to the side of the road.

There were two police officers talking to a man and a woman on the drive.

'That's Bella Freudmann,' Ruth said as they got out.

They walked along the verge and into the driveway.

Bella came over. Her face was streaked with tears, and her right eye seemed a little red and swollen.

'What's happened?' Ruth asked.

'Mark was here,' she exclaimed.

'When was this?'

'About half an hour ago,' Bella explained.

Ruth pointed to her face. 'What's happened to your eye?'

Bella was very agitated and jittery 'Mark hit me in the face.'

'Where is he now?' Nick asked.

Bella shrugged. 'I don't know. He came back here. He went through the house, grabbing all his stuff. Then he packed two suitcases with his clothes and put everything in the car. When I tried to stop him, he hit me.'

Ruth glanced over at the man leaning against the garden wall, smoking a cigarette. He had a mop of curly greying hair. She assumed it was Frank Collard.

Ruth gestured in the man's direction. 'Is that your brother?'

'Yeah, that's Frank,' Bella replied.

Hearing his name, Frank moved away from the wall and walked in their direction.

Ruth looked at him. He had a stern expression, which wasn't surprising after what had happened to his sister.

'Were you here when all this happened?' Ruth asked him.

'I was doing some work in the conservatory,' Frank explained. 'But I heard Mark come back.'

'Did you see him?' Nick asked.

Frank nodded. 'I thought Bella and Mark were having one of their usual rows. By the time I went to see what was going on, Mark was out on the drive, putting his stuff into the car.'

Okay. Someone else has now seen Mark Freudmann since he disappeared.

Ruth nodded. 'Did you say anything to him?'

Frank shrugged. 'I just asked him what was going on.'

'Did he say anything to you?' Nick said.

'He told me to mind my own fucking business and stay out of his way,' Frank replied.

Ruth looked at Bella. 'And then Mark left?'

Bella huffed. 'Yes. I just said that. I want to press charges for assault.'

'Okay,' Ruth said. 'Let's do one thing at a time. The first thing is to find Mark and ask him for his version of what's happened here.'

Bella glared at her. 'Are you calling us liars?'

'No, of course not. Is there anywhere you think he might have gone?'

'Maybe Susanna's,' Bella shrugged. 'Or he's flitted off to go and stay with Terry again.'

Ruth looked around. 'Did anyone else witness what was going on?'

Bella pointed to the small house next door. 'That nosey cow probably did. She's always snooping on us.'

. . .

RUTH AND NICK SAT AT VALERIE SIMPSON'S KITCHEN table, taking a statement.

Ruth gave her a kind smile. 'So, after you heard Mark and Bella rowing, can you tell us exactly what you saw?'

Val smiled back at her. 'Well, I was upstairs, folding up some washing. I heard the shouting, so I looked out. Mark had the boot of his car open and was putting suitcases inside.'

Thank God for nosey neighbours, Ruth thought to herself. *Don't know what we'd do without them.*

'And you're sure it was him?' Nick asked.

'Of course,' Val snorted. 'Who else would put suitcases into Mark's car?'

Ruth nodded patiently. 'Of course. But what we mean is, did you actually see Mark putting the cases into his car?'

Val frowned. 'Yes.'

'Okay,' Ruth said. 'Thank you.'

Nick looked up from his notepad. 'And this is when you saw Mark arguing with Bella?'

'That's right,' Val replied. 'She was going mad. In fact, she took some suitcases out of the car to try to stop him from leaving.'

'Did you see Mark leave?' Ruth asked.

'No,' Val shook her head. 'Someone rang my phone, so I had to go and answer it. It was bloody BT asking me if I wanted broadband. By the time I got back upstairs again, the car was gone.'

'And what about Frank?' Nick said. 'Did you see him at any point while Mark and Bella were arguing?'

'No,' Val said. 'I did see him talking to Bella on the driveway. She seemed very upset. And then the policemen arrived. I suppose that Bella must have called them.'

'Okay, thank you. You've been very helpful,' Ruth said as she and Nick got up to go.

Val pulled a face. 'Erm … there is something else. But …'

Ruth could see that whatever Val was going to tell them, it was making her feel uncomfortable.

Sitting down again, Ruth looked at her. 'Go on. Whatever it is, it might help us explain what's been going on between Bella and Mark.'

'I'm not sure quite how to put this.' Val frowned. 'The other night I was looking out. I can see down onto the decking and patio. And Bella had lit the fire pit, and she was sitting next to Frank and …'

There were a few seconds of silence.

'And …?' Ruth said with an encouraging nod.

'Well, they were kissing,' Val said as she blinked uncomfortably.

Ruth exchanged a look with Nick – *Okay, that is definitely strange.*

Nick frowned. 'When you say kissing …?'

'It wasn't kissing, like, you know, brother and sister.' Val squirmed. 'I mean, they were kissing. You know …'

Chapter 21

'Okay,' Nick said as he and Ruth drove from Llwydiarth towards DCC Susanna Freudmann's home. 'Bella and Frank kissing is seriously strange, right?'

'Yes,' Ruth agreed. 'Although I have encountered some pretty dark and weird stuff in my time. And we are in North Wales.'

Nick pretended to be offended. 'Hey, that's a cheap shot.'

'Come on, Nick,' Ruth joked.

'And there's me thinking that all Londoners were arrogant and judgemental, eh?'

'As if.' She laughed. 'I suppose if there was something going on between Bella and her brother, maybe Mark found out? It would explain why they had an argument last Thursday, and he left for a few days.'

'Maybe they weren't real brother and sister?' Nick said.

'You mean they were adopted or stepbrother and sister?'

'It would make it less strange and 'incesty',' Nick said.

Ruth frowned. 'I don't think *incesty* is a word.'

'Okay. You know what I mean, though.'

Ruth raised an eyebrow. 'I guess you'd need a few days to get your head around your wife having an affair with her own brother, however biological they are or aren't.'

'And then Mark returns to the family home to get his stuff,' Nick said.

'Bella is portraying herself as the wronged party in all this. Maybe it's the other way around.'

'At the moment, there is no crime that's been committed by Mark or Bella Freudmann,' Nick stated.

Ruth rolled her eyes. 'And we're back to square one with our severed foot and leg, aren't we?'

Ruth and Nick pulled up outside a large detached house with a white BMW on the drive. It had started to pour with rain, and Ruth cursed the fact that she had left her raincoat in the boot. As they got out of the car, she scuttled around the back to retrieve it. The wind was biting cold, and the intense rain felt like prickling thorns against her face. It felt icy against her neck, so she fastened up the top button.

As they jogged through the swirling rain towards the front door, Ruth noticed that she was feeling anxious. Susanna was an incredibly high-ranking police officer, and Ruth felt uneasy in the company of those types of authority figures. She reverted to feeling like a child, which she knew was ridiculous for a 52-year-old detective inspector.

Before they had even rung the doorbell, the door opened and a severe-looking woman with crow black hair, pointed features, dressed in her black police uniform frowned at them.

It was Susanna.

Gosh, she looks scary, Ruth thought.

'Have you found him yet?' she snapped.

Oh hi. How are you? Won't you come on in? Ruth thought sarcastically.

She and Nick exchanged a wary look.

'Not exactly,' Ruth said hesitantly as she cowered in the rain. 'Can we come in?'

'Of course.' Susanna gestured to the hallway. 'If you could take off your shoes, please. I have new carpets.'

Ruth and Nick dutifully took off their shoes, exchanged another wary look, and followed her into the house.

'What does *not exactly* mean?' Susanna asked in a withering tone.

'We've just come from his house in Llwydiarth,' Nick explained. 'Bella claims Mark turned up earlier, packed up his things into his car, and left.'

Susanna ushered them into the living room, which was neat and tidy, but a little soulless.

'No,' Susanna said adamantly. 'I don't believe that for one second.'

Why not?

Ruth frowned. 'Their neighbour watched Mark pack the car.'

Susanna fixed Ruth with a stare. 'My son hasn't called me for four days. There's something wrong. And if he was going to leave Bella and take all his stuff, he would have called me to talk it through.'

'I understand your concern,' Ruth said in a conciliatory tone. Given the evidence they had just given her, Susanna was being illogical. 'But we do have three people who just saw Mark at his home.'

Susanna pulled a face. 'Three?'

'Bella, her brother Frank, and her neighbour Valerie Simpson,' Ruth explained.

'The neighbour also saw Mark taking cash from a cashpoint at Tesco in Llancastell yesterday,' Nick said. 'Bella confirmed Mark had made the withdrawal.'

'I wouldn't trust anything that woman has to say to you,' Susanna sniped in a withering tone.

Ruth frowned. 'Sorry, ma'am. Do I take it you don't get on with Bella Freudmann?'

'No, I *do* not,' Susanna stated angrily. 'She's a ghastly woman. Marrying her was the worst thing that Mark ever did. He was happy until they got together.'

'Did your ex-husband feel the same?' Nick asked.

'Yes, absolutely,' Susanna said. 'We didn't agree on many things, but we certainly agreed on that. The Collard family are all pretty intolerable people. And don't think for a second it's some kind of class thing. What I mean is that their moral compass is very off, if you understand what I'm trying to say?'

'Yes, ma'am,' Ruth said, trying to be as tactful as she could be. 'We have several witnesses who have now seen Mark.'

'Then why hasn't he called me?' Susanna asked them in a tone that suggested it was their job to explain it.

'I can't tell you why your son hasn't phoned you,' Ruth said.

'Have you checked his phone records?'

Nick nodded. 'The phone company informed us yesterday that there had been no activity on his phone since last Thursday.'

'Well, that's impossible too,' Susanna snapped – she was getting emotional. Her voice was straining to hold back her anxiety. 'He's always on that bloody thing. There is something very wrong. I'm his mother, and I know my own son.'

'I can assure you that we will do everything we can to

track Mark's whereabouts,' Ruth said. 'And we will let you know as soon as we have any more information.'

Susanna nodded, but she was clearly now very anxious. 'Please find him, Inspector. He's my only child. And even though he's made many mistakes in his life, he is a good person at heart,' she said in a voice that finally revealed how she was truly feeling.

Chapter 22

Nick stirred in his sleep as he had heard a noise from somewhere inside the house. Opening his eyes, he peered over at Amanda, who was sound asleep with her back to him.

He rolled onto his side and checked the time. 4 am. Maybe he had heard something in his dream. In his head, he still had fragmented images from what had been a *drinking dream*. They were common in alcoholics and an almost nightly event when he was in early recovery. He had dreamed about a party in which he was desperately searching for alcohol. Finding a bottle of vodka, he secretly drank several mouthfuls, desperate that no one would see him. Waking from one of these dreams and realising that he hadn't picked up a drink was always such an immense relief. Although nothing like the blind panic that used to overwhelm him in the first few months of sobriety.

Another noise. It had come from downstairs. Someone was moving around, and he heard the soft click of a door.

Shit! It wasn't in my dream.

He knew that Fran had stayed over on the sofa again.

Even though they had had a nice evening, he couldn't get the nagging doubt about her involvement with Wayne Summers out of his mind. However, he knew that whatever his doubts were, he couldn't share them with Amanda.

A faint metallic rattle came from downstairs again.

What is that? Maybe I should just check?

With a slight sense of unease, Nick got out of bed and put on his dressing gown. For a split second, he worried that someone had broken into the house.

He padded quietly along the landing and pushed Megan's door open by a couple of inches. She was fast asleep, bathed in the light from her pink nightlight. The tresses of her blonde hair were spread out like tentacles across her pillow.

Reaching the top of the stairs, he descended quietly and made his way down the hallway.

Then another noise. Except this time, he recognised it was the sound of a drawer opening.

As he got to the living room, he peered in through the half-open door. He could see that Fran was searching through the drawers of the bureau where they kept stuff like passports, bank statements, and bills etc …

What the bloody hell is she doing? he thought angrily. *Is she looking for money?*

Although he was furious that Fran had betrayed their trust, he also felt vindicated in his concerns that she was untrustworthy.

Pushing open the door slowly, he stepped into the living room. 'Can I help?

Fran turned around, looking startled. 'Oh hi Nick,' she said, trying to sound casual.

'What are you doing?' Nick asked, trying to contain his anger.

'Oh,' Fran laughed. 'God, sorry. I'm not rifling through

your stuff. I'm just looking for painkillers. Sleeping on the sofa has played havoc with my back. I tried the kitchen, but I couldn't find anything. Do you know where Amanda keeps them?'

Nice try, but that's bullshit.

'Really?' Nick said sarcastically as he glared at her.

'I'm really sorry if you think I was having a nose round. I …'

'How's Wayne Summers?' he interrupted her.

Fran shrugged. 'I don't know what you're talking about.'

'I think you do,' Nick growled.

'What's going on?' asked a voice.

It was Amanda. She was bleary-eyed and tying the cord of her dressing gown as she entered.

Nick looked at her. 'I found Fran riffling through our stuff. She made some lame excuse that she was looking for painkillers.'

Fran seemed upset. 'Why are you being like this, Nick?'

'Being like what?' Nick asked.

'I can't believe you're calling me a liar,' Fran said, shaking her head.

Amanda was confused. 'Why were you looking for painkillers?'

Fran pointed. 'I have two fused discs at the base of my spine. I think sleeping on the sofa has made my lower back go into spasm.'

'Oh, God. Poor you,' Amanda said, pulling a face. 'I keep them in the cabinet in the downstairs loo.'

Fran gave Nick a wary look. 'Oh, sorry. That's why I couldn't find them.'

Nick looked at them both, aghast. 'You don't actually believe her, do you?'

'Shut up, Nick,' Amanda snapped.

Fran wiped a tear from her eye. 'Maybe I should just go home.'

Amanda nodded as she went over to her. 'Give me five minutes, and I'll drop you back. I'm really sorry, Fran.'

Nick shook his head in disbelief as he turned and walked out into the hallway and headed for the stairs.

Chapter 23

*T*hursday 28th January

IT WAS 9.12 AM AND RUTH WAS HURRYING DOWN THE corridor towards the CID office where her team was waiting for morning briefing to begin. Looking up, she saw Detective Chief Inspector Ashley Drake walking towards her. From his expression, she could see he was concerned about something. As her boss, Drake was normally fairly hands off when it came to the day to day running of Llancastell CID. He was a refreshing change from some of the micromanaging and bullying she had experienced from DCIs in the Met.

'I've had DCC Freudmann yelling down the phone at me,' he moaned. 'She claims that despite her fears about her son, you are no longer treating it as a missing persons case?'

'That's not exactly what I said, boss,' Ruth explained

with a frown. 'We have a sighting of Mark at a cashpoint at Tescos on Tuesday. And then, according to his wife, brother-in-law, and neighbour, he returned home, packed some of his belongings into his car, and left. I assured her I would still be looking for him, but it's not as if we can treat it as an emergency, is it?'

Drake rubbed his chin and looked at her. 'That's not quite how she explained it to me. She told me that Mark hasn't called her for a week, and he's never done that before.'

Ruth shrugged. 'I can't explain that, boss.'

'No.' Drake paused for thought. 'How reliable are the witnesses that claim to have seen him?'

'Bella and Mark's marriage seems to be on the rocks. We're not sure about her brother, who is staying with her. They could have lied, but my gut instinct is that they didn't,' Ruth said. 'As for the neighbour, she's seen Mark twice in two days. I don't see what she has to gain from lying about it.'

'Have you managed to track Mark down yet?' Drake asked.

Ruth shook her head. 'We've got an ANPR check out on his car. And his bank and phone company are going to be in contact if there's any more activity on his accounts. Otherwise, he's vanished.'

'What about the foot and leg you found?' Drake asked.

'We're back to square one with it, boss,' Ruth sighed. 'We're hopefully getting DNA back today or tomorrow. And we're hoping to get Mark's DNA so we can cross-match and rule him out. If it's not a match, then we have no other leads as to who they might belong to.'

Drake seemed perplexed, which was unusual. 'Nothing at all?'

'We've conducted a POLSA fingertip search of the

shoreline. The Canine Unit has been down there too. The Marine Unit can't find anything else. Nothing from the house-to-house or the hotel. No one saw anything.'

'But you've got a boot that belongs to Mark Freud-mann floating in the lake at the same time as the foot was discovered?' Drake pushed his glasses up the bridge of his nose by half an inch. 'Doesn't that strike you as very strange?'

Ruth gave a slow nod. 'Very. None of the evidence seems to add up. And it's incredibly frustrating.'

Drake looked at her and raised an eyebrow. 'Look, I can see this is proving to be anything but straightforward, but I wanted to let you know the DCC is on our case. And that's not a good thing.'

Ruth nodded. She knew that Drake would have her back and wouldn't be apportioning any blame. That just wasn't his style. He had the balls to protect his team, which is why the whole of Llancastell CID afforded him such loyalty. It wasn't uncommon for Ruth to overhear snatches of conversations from her team, such as *'Best bloody DCI I've ever worked for.'* It was true. And she'd been a copper for nearly thirty years.

Ruth pointed to the double doors that led into the CID office. 'You want to sit in on the morning briefing, boss?'

Drake nodded as his face softened. 'Actually, I will. It's been a while.'

Opening the doors, Ruth and Drake walked in. The atmosphere always changed a little when Drake entered the CID office. Not that he was in any way a frightening boss or a bully. It was just the same as when a head teacher appeared in a classroom or, she assumed, the staff room. He had a quiet authority.

'Right, guys,' Ruth said loudly as she marched to the end of the CID office. 'As you know, this investigation seems to twist backwards and forwards at a rate of knots. So, rather than us following any hypothesis, I want us to just concentrate on the evidence and analyse what that shows us. In terms of the suspects we have, it is trace, interview, and eliminate as usual. Nick, what have we got?'

'Nothing back from the handful of houses that overlook Lake Vyrnwy. Officers asked the occupants if they had seen anyone dumping stuff into the lake or anything at all suspicious in the last couple of weeks. They drew a blank.'

'What about the hotel?' she asked.

'Nothing there,' Nick replied. 'Staff and guests have been contacted, but again, no one has seen anything.'

'Anything on Mark Freudmann this morning? ANPR hits, traffic cameras, bank accounts, mobile phone?'

Garrow shook his head. 'Nothing, boss.'

Georgie looked over. 'Won't his car have one of those GPR trackers on it? Can we track it from that?'

'It depends on the GPS system,' Nick replied. 'If he doesn't want to be found, he might have turned it off. And some of the GPS systems only work if the car engine is on. But definitely worth trying, Georgie.'

'Can someone get onto the lab and hurry up the DNA they were going to get from the ankle bone?' Ruth said, thinking out loud. She looked at Georgie and Garrow. 'Can you two go to Bella Freudmann's this morning and get something that we can use for Mark Freudmann's DNA? Toothbrush, hairbrush.'

Nick glanced down at his phone and then pointed. 'Boss, I've got an email with the CCTV footage from Tesco's on Tuesday.'

Ruth pointed to the main office flat screen monitor that was up on the wall. 'Let's have a look then, shall we?'

Nick went over to a computer, logged on, went to his

emails, and then linked the computer to the main screen.

After a few seconds, CCTV footage from a high-angle camera showed a couple of people waiting in line for a cash vending machine. A time code and date were running along the bottom, which confirmed what Valerie Simpson told them she had witnessed.

A man of medium build walked into shot and joined the queue.

He was wearing a white baseball cap.

Ruth moved towards the screen as the CID team watched and gestured. 'This must be the man who Valerie Simpson identified as Mark Freudmann.'

'Yes, boss,' Georgie confirmed. 'She mentioned the white baseball cap.'

They watched for a few more seconds as the man got to the machine, inserted his card, and took out some cash.

As he turned, Nick froze the image.

The baseball cap was pulled low on the man's brow.

Ruth rolled her eyes, 'Well, I can't see anything from that. Can anyone else?'

'Yes, that could be anyone,' Drake agreed. 'We can't confirm Mark Freudmann's identity from that.'

'Maybe we should show it to DCC Freudmann?' French suggested.

'Especially if we believe that Bella Freudmann is in any way connected to her husband's disappearance,' Ruth added and then turned to Nick. 'Nick and I will take this to her in St Asaph.' Ruth looked out at her team. 'Everyone else, I want the missing persons register checked, ANPR and Traffic for Mark Freudmann's car. We'll reconvene here at five.'

As Ruth turned to go, she caught Drake's eye. He gave her a reassuring nod to show that he was happy that they were doing everything they could.

Chapter 24

Georgie and Garrow made their way out of Llancastell and headed out towards Llwydiarth. Her phone buzzed, and she glanced down at it. Yet another flirty text from DCI Kevin Finnan, whom she and Jim had met up with in Liverpool. Georgie had got his number from his card, and now they were texting each other and arranging to meet up.

Garrow seemed lost in thought as they traversed the narrow country lanes out towards Llwydiarth.

'Have you got a girlfriend, Jim?' Georgie asked, breaking the long silence.

'No,' Garrow replied. He seemed slightly taken aback by the bluntness of her question. 'Not at the moment.'

Garrow laughed as he looked at her.

'What?' she said with a slightly defensive expression.

'You really don't have any filter, do you?'

'I don't see the point.'

'Tact? Sensitivity? Subtlety?' Garrow suggested.

'Fuck that,' Georgie chortled. 'Life's too short to pussy-foot around.'

They turned the corner and pulled up outside Bella Freudmann's house.

There was a white transit van on the drive, which had *L&D Brothers Builders and Decorators* printed on the side in navy letters. Beside that was a smaller red escort van for a local carpet company.

Georgie pulled a face as they got out of the car. 'Strange time to get your house decorated and re-carpeted.'

Garrow shrugged. 'I guess it was a pre-standing arrangement.'

Walking up the garden path, Georgie saw that the front door was propped open to let the workmen and decorators come and go.

'Hello?' Georgie called as she and Garrow went in and stood in the doorway.

'Have you found him yet?' asked a voice.

Bella, wearing a long coat, appeared on the stairs and came down. She was wearing virtually no make-up, and her hair was scraped back under a sheepskin, trapper's style hat with long ear flaps. She seemed tired and drawn.

'Not yet, I'm afraid,' Garrow replied.

'Well, I hope he's crawled back under the rock he came from,' Bella said with a twisted mouth.

'Looks like you've got your hands full?' Georgie observed as one of the workmen passed her on the stairs.

'Oh, I know.' Bella rolled her eyes. 'With everything that's happened, I completely forgot they were coming. They've been booked in for months. Just a bit of prep work today and measuring up. Should be gone by lunchtime, thank God.'

Garrow gave her a look as if to say, *I told you.*

'What are you having done?' Georgie asked. Something told her that Bella was lying to them.

'Just the master bedroom,' Bella replied with a forced smile. 'Of course, the irony of the timing isn't lost on me as that twat has just left me … I'm just off to take the dogs for a walk, so is there something I can help you with?'

Garrow gave her an awkward look. 'I know you've been through a lot, but we are going to need something with Mark's DNA.'

Bella's face fell. 'Really? This is utterly ridiculous.'

'Sorry,' Garrow said with an apologetic shrug. 'It's just part of the procedure in an investigation like this.'

Bella narrowed her eyes. 'Essentially, you're calling me and my brother liars.'

As if on cue, Frank appeared from the kitchen and then looked at Bella. 'Problem?'

Georgie studied them for a second. Were they really involved in some kind of incestuous affair? The thought of it made her stomach turn. She peered at Bella and said in a polite tone that almost sounded sarcastic, 'Toothbrush, comb, something like that.'

'Fine,' Bella huffed and then disappeared up the stairs.

Georgie glanced over at Frank, who was fidgeting awkwardly. 'You and your sister must be very close?'

Frank frowned. 'Sorry?'

'We understand that you've recently been through a difficult divorce, and that's why you're living here? Which implies that you two must be very close,' Georgie said. She sensed Garrow bristle next to her and was aware that she might be sailing a little too close to the wind.

'She's my sister,' Frank said, pulling a face. 'That's what families do, isn't it? Help one another when there's a problem?'

Georgie didn't answer and then spotted Bella marching down the stairs. She was carrying a navy blue toothbrush.

'This was in the spare bedroom, so it must be Mark's,'

Bella sneered. 'He took the other one with him when he was here yesterday. Which makes all this a fucking joke.'

Taking an evidence bag from her pocket, Georgie opened it and smiled at her. 'If you could just pop it in here for me?' she said in the same overly polite tone.

Bella glared at her and dropped the toothbrush into the bag.

'Thank you,' Georgie chirped. 'I think that's all for today, so we'll get out of your way.'

Bella walked behind them to the door. 'I'd prefer it if you didn't come back here.'

Georgie turned, gestured to the evidence bag. 'I'm not sure we can guarantee that just yet.'

Bella turned and left.

Garrow looked at Georgie, who smirked. 'I thought at one point she was going to hit you.'

'Yeah,' Georgie grinned. 'She's one of those people that I can't help just winding up.'

Looking over at one of the workmen who was fishing around noisily for some tools in the back of the carpet van, Georgie had a thought.

'Hold this for a second,' she said as she handed the evidence bag to Garrow.

'Where are you going?'

'Back in a minute.'

With a quick check that neither Bella nor Frank were watching on from the house, Georgie wandered over to the workman.

'Must be nice to be booked up with work months in advance,' she said to him.

He frowned. 'Sorry, love, you've lost me.'

Georgie gestured to the house. 'It's just that Mrs Freudmann was telling me she'd had you guys booked in for months.'

The man was mystified and shook his head. 'Not us. This job only came in last week.'

Getting out her warrant card and showing it to him casually, Georgie asked, 'Can you tell me what day Mrs Freudmann booked the job?'

The man's face dropped as he saw her warrant card. 'I didn't know you were a police officer.' Maybe he was now regretting calling her *love,* Georgie wondered.

'If you can check for me?'

'Of course.' The man took out his mobile phone. 'Yeah, she booked us in last Thursday. Told us it was an emergency and needed doing straight away.'

'What was the emergency?' Georgie asked.

'Apparently, one of her dogs had some stomach bug. She said there was dog sick and diarrhoea everywhere. The carpet was totally ruined.'

'Did you remove the carpet from the bedroom?' Georgie asked, getting increasingly suspicious.

'No,' he replied. 'Mrs Freudmann and her brother had already taken it up and got rid of it. She said the smell was horrendous. But we're only here to measure up today. Carpet will go down beginning of next week.'

Georgie gave him a polite smile. 'Thanks. And it might be an idea not to tell Mrs Freudmann that we've had this little chat.'

The man shrugged as he grabbed a toolbag. 'Okay. Makes no difference to me.'

Garrow, who was now standing by the car, gave her a quizzical look as she approached. 'What was all that about?'

'Why would you lie about when you arranged to have carpets and decorating done?'

'What do you mean?'

'Bella told us she arranged for these guys to come in

months ago and had completely forgotten they were coming,' Georgie said.

'Okay.' Garrow was none the wiser.

Georgie gave him a dark look. 'Except she lied because she arranged for them to come last Thursday and told them it was an emergency.'

'Which means she is hiding something significant from us,' Garrow said.

Georgie gestured to the house. 'Yeah, so we're going to need a search warrant.'

Chapter 25

Nick and Ruth were driving along the A5 with the sea across to their right as they headed towards St Asaph.

'I never got to ask you if you've met Amanda's daughter yet,' Ruth said. 'Fran, wasn't it?'

Nick pulled a face. 'Yeah. That's a bit of a sore subject at the moment.'

'Why's that?'

'I think I know Fran from somewhere. You remember Wayne Summers?'

'I know the name.' Ruth searched her memory. 'Arson attack, wasn't it?'

'I remember her being mixed up with him,' Nick continued. 'Last night, I caught Fran going through all our stuff in the early hours. She made up some cock 'n' bull story about looking for painkillers.'

'You didn't believe her?'

'No, I didn't.'

Ruth pulled a face. 'I bet that went down well. What did Amanda say?'

'Not a lot, and she's now not talking to me.'

'Oh dear,' Ruth said. 'Not sure what the answer is there. Difficult one.'

Nick seemed keen not to continue the conversation as they pulled off the A5 and headed inland toward St Asaph Police Station. They parked up, went inside, explained why they were there and were shown to a meeting room.

Ruth knew very little about St Asaph except that it had the dubious distinction of being Britain's smallest city with a population of just over 3,000. The police station itself was a modern building. With its cladding, grey angular roof, and large windows, she thought it looked more like a secondary school than a police station.

Nick glanced over at her with a meaningful expression. 'I've been thinking.'

'Yeah, I thought I could smell burning,' Ruth quipped.

'Funny,' Nick said, rolling his eyes.

'Go on, then. What is it?'

'What if it's Frank Collard wearing Mark Freudmann's baseball cap in the CCTV?' Nick suggested.

Ruth thought for a moment. 'Okay. Nice theory, but it doesn't explain what Valerie Simpson saw from her window.'

Before they could continue, Susanna walked in. Her hair was pinned back tightly against her head, and she was wearing her black police uniform.

Without saying anything, Susanna went to the far end of the table and sat down. 'You have the CCTV from the cashpoint at the supermarket? Is that right?'

'Yes, ma'am,' Ruth said, feeling a little anxious.

Nick pulled out his laptop from his bag and flipped it open.

Susanna looked blank-faced at Ruth. 'I take it you've seen this footage?'

'Yes,' Ruth replied.

'What do you think?' Susanna asked. 'Is it Mark?'

'If I'm honest, I can't tell,' Ruth admitted.

Nick clicked on the relevant file to bring up the CCTV.

'What about you, Sergeant?' Susanna asked. 'What did you think?'

Nick gestured to Ruth. 'I'm in agreement with DI Hunter, ma'am. It's very difficult to see the man's face.'

'Show me then,' Susanna said coldly as she pointed towards the laptop screen.

Nick played the CCTV footage of the cashpoint. The man in the white baseball cap appeared in the frame and stood in the queue. He then went to the machine, put in a card, and withdrew cash.

As the man turned, Nick froze the image for Susanna to see.

'I'm afraid the man has this baseball cap pulled very low over his face,' Nick explained. 'It's very hard to see anything.'

'Yes, I can see that,' Susanna said sarcastically as she got up from her seat and came over. 'Play it again for me.'

Nick rewound the footage to where the man first appeared in the queue and then let it run to where he walked out of the shot.

Susanna frowned at them. 'That's Mark.'

Ruth frowned. 'Are you sure?'

Susanna pulled a surprised face. 'I'm his mother. I think I would recognise my own son, don't you?'

Ruth looked at her, wondering how to respond. 'Of course, ma'am. It's just that we don't see the man's face at any point.'

Susanna gave her a withering look. 'Do you have children, Detective Inspector Hunter?'

'Yes. I have a daughter,' Ruth said, feeling uneasy at Susanna's hostility.

'Well, I assume you would know her anywhere,' Susanna said. 'If you saw her at a distance, you would just know it was her. It's instinctive. And you wouldn't have to see her face clearly to know that it was her, would you?'

Ruth shrugged. She wasn't sure that she entirely agreed with Susanna's supposition. 'To be honest, I'm not sure.'

'Don't be ridiculous,' Susanna snorted and then pointed at the screen. 'I can tell from his body shape and the way he walks that it's my son.'

'Okay.' Ruth wasn't convinced. 'That's very helpful, ma'am.'

Susanna wasn't listening. Instead, she was staring at the screen. 'Can you play the footage back for me again, Sergeant?'

'Yes, ma'am.' Nick dutifully rewound the CCTV footage and let it play out again.

Susanna pointed suddenly. 'Freeze it just there.'

Ruth glanced at her. She had clearly seen something that concerned her. 'Everything all right, ma'am?'

Susanna went closer and pointed to a large, middle-aged man with a shock of steel-grey hair who was wearing a leather bomber jacket. He was standing to one side of the queue, looking on.

'That's Charlie Collard,' Susanna exclaimed.

What the hell was Bella's father doing standing beside a cash-point while Mark Freudmann withdrew money?

'Are you sure?' Ruth asked.

'Yes, positive,' Susanna said, as her eyes narrowed. 'I just don't understand.'

'Does Mark get on with his father-in-law?' Nick asked.

'God, no,' Susanna snorted as if this was a ridiculous question. 'They actively hate each other, as far as I know.

156

In recent years, they can hardly bear to be in the same room as each other at family functions. What the hell is he doing there? It doesn't make any sense.'

Ruth looked at Nick, wondering if the investigation had taken yet another bizarre turn.

Twenty minutes later, Ruth and Nick were hammering through Snowdonia, heading for Charlie Collard's main office at *Pig Meadow Farm*, a large free-range pig farm just outside Llanfyllin.

Ruth's phone buzzed with a text from Sarah. It was a little vague, telling her that she wouldn't be around later.

'Everything all right?' Nick asked.

Ruth nodded. 'Just a text from Sarah.'

'How's she doing?' Nick asked.

'Okay, I think,' Ruth replied. 'Given everything she's been through, she's doing really well. Unfortunately, she found out yesterday that her mum's got cancer.'

'Oh God,' Nick said. 'I'm sorry to hear that. Doesn't her mum still think she's missing?'

'Yeah, that's the problem. I don't think the PPS will let her see her now she's got a new identity.'

'God, that's really hard,' Nick said as they saw a sign up ahead – *Pig Meadow Farm – Free-Range Pigs*.

'Here we go,' Ruth said as they pulled into a space in the customer car park.

The area was surrounded by rolling fields on one side and woodland for as far as the eye could see on the other.

A young man in a high-vis green jacket approached with a smile. Ruth guessed he thought they were customers.

'Can I help?' the young man asked as he took off his gloves.

Taking out her warrant card, Ruth looked at him. 'DI Hunter and DS Evans. Llancastell CID. We're looking for Charlie Collard? Is he about?'

The young man's expression changed, as most people's did when seeing a warrant card. 'Erm, yeah. He's over in that far Portakabin.'

'Thanks,' Ruth said with a friendly smile.

Arriving at the Portakabin, Ruth knocked on the flimsy wooden door and, without waiting for an answer, went in. Inside, the cabin was set out like an office with a couple of computers, desks, and chairs. A middle-aged woman sat at the far end, talking quietly on the phone.

Over by the photocopier, a man was making tea.

As he turned, Ruth and Nick saw he was middle-aged, stocky, and grey-haired.

Charlie Collard.

If the man in the CCTV footage they had watched wasn't Charlie Collard, then he had one hell of a doppelganger somewhere in Llancastell.

Taking out her warrant card again, Ruth looked over at him. 'Mr Collard?'

'Yeah,' Charlie said as he stirred his tea, took the tea bag out with a spoon, and dropped it in the bin nonchalantly. He seemed completely unfazed by their presence in the office. 'Can I help?'

'DI Hunter and DS Evans from Llancastell CID,' Ruth said.

Charlie pointed to where he was standing. 'Kettle's just boiled if you fancy a brew?'

Nick shook his head. 'Thanks, but we're fine.'

Wandering casually over to his desk, Charlie sat down and gestured to two seats nearby. 'Grab a pew.'

'Thanks.' Ruth sat down.

He's a seriously cool customer.

'We're here about your son-in-law, Mark Freudmann,' Nick explained.

'Oh yeah?' Charlie gave an ironic laugh.

'We're trying to establish his whereabouts,' Ruth said.

'Last I heard, he'd packed up his stuff and left my daughter.' Charlie shrugged. 'And as far I'm concerned, that was bloody good riddance.'

Ruth frowned. 'You don't get on with Mark?'

She knew the answer to this, but she wanted to hear it directly from Charlie.

'Not really,' Charlie replied, rubbing his face. 'In fact, I'm not gonna lie to you. I can't stand the man.'

'Why's that?' Nick asked.

'He treated my daughter like shit. Gambled away her money, running around with other women,' Charlie growled. 'He was a feckless twat. But she said she loved him, so there wasn't anything I could do, was there? But I'm glad that he's out of her life now.'

'Can you tell us the last time you saw Mark?' Ruth asked.

Charlie moved his chair back and then crossed his legs. 'Must have been a couple of months ago. Maybe longer.'

Nick peered at him. 'You didn't see him last week?'

Charlie shook his head. 'No. Definitely not.'

Reaching into the laptop bag, Nick pulled out his computer and set it down on the desk. 'If you don't mind, I'm just going to show you something.'

Charlie shrugged. 'Go for it.'

As Nick tapped on the buttons, Ruth peered closely at Charlie's face. He didn't seem remotely concerned about what they were going to show him.

Nick played the CCTV footage, which showed the man in the white baseball cap at the cashpoint. 'This footage was taken at 1.15 pm on Tuesday afternoon at Tescos supermarket in Llancastell. We believe this man to be Mark Freudmann.'

Charlie leaned forward and peered at the screen. 'Hard to tell with that cap on, isn't it? Could be him.'

Nick then pointed to the figure standing to one side. 'And we think this man standing here is you?'

'What?' Charlie snorted with an ironic smile as he took a closer look. 'This fella here?'

'That's right,' Nick said.

'No, it's not me. Sorry.' Charlie frowned. 'Don't you think I would have noticed my own son-in-law standing right next to me in that queue?'

Ruth looked over at Charlie. 'Yes. But that man bears more than a striking resemblance to you, Mr Collard.'

'Yeah, he does,' Charlie agreed, seeming almost jovial. 'I'll give you that. Hey, maybe I've got a twin brother alive and well and living in Llancastell.'

'Can you tell us where you were on Tuesday afternoon?' Nick asked.

Charlie pointed at his desk. 'Sitting right here, like I always am, every day.'

'And you didn't go anywhere?'

'Not that I can remember,' Charlie replied. 'I certainly didn't drive to Tescos in Llancastell. I've just told you that.'

Ruth nodded. 'Okay, thank you for your help, Mr Collard.'

Chapter 26

I t had taken Sarah over three hours to travel by train from Llancastell to Doncaster via Chester and Stockport. With a few surreptitious messages, phone calls, and a trawl through social media for her extended family, Sarah had discovered that her mother was spending the day on the oncology ward at Doncaster's Royal Infirmary Hospital receiving chemotherapy treatment for her lung cancer.

As she marched down the platform at Doncaster station, she realised she hadn't been home by train for nearly twenty years. When she and Ruth used to visit her relatives in Yorkshire, they always drove up from London. Rebuilt in the 1930s, the station had a slight Deco feel to its architecture and a huge blue clock on its facade.

The journey took her back to her university days in the late 90s. She had taken a degree in sociology at Leeds Beckett University but had spent most of her time out socialising. The nightlife in Leeds was incredible, and after her quiet, rural upbringing in Hickleton – which all the kids renamed *Hicktown* – Sarah just needed to let her hair down.

Deciding that it was way too cold to walk the two miles from Doncaster Station over to the Royal Infirmary, she jumped into a taxi and began the journey across the town she used to call home. Named after the River Don that runs through the town, it was built by the Romans. Sarah used to love the fact that Sheffield and Leeds were only a stone's throw away and spent many weekends travelling to both cities as a teenager.

Passing the historic buildings such as Mansion House, which dated back to the 1780s, she felt nostalgic for the time she had spent there. On the right, she saw The Dome, or *The Donny Dome*, as it was known to locals. She remembered seeing the band *Suede* playing there in 1999 and singing her heart out to the song 'Trash'.

A few minutes later, the taxi pulled up outside the hospital, and Sarah jumped out. Her head was whirring. How would her mum react? It was probably going to be all too much for her. Was this the right thing to be doing? Was visiting her really going to put her in danger?

Getting into the lift, Sarah just stared into space as she lurched between the desire to see her mum and making sure that she was okay; or to play it safe and go, as the PPS had instructed her.

Coming out onto the third floor, Sarah marched towards the oncology ward. There was no going back now. She wasn't going to sit around in North Wales while her mum went through chemotherapy on her own. That just wasn't okay.

She walked gingerly into the Oncology Department, making sure that she gave the appearance that she knew where she was going.

Walking past two nurses hurrying the other way and

talking in loud voices, she spotted a large room to the right. Inside were several padded armchairs, with patients sitting attached to drips. She assumed they were receiving chemo-therapy.

To the left, she saw what appeared to be a little old lady wearing a baby pink headscarf.

It was her mum. It was Doreen.

Oh my God, she looks so old, Sarah thought in shock.

She moved very slowly towards her, hardly daring to breathe. Her mum was so frail and so unwell.

Taking a red plastic chair as she went, Sarah went warily to where her mum was sitting staring into space. Her stomach was tight, and her breathing was getting shallow.

Carefully putting the chair down to her side, Sarah sat down and looked at her.

For a few seconds, her mum didn't realise that anyone was sitting down next to her. Then she turned to look directly at Sarah.

'Hello?' Doreen gave a perplexed expression.

'Hello, Mum,' Sarah whispered.

For a few seconds, Doreen peered at her with a blank face as though she had never seen Sarah's face before.

'It's me, Mum,' she said. 'Sarah.'

Doreen frowned as though she was completely baffled. 'I … Sarah?'

Sarah reached out and gently took her bony hand.

Doreen's face was still aghast – it didn't make any sense to her.

'I don't understand,' Doreen voice shook. 'I …'

'I'm so sorry, Mum,' Sarah said, holding back the tears. 'I'm fine. I'm okay. And it's such a long story as to where I've been. But I am all right. And I wanted to see you.'

It was as if Doreen hadn't heard a word that Sarah had said. She just stared at her.

'I don't … understand.'

'I know. I'm so sorry, Mum.'

Taking her hand out of Sarah's, she reached up and very gently stroked her face as if she were a small child.

'Is it really you?' she asked as if this was some cruel joke.

'Yeah, it is me, Mum,' Sarah said. 'I came to see you because I heard you weren't well.'

'But you went missing,' Doreen said, shaking her head. 'We didn't know where you'd gone.'

'Yes, I know. I was taken away by some very evil men. And they kept me for years.'

Doreen narrowed her eyes. 'You mean like being kidnapped?'

Sarah nodded. 'Yeah. I was kidnapped.'

'What about police? Do they know you're okay?'

Sarah smiled at her. 'Yes. It's all okay, Mum. You don't need to worry about that.'

'What about Ruth? Have you seen her yet?'

'Yes, Mum. I'm living with her,' Sarah explained. 'She lives in North Wales now.'

'Does she?' Doreen asked, looking confused again. 'Are you going away again?'

Sarah shook her head. 'No. I have to give evidence against the men that took me. And that means that at the moment, no one can know that I've been to see you today. Do you understand that?'

Doreen blinked and then frowned. 'What do you mean?'

'You can't tell anyone that I've been to see you today.'

'Why not?'

'It's too complicated to explain,' Sarah said. 'But you need to promise me you won't tell anyone.'

'Yes. Don't worry; I'm not going to tell anyone.'

'Good.' Sarah smiled. 'But I'm going to write down my number just in case of emergencies.'

Doreen looked directly at her with watery eyes. She touched her cheek again. 'I thought I'd lost you. I thought you had gone forever.' Doreen pursed her lips as a tear rolled down her face. 'And now you're sitting here. It's a miracle.'

Sarah rubbed a tear from her face. 'It really is a miracle, Mum. You have no idea.'

Chapter 27

It had just gone five by the time Ruth had assembled the CID team together. The investigation was developing fast, but it was still proving to be incredibly confusing. Georgie and Jim had revealed what they had found at Bella's home and the lie she had told about calling in the carpet firm and decorators. She agreed with them it was highly suspicious, and she had asked Drake to talk to a local magistrate to secure a Section 18 Search Warrant for the property.

'Right, listen up, everyone.' Ruth went over to a computer and put the CCTV footage from the cashpoint onto the main monitor that was attached to the wall in the CID office. 'Just to keep you up to speed because events seem to be moving fast in this investigation. Nick and I showed this footage from the cashpoint to DCC Freudmann. She is convinced that the man here in the white baseball cap who withdrew money is her son Mark.'

Garrow frowned. 'But you can't see his face, boss?'

'I know.' Ruth shrugged. 'And I did point that out to

her, but she claims that from his body shape and the way he moves, she could identify the man as her son.'

'Maybe she just wants it to be him,' Georgie suggested.

'That's a possibility. The other development is that the DCC spotted a figure just here in the CCTV who very closely resembled Charlie Collard, Bella's father,' Nick explained.

'What? That doesn't make any sense,' Garrow said.

'We went and confronted Charlie Collard with the CCTV,' Ruth said. 'He categorically denies that it was him.'

'Does it look like him?' Georgie asked, pointing to the image on the monitor.

'Either Charlie Collard has an identical twin, or he's lying to us,' Nick said dryly.

'What was he doing there with Mark Freudmann?' Garrow asked.

Ruth nodded. 'You're right. They hate each other's guts. But what if this man here is actually Frank Collard?'

Georgie raised an eyebrow. 'Now I'm really confused.'

'Frank is wearing Mark Freudmann's distinctive white baseball cap. Now that *would* explain why Charlie Collard might be standing just over here.'

Garrow raised an eyebrow. 'But Valerie Simpson told us she saw Mark Freudmann at the cashpoint.'

Nick shrugged. 'She was in her car. And what she saw from a distance was a man who was a similar age and build to Mark, wearing his baseball cap low over his face, at the cashpoint. She could have been mistaken.'

'She also told us she saw Mark packing the car and arguing with Bella on the drive,' Garrow said.

'Except she saw that from the first-floor window and probably a hundred, if not a hundred and fifty yards away.'

Ruth's hypothesis cleared in her mind. 'What if she saw Frank Collard wearing Mark's white baseball cap?'

There were a few seconds as the CID team processed this.

Ruth went over to the scene board and looked out at the room. 'Okay, let's play this out, shall we? Last Thursday evening, the 21st, Bella and Mark were sitting outside on the patio beside a fire pit. They begin to have a row. Possibly it's to do with Mark's gambling or womanising. It might even be to do with whatever relationship Bella has with her brother Frank. The row gets violent, and Bella throws a glass at Mark. Frank comes out and tries to calm things down. The row continues inside the house. Maybe Mark goes up to the master bedroom to pack his things because he's leaving Bella. She attacks him in the bedroom with something sharp like a knife and kills him. There are now bloodstains on the carpet and walls. She asks Frank to help. In the next 24 to 48 hours, Bella and Frank decide that they have to dismember Mark's body and get rid of it. They decide they are going to dispose of it in Lake Vyrnwy. They take up the bloodstained carpet, paint over any bloodstains on the walls, and then contact a carpet and decorating company to cover their tracks. They continue to act as if everything is normal.

On the Friday, Susanna Freudmann contacts Bella to ask where Mark is. He's not answering his phone. Bella tells her that Mark has done one of his disappearing acts again.'

Garrow looked over. 'Why did we just find a foot and half a leg, boss?'

Nick sat forward in his chair. 'If they wrapped up Mark's body and attached weights before dropping it into the lake. For some reason, his left foot and leg came loose and floated to the surface. The rest is still sitting on the bed of the lake.'

'Sounds plausible,' Ruth said. 'Susanna continues to try and contact Mark all weekend but doesn't get an answer which is completely out of character.'

Georgie nodded. 'But they didn't count on us finding the foot or the wellington boot in the lake. Which is why Frank had to pretend to be Mark so that we would still think that Mark was alive.'

'I'm thinking by this point, Bella might have contacted her father Charlie to tell him what's happened,' Ruth said. 'Frank Collard is banned from driving, so Charlie took him into Llancastell. Maybe Frank is wearing Mark's clothes. We know he was wearing Mark's white baseball cap. Frank used the card for their joint account to take out money. Bella knew that we'd look at the CCTV when she flagged up that Mark has used the cashpoint and just hoped that we'd ask her to confirm that it was Mark in the CCTV footage. She didn't count on Valerie Simpson driving past and seeing Frank at the cashpoint in Mark's clothes and cap.'

Nick raised an eyebrow. 'It actually helped her out in the short term.'

'And then Bella and Frank manufacture this big row on the drive, with Frank putting suitcases into his car,' Georgie said.

Ruth nodded, 'Exactly. They know that Valerie Simpson is a nosey neighbour, and she'll be watching from her first-floor window. Now they've got an independent witness to the fact that Mark has come home, packed his bags, and left.'

'Bloody hell.' Nick sighed.

Ruth pulled a face. 'The only problem is that this is

complete supposition. Unless we can find some hard evidence, then the CPS aren't going to be interested in charging them.'

Garrow looked over and winced. 'Good news and bad news on that one, boss. Good news is that the lab have finally extracted decent DNA from the ankle bone of the foot. Bad news is that the toothbrush Bella gave us has nothing on it we can get DNA from. In fact, the lab suspect that it's a brand new toothbrush that's never been used.'

'Of course, it's a new toothbrush,' Nick said dryly. 'She's not stupid. She's buying time.'

Drake appeared at the door, holding a document. 'Ruth, I've got your Section 18 Search Warrant signed off.'

'That's great, boss.' Ruth approached him and took it.

Drake gave her a dark look and said quietly. 'Remember that this is the DCC's son we're dealing with. We need everything done by the book and with the utmost sensitivity.'

'Of course,' Ruth replied sombrely.

Ruth walked back across the CID office. She needed to arrange for the SOCOs to meet her down at Bella Freudmann's house ASAP.

Georgie glanced up from her desk, where she was looking at her computer screen, and said with a sense of urgency. 'Boss?'

'What is it?' Ruth asked as she turned and went back the way she had come.

'Mark Freudmann had a brand new Land Rover Discovery,' Bella explained. 'I spoke to the dealership who were going to see if they could use the car's GPS to get a location on where the car is now.'

'And?' Ruth asked.

'According to the GPS co-ordinates, Mark's car is

sitting at their home in Llwydiarth. I didn't see it earlier, so it must be hidden away.'

Ruth nodded. 'Okay. Good work, Georgie. I'm calling the SOCO team now. And then I want you and Jim to accompany me and Nick to Llwydiarth. I think Bella Freudmann's luck just ran out.'

Chapter 28

Glancing up at the monitor on platform 3 at Chester Station, Sarah saw she had ten minutes before her train left to take her across the Welsh border to Llancastell General. The journey only took twenty minutes, and Ruth had sent a text to say that she would work most of the evening. She had decided not to tell Ruth that she had been to Doncaster to see her mum. Even though Ruth would probably understand, she would also be furious. For starters, breaking the agreement she had signed with the PPS could lose Sarah her new identity and her home. They had made it very clear that if she attempted to contact a member of her family before she had given her evidence, they could withdraw their protection, and she would be on her own. She didn't care. Her mum was seriously ill and, even though the treatment was working, there was no guarantee that she would live long enough for Sarah to wait for any trial to finish.

Sarah wandered down to the small café and shop that was halfway down the platform, ordered a café latte, and grabbed a peanut KitKat. A middle-aged man came in behind her. He was tall, Eastern European looking, with a shaved head and piercing blue eyes. Taking a packet of crisps with his gloved hands, he joined her at the counter and gave her a curious smile.

That was weird.

'Coffee, black,' the man said to the woman who was serving. His accent was definitely Eastern European, maybe Polish. It wasn't that surprising as there was a large Polish population in North Wales, but it still spooked her. Maybe it was because his voice and accent reminded her of Sergei Saratov.

The woman handed Sarah her coffee. 'Here you go. Mind it's not too hot, dearie. We've got some of those sleeves over there if you need one.'

Sarah smiled. 'Thank you.'

Before she could turn to go, the man had peered over at her with a frown and asked, 'Don't I know you from somewhere?'

Sarah shook her head as her pulse quickened a little. *Is he hitting on me, or is this something more sinister?*

'No, I don't think so.'

'Sorry. I know that sounded like some terrible line,' the man said with a smile. 'It's just that I think I've met you somewhere before. I am normally very good with faces.'

Now on her guard and feeling uneasy, Sarah gave him a forced smile. 'I don't remember. Maybe it was someone else?'

'Ever been to Russia?' he asked.

'Yes,' she said and then wondered why she hadn't just lied.

'Oh, okay. Whereabouts?' he asked as the woman behind the counter handed him his black coffee.

'Moscow and St Petersburg,' she replied, trying to back away slowly to indicate she wasn't really in a chatty mood.

The man grinned. 'Really? I'm from St Petersburg. Although so are five million other people.'

Sarah indicated outside to the platform. 'Anyway, I'd better go and wait for my train.'

'Oh, you're getting the same train as me,' the man said. 'Going to North Wales?'

Sarah nodded as she took two steps towards the door. She was now feeling frightened. 'Yes.'

'Well, it was nice to meet you,' the man said. 'I didn't get your name?'

Sarah's pulse was racing. 'Nice to meet you too. I'm going out here now.'

'Okay, bye then,' he said. 'My name's Vitali.'

Coming out into the cold air outside, Sarah marched down to the end of the platform, not daring to look back. Her pulse was racing.

What the hell was all that about? Was he just being friendly? Am I just totally paranoid?

She stopped and glanced down the platform to see her train coming around the bend and then draw level with the platform as it slowed to a stop. Then she spotted the man, Vitali, coming out of the café. He looked over, gave her a cheery wave, and then got on the train as the doors opened.

What am I going to do? I don't want to be trapped on this train. What if he actually knows who I am?

Taking a deep breath, she stared down the platform to check that the man had boarded the train.

As the electronic beeps sounded to warn passengers that the doors were closing, she made her decision.

She took two steps back from the train. She would wait for the next one.

Chapter 29

I t was dark by the time Ruth and Nick sped into
Llwydiarth and pulled up outside Bella Freudmann's
home. Georgie and Garrow were following behind,
along with two patrol cars and four uniformed officers who
were going to help secure the premises and support the
search. The SOCO van had already arrived and was
parked close to the far side of the drive.

Feeling a slight burst of adrenaline, Ruth got out of the
car and noticed that Bella's white Porsche Cayenne wasn't
parked on the drive. Did that mean she was out? Was
Frank Collard in the house on his own? Either way, given
the serious nature of the crime they were investigating,
they could execute the search warrant, whether Bella was
at home or not.

As Ruth and Nick marched up the drive, the gravel
crunched under their shoes.

'You think she's out?' Nick asked as they reached the
front door.

'Possibly,' Ruth replied. 'If she is, we're going in
anyway.'

'Georgie told me to watch out for the dogs.'

Ruth hadn't thought of that. 'If there's a problem, we'll have to get the Canine Unit down here.'

Pressing the buzzer, she stood back from the front door and opened up the search warrant to show whoever opened the door.

It was complete silence as they waited.

Nick turned to her. 'No dogs?'

'Maybe she's taken them for a walk,' Ruth suggested.

Ruth pressed the buzzer again several times. She was now convinced that no one was at home. That would certainly make their search of the home easier.

After waiting for another minute, she signalled to two burly uniformed officers who were holding a black steel battering ram.

'Constable, can we have this door open, please?' she asked as she and Nick stepped back to allow them through.

With an almighty swing, the Constable smashed the battering ram hard against the lock of the front door.

CRASH!

The front door flew open, and they made their way in.

'This is a police raid!' shouted one of the officers as they marched into the hallway. 'Make yourself known!'

Nothing.

'Doesn't look like anyone's home, ma'am,' the officer said.

Ruth nodded, 'Thank you, Constable.'

'Morning, everyone,' said a cheerful voice.

It was Tony Amis, the chief SOCO standing behind them on the driveway.

He was dressed in a white forensic suit, blue gloves, and a nitrile mask.

Ruth gave him a laconic smile. 'Morning, Tony.'

'Where do you want us, Inspector?' he asked, pointing to the interior of the house.

'We think that the master bedroom upstairs might be a scene of crime,' Ruth explained. 'I'd start there.'

'Might I suggest officers limit themselves to the ground floor at the moment. I'll use forensic suits and stepping plates upstairs,' Amis said. 'If we find anything significant in the bedroom, then the entire house will need properly securing as a crime scene.'

'Sounds sensible, Tony.' Ruth saw Georgie approaching the front door.

'I think I've found something, boss,' she said, gesturing outside.

Ruth looked at Nick, and they followed her out.

Georgie marched over to the left of the house, where there was a double garage. Both doors were closed, as was the side door.

'What are we looking at, Georgie?' Nick asked.

'It's all locked up,' Georgie replied as she then gestured to the side door. 'But there's a slight gap in the frame. I think there's a black car inside this garage.'

Ruth knew that Mark Freudmann owned a black Land Rover Discovery, and the GPS signal had indicated that it was at the house somewhere.

Going to the double doors, Ruth could see they were secured with a padlock.

Nick signalled to a uniformed officer who was reeling out some police evidence tape to secure the site.

'Constable?' Nick said. 'You don't happen to have a pair of bolt cutters in your vehicle, do you?'

The constable gave him a wry smile. 'I do indeed, Sarge.' Putting down the roll of tape, the constable jogged over to the patrol car.

Ruth looked at Nick. 'Good thinking, Batman.'

'Hey, not just a pretty face,' Nick joked.

Georgie frowned. 'Don't you mean not *even* a pretty face?'

Nick gave her a sarcastic smile as the constable jogged over and handed him the bolt cutters. Nick opened them, walked over to the garage doors, and snapped the metal lock with a snip.

Crouching down, Nick took the padlock out of the lock, grabbed the up-and-over garage door, and pushed it up.

With a metallic rattle, the door slid up to reveal what was inside the garage.

A black Land Rover Discovery.

Georgie grinned. 'Bingo!'

'Nice work, Georgie.' Ruth entered the garage.

'Thanks, boss,' Georgie said, trying to sound less delighted than she actually was. 'That's the right registration.'

Going to the rear of the vehicle, Ruth cupped her hands and peered into the boot. There were two large suitcases and a holdall sitting there.

'We've got luggage in the back,' she said.

Georgie gave her a concerned look. 'Boss, I've had a nasty thought.'

'No surprise there,' Nick joked.

'What is it?' Ruth asked.

'I spoke to the carpet-fitter earlier,' Georgie explained. 'I asked him not to mention it to Bella, but if she had any inkling that I had quizzed him about when she had called, then she might have panicked. She and Frank aren't at home. The car and dogs have gone. What if they've done a runner, boss?'

It was a good point and not something that Ruth had considered up to that point.

'Let's see what the SOCOs turn up,' Ruth said as she gestured to the car. 'I think we've got enough to arrest both Bella and Frank now. And if we can get an arrest warrant, then we can mobilise North Wales Police to find them.'

Making her way back over to the house, Garrow came out of the front door and gave her a look. 'Boss, Amis wants you to suit up and go upstairs.'

That sounds ominous, she thought.

'Okay,' Ruth said, entering the house. 'Did he say why?'

Garrow gave a wry smile. 'No. But he did use the French phrase *tout de suite.*'

'Yeah, my French is a bit rusty if I'm honest, Jim,' Ruth admitted as she went to grab a forensic suit, shoe covers, and a mask.

'It means 'immediately', boss,' he explained.

Ruth smiled as she pulled on her forensic suit. 'Yeah, Jim, I got the gist of it.'

Putting the mask over her nose and mouth, she realised that even after all these years, it still made her feel a little claustrophobic.

She climbed the stairs and saw there were now four SOCOs on the landing and the passageway that led down to the master bedroom.

As she got to the top, she looked at the nearest SOCO. 'Professor Amis?'

The SOCO pointed. 'Down there. Second door on the right, ma'am.'

As she made her way towards the bedroom, she could already see that there was blue UV light leaking out of the room across the carpet.

Getting to the doorway, she saw Amis crouched down on the far side of the bedroom. He was wearing goggles and using a UV light.

'Something to show me, Tony?' she asked as she trod on the aluminium step plates going in.

Pushing up his goggles, he gave her a dark look. 'There is blood everywhere.'

Ruth frowned, but she wasn't hugely surprised.

He handed her a pair of UV sensitive goggles. 'Come and have a look.'

Shining the torch on the bare floorboards, it was clear to see that the floor had been washed and scrubbed. There were, however, still black flecks of blood residue, not visible to the naked eye, across a large area, especially dark around the joins in the floorboards, where the blood would have pooled.

'Whoever tried to clear all this up has done a pretty shoddy job,' Amis said as he then shone the UV light onto the far wall. 'Someone has repainted this very recently. In fact, the paint is still a little sticky in places, so only a couple of days.'

'That fits in with our timescale.' Ruth peered at the wall. There were spots and flecks of blood all the way to the top of the wall. 'How the hell is there blood up there?'

Amis raised an eyebrow. 'I'm no blood splatter expert, but even I can see your victim had an artery severed in the attack.' He pointed to the side of his own neck. 'Probably one of the carotid arteries on either side of the neck. He or she would have been dead in less than a minute.'

'Jesus,' Ruth muttered under her breath. 'We believe that our body was dismembered before leaving here, so can you guys check to see if you can find signs of where that might have happened.'

Amis' eyes widened. 'The foot?'

'Sorry?'

'The foot and leg we found at Lake Vyrnwy,' Amis said

with a smile. 'You think they originate from whoever was murdered in this room?'

'I do now. I just wasn't sure.'

'Right,' Amis said with a fascinated nod. 'Well, if they've done as bad a job of clearing up wherever they dismembered the body, then we won't have a problem finding it.'

'Thanks, Tony,' Ruth said as she turned and made her way out of the bedroom.

For the briefest of seconds, she got a flash of what had happened in that bedroom when Bella had attacked and killed Mark. It sent a shiver down her spine as she reached the top of the stairs.

Waiting for her at the bottom was Garrow, who was holding an evidence bag. 'What have we got up there, boss?'

'A lot of blood,' she said as she stood to one side and took off her forensic shoe covers 'I need you and Georgie to get everyone out of this house now. It's a murder scene of crime. Anyone coming back in needs to be wearing full forensics. And ask the SOCOs to put down step plates on the ground floor. I don't want any fuck ups. Get someone in uniform to extend the cordon around the house to include the road. I need someone to run a proper duty log and any spare bods to start house-to-house interviews with everyone within a mile either way of here.'

'Yes, boss,' Garrow nodded.

'What have you got there?' she asked, pointing to the evidence bag.

Garrow raised a knowing eyebrow as he held up the bag and turned it around so Ruth could see what was inside.

A white baseball cap that looked identical to the one they had seen in the CCTV footage.

'Nice one,' she said. 'Where did you find that?'

'SOCOs found it rolled up in a towel inside the wheelie bin,' Garrow explained.

Ruth looked at him. 'In the old days, we used to say that we've got them *bang to rights.*'

Garrow gave her a darker look. 'There is some bad news though, boss.'

'Which is?'

'There's a secure gun cabinet under the stairs there,' Garrow pointed to the small, open wooden door which she could only see the back of. 'It's been unlocked, and the gun and ammunition have been taken.'

Chapter 30

Ruth glanced up at Drake, who was sitting at his desk and smoothing his hand over his goatee.

'What about DNA?' he asked.

'SOCOs found several toothbrushes and a man's comb,' Ruth replied. 'We're convinced that we can get Mark Freudmann's DNA from one of them. Then we can see if we can match that to the blood samples from the house and the foot and leg that we found.'

Drake nodded his head slowly. 'Okay. We won't get a meeting with the CPS today, but I'll insist we meet with them first thing tomorrow. If we can match the DNA, then we have enough to arrest and charge Bella for her husband's murder.'

'And Frank Collard for conspiracy,' Ruth added.

'We're going to have to drag the lake,' Drake said. 'And someone is going to have to go and talk to the DCC before the press gets wind of what's going on. The press office is getting calls about our operation in Llwydiarth today.'

'I'll go and talk to her on the way home,' Ruth said

with a serious expression. It wasn't something that she was looking forward to, but it was the right thing to do.

'Are you sure?' Drake asked. 'I'm happy to do it.'

Ruth shook her head. 'She knows I'm the SIO, boss. It's going to seem strange if you rock up on the doorstep. I'd prefer to talk to her myself.'

Drake nodded and sighed. 'How convinced are you that they've gone on the run?'

'We have a uniform patrol sitting just down the road from the house,' Ruth explained. 'I think Bella knew we were going to turn up with a search warrant eventually.'

'What about a press conference?' Drake asked.

'Once we have that DNA match, then I think that's an excellent idea,' Ruth agreed.

'I'm guessing that you're checking their phones and bank details?' Drake asked.

'Yes, boss,' Ruth replied. 'Bella has a brand new Porsche Cayenne. A car like that will have a top-end GPS tracker fitted to it.'

Drake raised an eyebrow. 'Unless they've had the sense to turn it off.'

Ruth pulled a face. 'After the botched job they did of clearing up the crime scene, I'm not sure that would even occur to them. We're not exactly dealing with criminal masterminds here.'

'I hope you're right.' Drake said with a dark expression. 'I can't imagine the fallout if we allow Mark Freudmann's killers to roam around North Wales for very long. The DCC will be all over us like a rash.'

'Yeah, that's true. We'll be on the hunt for Bella until we find her, boss. There is something else that makes it all the more serious.'

Drake didn't like the sound of that. 'Which is what, Ruth?'

'We think they might be armed,' Ruth replied. 'They had a secure gun cabinet. Except when we got there, it had been cleared out.'

Drake sat back in his chair – it wasn't good news.

By THE TIME RUTH PARKED UP OUTSIDE THE DCC's house, the ink-black sky was clear and sprinkled with stars. Over to the east, a full moon hung ominously over the top of the trees that traversed the horizon. Ruth had heard that it was known as a *Wolf Moon,* as it was the first full moon of January. The radio had claimed that its origin came from Native Americans who often heard the howling of wolves during the icy cold nights at this time of the year. Given the conversation Ruth was about to have with DCC Susanna Freudmann, it seemed an appropriately ominous symbol in the sky.

Looking down at the phone, Ruth sent a quick text to Sarah to tell her she would be home in just over an hour. For a moment, she remembered Sarah's news about her mother and wondered how she was dealing with it. She thought of her own mother, who died from breast cancer in 2011. Her mother had been a slightly bitter woman who seemed to keep an emotional distance from everyone around her. She even found giving someone a hug challenging. Ruth had often wondered what had happened to her mother to make her that way. As she thought of her, it seemed so sad that she had never talked about why she felt the way she did. And as a result, she had lived her whole life with this detached fragility that seemed to continually preoccupy her. Then Ruth realised it was the same brittleness that Susanna Freudmann exhibited. A frosty indifference that was no doubt some form of coping mechanism.

Ruth's train of thought was broken as a light came on at a downstairs window.

Time to get this over and done with, she thought, now with a heightened sense of empathy for Susanna.

Walking up the garden path, she noticed the lack of plants and flowers in the front garden. There was a small, neat lawn, and everything else had been patioed.

Taking a deep breath, Ruth used the silver knocker to bang on the door. She then took a step back to allow an appropriate distance for when Susanna opened the door.

After nearly a minute, the door finally opened, and Susanna peered out at her. Her hair was pulled back into a ponytail, and she was wearing a sweatshirt and jeans.

Blimey, Ruth thought. *She actually looks kind of attractive like that.*

'Sorry for calling so late,' Ruth said apologetically.

'That's fine. I've had a report that you've called SOCOs into the house?'

'That's right.' Ruth then looked at her. 'Is it okay if I come in?'

'Yes,' she said, opening the door wider. 'I suppose you should.'

Ruth followed Susanna into a living room where there was a log fire burning and some classical music playing very quietly.

'Sit down, Ruth,' Susanna said, pointing to a large, teal-coloured sofa. 'Any more developments in finding Mark?'

'I'm afraid not, ma'am.' Ruth hesitated for a few seconds. 'But we have made some significant discoveries at the home today.'

Susanna stared directly at her. 'How significant?'

'Significant enough for myself and DCI Drake to meet

with the CPS first thing tomorrow and issue an arrest warrant for Bella Freudmann and Frank Collard.'

Susanna sat forward and nodded almost imperceptibly. 'You're going to arrest them for Mark's murder, aren't you?'

'I'm afraid so,' Ruth said.

There were a few seconds of silence. The crackling noise of the open fire and burning wood seemed to intensify with the solemn atmosphere.

'What did you find?' Susanna asked eventually in a soft voice.

'SOCOs found a substantial amount of blood in the master bedroom,' Ruth said. 'We also found Mark's car in the garage.'

Susanna's eyes roamed around the room as she took in the news. 'What about the CCTV of the cashpoint?'

'We believe that was Frank Collard posing as Mark,' Ruth said. 'That would explain why Charlie Collard was standing to one side. Frank Collard is banned from driving, so Charlie Collard must have given him a lift.'

Susanna frowned. 'What about Mark and Bella's argument that was witnessed by their neighbour?'

'Frank and Bella staged it so that people would believe that Mark was still alive.'

'And you believe Bella murdered Mark in that bedroom last Thursday?' Susanna asked.

'Yes, ma'am.'

'Do you have any doubts that Mark is dead?'

'No, ma'am,' Ruth said gently. 'I'm so sorry.'

Susanna took an audible breath, but her face revealed nothing more than she was deep in thought. The pain of learning that her son had been murdered seemed to have been buried deep within.

Getting up from the armchair, Susanna gave her a

meaningful look. 'It was very good of you to come here tonight and tell me what you had found.'

'I'm so sorry for your loss.' Ruth got up from the sofa.

Susanna frowned. 'And where are Bella and Frank Collard now?'

'We think they've had gone on the run,' Ruth said.

'Right.' Susanna straightened her back. 'I would appreciate it if you did everything within your power to bring them to justice.'

Ruth looked directly at her. 'I promise I will. I really mean it.'

'Yes, I can see that you do.'

As Ruth went to go, she remembered something. 'Just one last thing, ma'am.'

'Yes?'

'We found a gun cabinet under the stairs in the house.'

'Yes. Mark used to go on shoots with the great and the good sometimes. Not my sort of thing.'

'So, there should have been a shotgun in there?'

Susanna gave her a dark look. 'I take it there isn't?'

'No. The gun cabinet had been cleared out,' Ruth informed her.

'Oh, dear. That does make everything far more serious.'

Chapter 31

The CID office was buzzing with the kind of excitement that comes with being on the verge of cracking a murder case. The air was thick with coffee fumes and bacon rolls. Ruth glanced at her watch. It was 1 am, but Bella and Frank were on the run, and there was no time to lose.

Walking to the front of the office, Ruth put down her coffee and perched on a nearby table. 'Right guys, let's get cracking. We've got a lot to get through. As most of you know, later today, we will be getting an arrest warrant for Bella Freudmann's arrest on suspicion of the murder of her husband, Mark.'

There was a murmur as some detectives made their thoughts known to each other.

'We will also be arresting Frank Collard for conspiracy. Myself and DCI Drake will be meeting the CPS this morning to get them up to date with what we have.' Ruth explained. 'However, the fact they have at least one firearm with them does make our search for them far more serious, and we will have to use Authorised Firearms officers when we eventually track them down.'

The doors to the office opened, and Nick marched in holding a computer printout. He seemed energised as he approached.

'Oh, nice of you to join us this morning, Nick,' Georgie joked.

'I haven't been home, smart-arse,' Nick replied before pointing to the paper he was holding. 'We've got her.'

'What is it?' Ruth asked.

'DNA results, boss,' Nick explained. 'The DNA found on Mark Freudmann's comb and toothbrush matches the DNA of the blood in the bedroom and the severed foot and leg.'

Ruth gave a smile of relief. 'Brilliant.'

There were more murmurs around the office. Everyone knew that this was now an open-and shut-case.

'Bella Freudmann is going to prison for a very long time,' Nick said.

Ruth raised an eyebrow. 'We've got to find her first.'

Garrow looked over. 'Boss, SOCOs report shows there were no passports found at the property.'

Ruth frowned. 'Maybe they're planning on going abroad? Jim, update the PNC and indicate that Bella Freudmann is wanted. I'll organise an 'All Ports Warning'.'

'We need a trace on that car ASAP' Nick said. 'The registration is already logged with traffic and the ANPR unit. I'll talk to the Digital Forensics and chase getting the GPS signal tracked.'

Ruth turned to the map on the scene board. 'Nearest airport is Liverpool or Manchester, isn't it?'

Garrow glanced over. 'There's an airport on Anglesey, boss.'

'How long would that take?' Ruth asked.

'It's about seventy miles from here, so an hour and a half. Maybe two hours on those roads,' Garrow said.

Ruth nodded. 'Are there just domestic flights?'

Garrow shook his head. 'No, boss. If I remember correctly, you can fly to Dublin, a few places in France and maybe Spain.'

'Great,' Ruth said dryly. 'Give their security a ring and give them a description. I do not want them flying out of the country. And then ring Liverpool and Manchester, talk to officers there, and do the same.'

'Yes, boss,' Garrow said.

'Right. I need Bella and Frank's bank accounts, phones, and social media monitored. If they make a transaction, take out cash or make a phone call, we need to know immediately.'

French looked over. 'Got something, boss. Frank Collard's account shows a payment from yesterday of £215 to a Hafod Boarding Kennels.'

'Right, so wherever they're heading, they're not taking the dogs with them,' Ruth said, thinking aloud.

A phone rang on one of the desks, and Georgie went over to answer it.

Nick looked over at her. 'Do we think Charlie Collard is involved, boss?'

'Possibly. I noticed they have CCTV cameras at the *Pig Meadow Farm* site. I want all the footage going back to Thursday 21st. Check Bella's phone records and see if she called the farm or her father's mobile at any point on the 21st or after,' Ruth said. 'I'm holding a press conference at 9 am. Bella and Frank are on the run somewhere, and someone must have seen them.

Georgie put down the phone. 'Boss, that was the Underwater Search and Marine Unit. They've been dragging the lake and using sonar. They've found something significant.'

THE SKY WAS A DARK BLACK CANVAS FULL OF CLOUD COVER as Ruth and Nick arrived at Lake Vyrnwy. As they turned the corner, Ruth could see the blazing halogen lights that the North Wales USMU had erected to help with the search of the lake. As they got out, there was a soft, musty rain in the air which swirled in the vanilla halogen beams that arced and fell across the water.

Ruth glanced at her watch. The sun wasn't going to rise for another two hours. The rain was getting heavier. As they approached, she could see a boat which was two hundred yards from the shore. Its diesel engine throbbed in a low rhythmic tone. Close by, two officers were looking at a tiny sonar screen. She assumed that the sonar equipment was on board the boat.

'What have we got, Sergeant?' Ruth asked as she approached, and she and Nick showed their warrant cards.

'We located an object on the lake bed.' He gestured to the boat, which had turned and was heading across the lake to where they were standing. 'My men have just winched it on board.'

'Did they say what it was?' Nick asked.

'I'm not sure. They said that whatever it is, it stinks to high heaven,' the Sergeant explained.

Ruth exchanged a look with Nick – could be Mark Freudmann's remains.

'Anyone seen the SOCOs yet?' Ruth asked, and as if on cue, the SOCO van arrived and parked next to their car.

For a few seconds, Ruth just watched the USMU boat

moving slowly, its harsh floodlights glaring in the rain, carrying its grim cargo towards them.

'Is that the rest of him?' asked a voice.

It was Tony Amis, and he was already dressed in a forensic suit.

'We don't know yet, Tony,' Ruth said in a deliberately sombre tone.

Thirty seconds later, the boat arrived, and two USMU officers jumped off and secured the boat to the shore. Another officer went to the back, and with the help of another, they lifted whatever they had found at the bottom of the lake and carried it, dripping with water, over to a flat piece of ground.

Ruth peered at it, trying to work out what it was.

'It looks like an old chest freezer, boss,' Nick said.

'Is it?' she asked as she looked again.

Amis walked a few steps to the left, moved one of the halogen lights so that it shone on the freezer, and then ambled over.

'Yes, it is,' Amis agreed.

In the glare of the light, Ruth could see that it was indeed an old chest freezer. It had been crudely wrapped in black and brown gaffer tape. Around its middle was a thick chain which had what appeared to be gym barbell weights attached to it.

Putting on his gloves, Amis pulled up his mask and winced. Whatever was in there was making a terrible smell. Pulling at the handle, the lid of the freezer rose by about six inches, and then the taut chain prevented it being opened any further.

Amis glanced back at one of the SOCOs.

'I'm going to need a bolt cutter,' he shouted over.

One of the USMU officers went over to the boat,

jumped on and then returned with large bolt cutters which he then went and handed to Amis.

With a quick snip, Amis cut the steel chain, which then fell away from the freezer and landed with a metallic clang on the ground. Taking out a knife, Amis went to work on the gaffer tape, tearing it noisily from the surface of the freezer.

He grabbed the handle, lifted the lid of the freezer so that it was fully open, and peered inside. He took out a torch, peered carefully inside, and then glanced back at Ruth.

'What have we got, Tony?' she asked.

'It's your man,' Amis said quietly. Even Amis seemed stunned by what he had seen. 'Minus a foot and a leg, obviously.'

Ruth went over to the SOCO and gestured. 'I'm going to need a suit.'

Amis was continuing to rummage a little as Ruth put on a forensic suit, mask, and shoe covers and then walked over towards the freezer.

'That explains it,' Amis said as she arrived. The smell was overwhelming. If she wasn't careful, she was definitely going to vomit.

'Explains what?' Ruth was trying to keep her distance and breathe through her mouth.

'There was a six-inch gap where the lid wasn't fully closed.'

'So what?'

'My guess is that every time there was a strong current, the freezer was tossed around on the lake bed. And when that happened, its contents were shaken around, and some of them escaped,' Amis explained.

Ruth nodded. 'Which is why we found the foot, the leg, and the boot at different times.'

'Exactly.' Amis said as he continued to look at Mark's remains. 'I've got some good news and some bad news.'

'Good news,' Ruth said.

Amis turned around and held something up. 'This was taped to the bottom of the freezer.'

Ruth peered at what he was holding. It was a large hunting knife with a serrated blade. 'Looks like we've got our murder weapon. That is good news.'

Amis looked at Ruth and gestured to the inside of the freezer. 'The bad is we're missing a head and hands.'

Chapter 32

Opening the door to the conference room, Ruth went inside and made her way to the table at the front. The room was already buzzing with journalists. She sat down and took a sip of water. There were a few minutes before the briefing was due to start, and she wanted to run through what she was going to say.

Glancing out at the packed room, she knew that the search for Bella Freudmann and Frank Collard was going to be major news.

Ruth's phone buzzed, and she read her most recent update.

BBC Wales @ BBC Wales Breaking News

Sources claim that the murder victim is Mark Freudmann, son of Welsh police chief, Susanna Freudmann. Police are now hunting for his wife, Bella, in connection with his murder.

Ruth had to admit that any social media explosion was probably going to help them catch Bella and Frank. She wondered if they would be smart enough to change their appearance. In the sparsely populated region of Snowdonia, they would be fairly recognisable, especially in her top-of-the-range white Porsche.

Checking her watch, Ruth stared out at the assembled journalists. A figure marched up the side of the room towards her. It was Kerry, the Chief Corporate Communications Officer for North Wales Police, who had come across from the main press office in St Asaph. Ruth had met her on various occasions over the last four years and continued to find her odious.

Kerry sat down next to her. 'Morning, Ruth. I love what you've done with your hair.'

What? I haven't done anything with my hair. Why is she being nice?

Ruth tried not to look confused. 'Oh, right. Thanks. How are things at St Asaph?'

'Good. Overworked and underpaid, but that goes with the job,' Kerry said with a cheerful smile.

Either she's having incredible sex with someone new, or she's had a personality transplant.

'Too right,' Ruth agreed, wondering if this was some kind of ruse to get her to drop her defences. 'I was down at St Asaph a couple of days ago.'

'I heard,' Kerry said with a serious face. 'I feel so sorry for Susanna. Mark was her only child, and she really doted on him. And the way he was killed and then discovered is going to be all over the tabloids. It's horrendous.'

'It's very sad,' Ruth agreed. 'I guess if we can find Bella and Frank and put them away for a very long time, there will be some kind of justice for Susanna and Mark.'

Kerry smiled at her. 'I have every faith that you'll do that, Ruth.'

Okay, she is still being weird. Maybe it's industrial-strength HRT?

Glancing down at the microphones and tape recorders, Ruth realised it was time to start.

'I'd better get on with it.' Ruth gave a subtle gesture to the waiting media. 'Good morning, I'm Detective Inspector Ruth Hunter, and I am the Senior Investigating Officer for the investigation into the murder of Mark Freudmann. This press conference is to update you on the case and to appeal to the public for any information regarding his death. We are currently looking for Bella Freudmann, Mark's wife, and his brother-in-law Frank Collard in connection with Mark's murder. If you have any information about their whereabouts, please contact us on the North Wales Police helpline. We believe that Mark was killed at his home in Llwydiarth, Snowdonia, last Thursday, the 21st January. We are looking for anyone who was in the area at the time, or saw anything suspicious, to come forward. At this stage of the investigation, our main focus is to find Bella Freudmann and Frank Collard, who we believe were in the house at the time of Mark's murder. Now, I do have some time to take questions, if there are any.'

A reporter peered up at her from the front row. 'James Peake, Mirror Group. Can you confirm that Bella Freudmann and Frank Collard are now suspected of murdering her husband.'

'I'm not prepared to discuss the exact details of our investigation. What I can say is that we are very keen to talk to Bella and Frank and we hope they can help us with our enquiries,' Ruth explained calmly.

A television journalist made a gesture from the back of the room, and Ruth nodded.

'Sophie Pemberton, BBC News. Detective Inspector, can you confirm you found a severed foot in Lake Vyrnwy last Sunday, and can you tell us if you believe this is connected to Mark Freudmann's murder?'

'As I said, at this stage, I'm not at liberty to discuss the case in detail. But what I want to reiterate is that Mark Freudmann was an innocent man who was attacked and killed in his own home. We would like to hear from anyone who was in that area last Thursday evening; or from anyone who has information about the whereabouts of Bella and Frank. Thank you. There will be no more questions at this time.'

Ruth was pleased with how she had handled the press conference. She stood, gathered up her files, and looked over at Kerry.

'Handled like a true pro,' Kerry said with a smile. 'As always.'

'Thanks, Kerry,' Ruth said, still astounded by the transformation in her attitude and character.

This is very surreal. I feel like I'm having an out of body experience.

'Next time you're in St Asaph, pop in for coffee, and we can have a catch up,' Kerry suggested, as though they were the best of friends.

Ruth gave her an uncertain smile. 'Thanks. I will. Take care, Kerry.'

Yeah, that will never happen. And I need to go outside, have a ciggie, and rejoin Planet Earth.

RUTH SWIGGED AT HER LUKEWARM COFFEE AS SHE SAT BACK in her office chair. She didn't care. She had lost count of how many hours it had been since she last slept, so any caffeine was welcome. For a moment, she thought of Sarah. She couldn't wait for the case to be over so they could spend some time together. They had traded a few texts, but she knew Sarah would be frantically worrying about her mother.

Grabbing some folders, Ruth got up and wandered out into the CID office, which was a hive of activity in the search for Bella and Frank. There were two ways of looking at the situation, Ruth thought, given her experience of chasing down suspects on the run. Statistically, the longer Bella and Frank were on the run, the more likely they were to make a mistake and get caught. However, there was also a downside. They would also become desperate, and so it might make them dangerous. If they had a shotgun, that put the operation into a whole different arena. The more time they had, the more chances they would have to find a way out of the country, if that was their plan. She just needed them to make a mistake.

'Anything on their bank accounts, phones, or social media?' Ruth asked to the collective room.

Garrow glanced over and shook his head. 'Nothing, boss. But according to the bank records, Bella took out a thousand pounds in cash from the HSBC in Dolgellau last week.'

Ruth frowned. 'When was that?'

'Friday morning,' Garrow said.

'If we think Mark was murdered on Thursday night, then my guess is that she was starting to prepare things in case she had to go on the run,' Ruth said, thinking aloud. 'Have we got the CCTV from *Pig Meadow Farm* yet?'

'Uniform have picked it up, boss,' Georgie replied. 'I'm trying to get a trace on Charlie Collard's mobile phone. If Bella and Frank are smart enough to buy an untraceable burner phone to call him, we might get their location from that?'

'Good work, Georgie.' Wandering over to the map of

North Wales, Ruth peered at it. 'Where the bloody hell are you?'

Garrow looked over. 'Boss, airport security at Anglesey, Liverpool, and Manchester have been alerted to the fact that they might be trying to get a flight. And the HMPO are putting a flag on their passports, but they said that can take several hours to go live.'

The HMPO stood for Her Majesty's Passport Office.

'Thank you, Jim,' Ruth said. 'What about ferries? If they go to Anglesey, they can get a ferry to Ireland.'

'All ports warning is in place.' Nick went over to his computer. 'The Border Force know they are persons of interest to us. The only problem we have is that there isn't always a passport check for foot passengers travelling to Ireland from Holyhead.'

'I wonder if they know that,' Ruth asked, thinking out loud.

'Bingo!' Nick exclaimed. 'Boss, we've got a GPS hit on Bella Freudmann's Porsche. Come and have a look.'

Ruth walked over to Nick's computer which showed the 'active map' of North Wales. A small red digital pin showed where the Porsche was located.

Ruth nodded. It could be the break that they needed. 'Where is that?' Ruth asked as she studied the map.

'It's just out by Moel Siabod. Basically, it's the middle of nowhere.'

Moel Siabod was a solitary mountain, isolated from all the other enormous peaks of Snowdonia in its own space to the north of the national park.

Ruth pointed up to the map. 'We need an Armed Response Vehicle to block off this track at the top. And we need AROs on either side of this track in case they make a break cross-country. I want a dog unit on both sides.'

'We've got two helicopters out on Snowdonia,' Nick said, thinking out loud.

'Jim, contact Air Support. Tell them to keep well away from the area but to be on standby if Bella and Frank make a move. I don't want them spooked.' Ruth thought for a moment and then pointed at the map. 'And we need marksmen here, just to be on the safe side.'

Chapter 33

The winter sun was dropping low towards the horizon as Ruth and other officers from Llancastell CID moved into positions overlooking the disused farm buildings. She immediately spotted the white Porsche Cayenne parked to one side. The intel had been correct. It seemed very likely that Bella and Frank were holed up inside. Her stomach was tense and adrenaline pumped hard through her veins.

The late-afternoon sky flared an incredible flamingo-pink, and the wind off the nearby mountains was bitter on her face and ears. Behind the buildings, at 2,600 feet, loomed the grey and purple peaks of Moel Siabod, the highest point in the Moelwynion mountain range.

As Ruth moved forwards, she was accompanied by AROs dressed in their black Nomex boots, gloves, and Kevlar helmets over balaclavas. Carrying Glock 9 mm pistols, the AROs moved purposefully behind some old, rusty farm machinery. Their movements were well-rehearsed. ARO training was repetitive, thorough, and precise.

Ruth adjusted the thick stab vest that she and the other CID detectives were all wearing. It was too small, or maybe she was putting on weight. No one was taking any chances with suspects who had a firearm. Bella had committed a brutal, cold-blooded murder. She and Frank were armed, and they might now believe that they had nothing to lose by killing others.

Ruth motioned silently for the CID officers and the AROs to begin heading for the farm buildings, guns trained on the weather-worn doors and broken windows.

Ruth murmured into her radio, 'Three-six to Gold Command. Officers in position two at target location, over.'

The radio crackled back. 'Three-six received. Units to proceed to position one, over.'

Ruth gestured, and the officers moved quietly over the final few yards of icy grass and gravel, which crunched under their feet. There were two large wooden doors at the front of the main building that had been padlocked closed. Ruth noticed the padlock was rusty and looked like it had been there for years. If Bella and Frank were in the building, they hadn't come in this way.

Ruth motioned, and four AROs moved away from them, heading for the sides and back of the building. Then two AROs stepped forwards with what they liked to call 'The Enforcer', a steel battering ram that would knock the door open in one hit.

Ruth clicked her radio. 'Three-six to Gold Command. All units are at position one.'

There was an anxious moment as they waited, and then, 'Three-six received. Gold Command order is go.'

Ruth nodded at the AROs and moved back against the grey stone wall. It was cold and hard, even with the vest on. Where were they? Were they lying in wait, or were they oblivious to the operation?

Bang!

Ruth flinched as the doors smashed open with an almighty crash, and the AROs moved in, weapons trained in front of them.

'Armed police!' they bellowed as they stormed into the building. 'Armed police!'

Ruth followed, her heart pounding in her chest. She scanned left and right into the darkness of the building. Were they going to have to play a tense game of hide-and-seek to smoke Bella and Frank out?

The building smelt damp and musty, and the floor was covered with straw and dry mud. As the wind picked up outside, the roof timbers creaked with an eerie groan. Ruth continued moving, heart thumping, eyes searching left and right for any movement. CID officers and AROs had fanned out throughout the building, clearing the stalls.

'Armed Police!' the AROs bellowed as they moved on through.

Ruth's heart started to sink. There was nothing. Bella and Frank were nowhere to be found, and there weren't any places left to hide.

Nick appeared at her side and shook his head. 'Nothing here, boss.'

'Shit!' Ruth muttered to herself. She told herself that Bella and Frank could still be in an outbuilding on the other side of the yard, but the AROs would have swept through that in seconds. She would have heard something.

Ruth glanced up as a senior ARO came through the main doors. 'Sorry, ma'am. We're been through the whole site. There's no one here.'

Chapter 34

It was late morning, and the whole of CID had regrouped back at Llancastell nick. After the failure of the morning's raid, there was a palpable sense of disappointment in the room, which wasn't helped by growing fatigue and frustration. Officers were running on adrenaline, coffee, and virtually no sleep. Some of the DCs had managed to slope away for three to four hours and a shower. However, Ruth was going nowhere until Bella and Frank were in their custody.

Standing up in her office, she gave a mighty yawn and stretched out her back. It wouldn't be long before she was heading downstairs to the canteen for a double espresso and then a crafty ciggie outside.

Taking a few steps, she came out into the CID office – her team were tired.

Garrow put the phone down and looked over at her. 'Boss, I've just spoken to the local gun club. Mark Freudmann had a shotgun registered there.'

'Did they say anything else?' Ruth asked.

Garrow pulled a face. 'Yeah. The bloke made some

joke that everyone knew Mark at the gun club because he owned a …' Garrow peered down at his notepad and read. 'A Mossberg 590 12 gauge shotgun with a ten round box magazine.'

'Jesus! Does that mean it holds ten rounds?' Ruth said. An ordinary shotgun held only two before it needed reloading. Having ten meant that they posed a far more serious danger.

'I'm afraid so, boss,' Garrow replied.

'Anything from the airports yet?' she asked.

Garrow shook his head. 'Nothing. The flags on their passports should be in place by now, so if they try to get through security, they'll be immediately arrested.'

Ruth nodded. 'Fingers crossed.'

At that moment, Georgie approached with some open folders and printouts. 'Boss, I've done some digging on Bella Freudmann. Both she and Frank were adopted when they were only babies. Bella in 1981 and Frank in 1983.'

Ruth raised an eyebrow. 'So, they're not biologically related.'

'No,' Georgie said. 'And they didn't even spend that much time together as kids. Bella was sent to an all-girls boarding school in mid-Wales until she was eighteen. Frank went to an all-boys boarding school in Shropshire.'

Ruth frowned. 'Maybe Valerie Simpson did see Bella and Frank kissing on the patio? If they had completely different birth parents, maybe they didn't think it was that weird to be with each other.'

Georgie pulled a face. 'It's still pretty weird, boss.'

'I've encountered a lot weirder,' Ruth said with a shrug. 'If they started some kind of relationship when Frank moved in after a failed marriage, that would provide a motive for them to plan and kill Mark.'

'Yes, boss,' Georgie agreed and then pointed to another

folder. 'I pulled Bella's medical records. She's had three spells in the South Manchester Psychiatric Hospital, which is usually known as The Priory.'

'Does it specify why?'

'Depression, anxiety, and suicidal thoughts,' Georgie said as she read from the file. 'That was 2010, 2012, and 2015. But, then in 2018, she spent two months in a psychiatric unit just outside Llangollen. Her GP has recorded that she was suicidal.'

'Okay, so it doesn't sound like she is mentally stable. And now she's armed with a pump-action shotgun,' Ruth said, shaking her head.

'It does explain why Terry Fowles described her as *a psycho*. He told us she had terrible mood swings.'

'And we know she attacked Mark with a baseball bat last year, broke his jaw, and put him in hospital,' Ruth said. 'Bella told me that Mark had threatened her with a shotgun, but it might be just that she was having some kind of breakdown.'

'If my husband was gambling away all my money and shagging women behind my back, I might have a breakdown and go for him with a baseball bat,' Georgie joked.

'Yeah, but you wouldn't murder him, chop him up and chuck him in a lake,' Ruth said.

Georgie shrugged with a grin as she went back to her desk. 'That all depends.'

Ruth laughed. 'Yeah, I guess we all have our breaking point.'

'Boss.' Nick looked over from the computer. 'I've just got that CCTV footage over from *Pig Meadow Farm*. I've just had a whizz through.'

'Anything interesting?' she asked.

'Yes, boss,' Nick replied, giving her a meaningful look. 'I think you need to see this.'

Ruth pointed to the monitor up on the wall. 'Can you get it up there so we can all have a look?'

'One second,' Nick said as he tapped away at his computer.

A second later, the monitor burst into life with the grainy image of some CCTV. The camera was high, and it was a bird's-eye view of the customer's car park at the farm. The date stamp at the bottom read *Thursday 21st January* and the time stamp read *23.28*.

'Okay, so as you can see, this is the customer car park at the farm. It's the only place they have CCTV.'

Ruth pointed to the screen. 'What are we looking at?'

'This is 11.28 pm on the evening that we believe Bella murdered Mark,' Nick said. 'And then this vehicle arrives in the car park.'

As the CCTV footage played forward, Ruth could see a large Toyota pickup truck pull into the car park and stop. She could clearly make out the registration.

'I've done a PNC check,' Nick explained. 'This pickup is, surprise surprise, registered to Charlie Collard. And then as I play it forward, this happens.'

Ruth watched as Nick played the CCTV footage on. It showed Charlie Collard getting out of the car and walking slowly across the car park. Then a figure appeared from out of the shadows at the right-hand side of the screen. They were wearing a hoodie and baggy clothing.

'Then this person here comes out, and Charlie has an animated conversation with them,' Nick said.

Ruth frowned. 'What is that person carrying?'

'I'm not sure, but isn't that a black bin bag?' Georgie suggested.

'I think it's clearer as I play it forward again,' Nick said.

The CCTV footage played again. The figure handed what appeared to be a heavy rubbish bag to Charlie, who took it. The figure turned and exited the screen. Charlie then made his way back across the car park, holding the rubbish bag, heading for the farm's main reception before disappearing out of sight.'

'Do we think that's Bella?' Garrow asked.

'I've managed to grab a still and zoom in a bit,' Nick said as he clicked a button to reveal a freeze frame. It showed the figure as they turned.

Ruth examined the grainy face that was partially covered with a hoodie. 'Yeah, I think that is Bella.'

'I agree,' added Georgie.

'What's in the bag?' Garrow asked.

Ruth pulled a face. 'I've got a horrible feeling that it's Mark Freudmann's head and hands. They were missing from the freezer that we dragged from Lake Vyrnwy. And if you want to hide the identity of a body, take the head and hands.'

Nick nodded. 'No fingerprints, no dental records.'

Georgie frowned. 'So, where is Charlie Collard going with that bag?'

Then something occurred to Ruth as she looked at them. 'There's dozens of pigs out the back. Maybe Charlie fed them the head and hands.'

'I thought that was just a myth?' Nick said.

Garrow shook his head. 'Pigs will eat anything, including human flesh and bone.'

'Jesus.' Georgie grimaced. 'That's disgusting.'

'I'll talk to Drake and get a search warrant for the farm,' Ruth said. 'We'll get the SOCOs down there. But first, we need to find Bella and Frank.'

Garrow moved his chair from his computer and looked at them with a smirk. 'I think I've got it.'

'Well, I don't want it,' Georgie joked.

Garrow pointed to his computer screen. 'These are

Frank Collard's bank records. I've searched back, and in November of last year, he booked a vehicle and two passengers onto a ferry travelling from Holyhead to Dublin. And guess when that ferry is?'

Ruth looked at him. 'I'm really hoping you're going to say in a few hours rather than this morning.'

Garrow nodded with a smile. 'Ferry leaves Holyhead at 5.25 pm. It's the last one of the day.'

Glancing at her watch, Ruth saw it was now 3.45 pm. It would take them nearly 50 mins to get to Holyhead if they left right now – so they would get there about 4.35 pm. Just enough time to talk to security, the port police, and make sure that Bella and Frank didn't get onto the ferry.

'How are they getting there?' Georgie asked. 'Given that they abandoned the Porsche.'

It was a good point, Ruth thought.

'Maybe they switched cars at the place we raided?' Nick suggested.

'Have we checked if Frank Collard owns a car?' Ruth asked.

Garrow nodded. 'He was banned for drink-driving, but he owns a Jaguar F-type. Black. I've got the reg.'

'Let's assume they are now in that car. Text me the reg, Jim.' Taking the car keys from her pocket, she tossed them to Nick. 'Come on, we'd better get going.'

'Yes, boss.' Nick grabbed his jacket from the back of his chair.

'Oh, and Nick?' she said with a grin.

'Yes, boss?'

'You drive; I'll smoke.'

Nick laughed. 'You haven't said that for ages.'

'I thought it seemed appropriate,' Ruth said as they headed out of the door.

Chapter 35

An hour later, Nick and Ruth pulled into Holyhead Ferry Terminal. Ruth had rung Sarah to explain that she was still working on the case and had no idea when she would be back. Sarah had seemed a little distracted, but Ruth knew that she was struggling with adjusting – she just needed patience and time.

Ruth had also informed Drake of what they were doing, and had asked Anglesey Police Force to provide two uniformed units as backup in case Bella and Frank tried to escape.

As they made their way towards the Customs and Immigration Office, Ruth gazed up into the greying sky. Two gulls dived and flapped overhead; their loud rhythmic squawking was unsettling. The air was thick with diesel fumes and the smell of the sea.

Arriving at the office, Ruth and Nick showed their warrant cards and were directed to Caitlin Jones, Head of Operations.

Caitlin, 30s, petite and blonde, sat in a tidy office eating a sandwich and nursing a large bottle of water. 'I understand that you guys are over from the mainland. Anything we can do to help?'

'We've got two murder suspects we think are going to board the last ferry out of here to Dublin,' Nick explained.

'Oh, God.' Caitlin seemed surprised. 'Erm … You can have a look at the passenger lists.'

'We think they're in a car,' Ruth said.

Caitlin went to her computer. 'Got the make and registration?'

Ruth glanced at her phone. 'Jaguar F-type. Registration: Foxtrot, Charlie, seven, five.'

After a few seconds, Caitlin frowned. 'I can't find it on here.' She hit the printer, and a moment later, it whirred into action. Getting up from her desk, she retrieved the printout.

'That's the passenger and vehicle list for tonight's ferry,' Caitlin said as she handed them over.

Ruth smiled. 'Thanks.' She was worried that the vehicle wasn't on the computer. What if they were travelling in another vehicle?

'We're looking for a Bella Freudmann and Frank Collard,' Ruth informed Caitlin, who went back and sat at her desk again.

'That's right. You did a press conference yesterday, didn't you?' Caitlin asked, her eyes widening. 'I read about it on Twitter. Isn't she meant to have murdered her husband?'

'We can't really discuss the investigation at this stage.' Ruth said as she ran her finger slowly down the vehicle list. There were no Jaguars listed. Maybe they weren't getting on the ferry. Maybe they had booked the tickets to act as a diversion while they made their escape from somewhere else. Were they that clever and calculating to pull something like that off?

'Anything?' Nick asked as he read through the second half of the printout.

'Nope. Nothing even close,' Ruth admitted. 'You?'

Nick shook his head. 'No, nothing. Nothing on the list of foot passengers.'

Caitlin peered over from her desk. 'At the risk of making things difficult, there will be some last-minute foot passengers who don't appear on that list.'

Nick and Ruth looked at each other – that *did* make it more difficult.

'How far is Anglesey airport from here?' Nick asked.

'Five or six miles,' Caitlin replied.

Ruth pulled a face at him. 'Are you thinking the same thing as me?'

'They booked the tickets knowing that we would look at Frank's bank account. And that would lead us to think they are getting this ferry, so all our officers and resources are here. Meanwhile, they're heading for an airport.'

'Except there should be a stop on their passports,' Ruth said.

'I bloody hope so.' Nick pulled a face. 'To be fair, boss, they could have travelled to any port or airport in the country.'

'I know,' Ruth sighed as she looked over at Caitlin. 'Thanks for your help, but I think we've been outmanoeuvred.'

'Hope you catch them,' Caitlin said as they left the office and headed out towards the dockside.

Ruth was feeling exhausted and deflated. 'I'm starting to think we're not going to stop them leaving the country.'

Nick gestured over to the ferry. 'Let's just make sure.'

They made their way quickly over to the foot passenger

entrance for the 5.25 pm ferry and identified themselves to the ticket collectors and immigration officers.

For the next ten minutes, they watched the stream of passengers queuing and showing their tickets and passports before boarding. However, there was no sign of Bella or Frank.

As the queue shortened, Ruth gave an exasperated sigh. 'We can't let them get away.'

'We're running out of passengers,' Nick said, gesturing to the dwindling queue.

Ruth knew that the chances of finding them now were diminishing fast. Gazing up at the ferry, she wondered how they had got it so wrong.

Out of the corner of her eye, Ruth spotted a woman leaning with her back against the ferry's guard rail. As she turned sideways, Ruth noticed her hat. A sheepskin, trapper's style hat with long ear flaps.

For a moment, she wondered where she had seen the hat before.

Then it clicked.

Bella Freudmann was wearing one. Bloody hell.

'You okay?' Nick asked.

'Up there,' Ruth said, pointing.

'What am I looking at?' Nick asked, putting her hand over her eyes to block out the fading sunlight.

Then suddenly, in the same place where Bella had been standing, a man looked over the rails. He was wearing a black baseball cap and sunglasses, but even from a distance, Ruth recognised him.

Shit! Frank Collard!

'They're on the ferry!' Ruth cried out.

'What?'

'Come on!' Ruth took Nick by the arm, and they both broke into a run.

As they sprinted over to the ferry, Ruth noticed that there were no more passengers to get on, and the check-in point was now closed.

They showed their warrant cards and boarded.

A deep, thunderous blast of a horn sounded.

Ruth glanced over at movement on the dockside as one of the enormous steel mooring chains began to be wound in noisily.

She glanced at Nick. 'Looks like we're going to Dublin.'

Chapter 36

R uth and Nick had been searching the ferry for over ten minutes but hadn't seen any sign yet of Bella or Frank. They walked back through the huge lounge and bar on the upper deck. With 1,500 passengers on board, their search wouldn't be easy.

'And you're sure it was her?' Nick asked.

Ruth gave her a scornful look. 'Yes. Didn't you see them both?'

'Actually, if I'm honest, the sun was in my eyes, boss.'

'Well, I'm not seeing things,' Ruth snapped. The exhaustion was getting to her, and the mind can play all sorts of tricks when you're that tired.

Nick nodded and went over to the central concourse where there was a deck plan of the ferry. 'It's just that we've been everywhere, haven't we?'

By now, Ruth doubted what she had seen.

'What about the actual car deck?' Nick suggested, pointing to the plan. 'It's the one place we haven't looked.'

They turned and headed for the central stairwell, where they could access the lower decks.

'At least we know she hasn't got that bloody shotgun anymore,' Ruth said as they clattered down the stairs at speed. There was no way of getting a shotgun through the metal detectors at the gates.

At the bottom of the stairs, they ran straight ahead and took the door to the car deck.

A security officer in a high-vis jacket gave them a quizzical look and put up his hand. 'Sorry, guys. Vehicle deck can only be accessed once we've docked in Dublin.'

'We're police officers. We think there might be two suspects hiding down here,' Nick said as he showed his warrant card and gestured into the steel doorway.

'Call security and tell them to look out for a middle-aged couple,' Ruth said to the man. 'The man is wearing a black baseball cap and possibly sunglasses. The woman is wearing a hat with ear flaps.'

'Okay …' the man stammered, looking terrified. 'What have they done?'

'They're wanted for murder,' Nick said as they pushed past him.

Feeling the tension in her stomach, Ruth opened one of the steel doors very slowly. The air inside was thick with petrol and diesel fumes.

Moving forward into the car deck, Ruth began to walk along the long lines of cars. Her and Nick's boots clanged and echoed on the steel floor. Scanning left and right, it was difficult to see behind some of the larger vehicles.

Suddenly, two figures moved from behind a Range Rover and headed for an exit further down the car deck.

It was Bella and Frank.

Ruth pointed. 'Over there!' she yelled, glancing over at Nick.

They broke into a run and, a few seconds later, Ruth smashed through the exit doors with Nick just behind her.

They looked left and then right.

Nothing.

'Where are they?' Nick yelled.

Ruth saw Bella and Frank heading back towards the stairwell.

'There!' she said, and they set off again.

By the time they got to the stairs, they had disappeared again. However, Ruth could hear the sound of running feet above them.

'Up this way!'

Leaping up the steps, two by two, Ruth felt the muscles in her thighs begin to burn.

Jesus, this is starting to really hurt.

Reaching the middle deck, she glanced both ways. Nothing.

The sound of running feet came again from above.

'Come on,' Nick urged as he took over the lead.

Dragging in air, they arrived on the upper deck. Glancing around, there was no sign of them, but there was a door about ten yards away that led outside.

Nick ran to it, opened it, and Ruth followed.

The wind whipped around their faces as they ran down the deck towards the stern.

They spotted Bella and Frank up ahead.

He was dragging her by the hand as other passengers jumped out of their way with irate glances.

Ruth and Nick followed after them.

'OUT OF THE WAY! POLICE!' Nick yelled.

The fugitives had now reached the end of the deck.

Right! Now they're trapped!

However, Bella and Frank climbed rather awkwardly over the safety rail onto the final ten-foot of deck beyond. Nothing now protected them from a fifty-foot drop into the white, swirling depths of the Irish Sea.

Ruth and Nick stopped at the rail, breathing heavily.

'What are you doing?' Ruth yelled at them both before climbing over the rail.

Nearby passengers were looking on in shock.

'Stay where you are!' Bella yelled, moving backwards.

Oh God, if she slips now, she's going into the sea.

'You need to come with us, Bella,' Ruth said gently.

'I can't,' Bella replied as she glanced backwards and saw that the heels of her shoes were now only a foot from the edge. 'You don't understand.'

'Okay. You're right. I don't understand, but I don't want you to die,' Ruth said as she pointed to the sea.

Ruth climbed over the rail. The slight rolling of the deck, and the battering wind, made it feel very precarious.

Bella shrugged. 'What's the choice?'

'You can't believe that jumping off there is the only choice you have?' Nick asked.

'I will spend my life in prison. So will Frank, and I don't want to live without him.' Bella turned to Frank. 'I don't want to be without you.'

'I can't do this, Bella,' he said quietly. 'I'm so sorry.'

With that, Frank turned and prepared to jump into the sea below.

'NO!' Ruth said, making a dive to stop him.

It was too late.

Frank had already stepped out into the abyss and was falling feet first into the icy sea below.

Oh, my God!

By now, several of the ferry's security officers had arrived and were moving passengers back and out of the way.

Ruth lunged at Bella as she tried to jump in after Frank, grabbed her arms, and handcuffed them behind her back. 'Bella Freudmann, I am arresting you on suspicion of the murder of Mark Freudmann. You do not have to say anything, but it may harm your defence if you do not mention, when questioned, something which you later rely on in court. Anything you do say may be given in evidence.'

Chapter 37

Having debriefed Drake on the events over at Holyhead, Ruth made her way back to the CID office, where the team were working away busily. The news that Bella Freudmann had been arrested and was now in custody had given everyone a huge lift.

Wandering over to the scene boards, Ruth moved a strand of hair from her face.

God, my hair is so greasy. I'd give anything for a shower, she thought. She hadn't slept for so long, and she felt grubby.

Casting her eyes over the evidence, she peered at the smiling photo of Mark Freudmann. What a terrible and violent death he had suffered at the hands of his wife. Even though they had his dismembered remains that had been discovered in the chest freezer, they still hadn't found his head or hands. As unpleasant as it sounded, Susanna would want to bury her son with all his remains in a coffin. That meant they needed to find out what Bella had taken to her father's farm on the night of the 21st January.

Turning around, Ruth perched herself on a table and glanced down at her watch. It was 9 pm.

'Right guys, listen up,' she said, aware that she just didn't have the energy to raise her voice. 'As you all know, we have Bella Freudmann in custody, and she will be charged with Mark's murder tomorrow.'

There were mutterings, cheers, and some applause. They had got the result they all wanted.

'And I hope that will get justice for Mark and his family. Especially the DCC, as she is one of us,' Ruth said.

'Well done, boss,' French said. 'Although the next time you and Nick sod off to Dublin, can you bring us back some duty-free?'

There was laughter from some of the detectives.

'Very funny, Dan.' Ruth grinned. 'On a more serious note, Frank Collard decided to jump from the ferry, and although his body hasn't been retrieved, the coastguard has told me that there is no way that he could have survived.'

'Have we got a search warrant for *Pig Meadow Farm* yet, boss?' Georgie asked.

'We'll have one first thing in the morning,' Ruth said. 'And however gruesome it is to think about, we owe it to the family to find out exactly what happened to Mark and to retrieve all his remains so they can be buried together.'

The atmosphere in the office became a little more sombre as they thought of what Ruth had said.

She glanced at her watch again. 'It's nine o'clock and you've all worked incredibly hard on this case. I'm so proud of the work you've done on this so far, but we still have loose ends to tidy up before Bella Freudmann goes to trial. So, I want you to go home, shower; because some of you are starting to smell, and get some sleep. And remind whoever you live with that you still exist.'

'Thanks, boss.' Georgie grabbed her jacket. 'To be honest, I'm fucked, and not in a good way.'

Ruth laughed. 'Yeah, well, I don't think any of us have got the energy for that.'

More laughter as the CID team turned off computers, tidied desks, and started to make their way out.

'Back here at six, please!' Ruth shouted as they disappeared.

As she parked her car, Ruth was relieved to see that Sarah's car was on the other side of the house. She couldn't wait to see her and fill her in on all that had happened in the past forty-eight hours, especially the aborted ferry trip to Dublin.

Walking around to the boot, Ruth grabbed a shopping bag. Inside, she had a chilled bottle of wine, a large lasagne, and ice cream. As she went to the front door and took out her key, she knew what she really should do is shower and go to bed. But she needed to catch up with Sarah, and as long as she got six hours sleep, she knew she'd be okay.

She came into the warm, cosiness of the house expecting to hear the television or Sarah pottering around somewhere. Instead, the house was in virtual darkness.

That's weird, she thought. *It's still early.*

'Hello?' she called out as she switched on the hall light and made her way to the kitchen, where she began to unpack her shopping.

Taking two glasses from the cupboard, she twisted the top off the wine and poured herself an enormous glass. Leaning back on the work counter, she wondered where the hell Sarah was.

She blew out her cheeks and thought, *What a bloody couple of days it's been* before taking two large mouthfuls of wine.

That's better, she thought, as she felt the tension beginning to seep out of her body. It had occurred to her that there was something strange about the first glass of wine of the day. She began to feel relaxed as soon as she had swallowed the first mouthful or two, which made no sense as the alcohol hadn't had time to take any effect. It must be psychosomatic, she assumed.

'Hello?' she called again and started to feel a little uneasy.

Where the hell has Sarah got to?

Walking back into the hallway, Ruth stopped and listened.

Silence.

Then she saw a tiny chink of light through the gap in the door of the living room. She went over, opened it, and saw that one small light was on in the corner.

And Sarah was lying asleep on the sofa.

Ruth looked at her. She was in such a deep sleep that it was hard to see that she was breathing.

Then, after a second, Sarah stirred and turned her head a little.

Aww bless. Maybe I should just cover her in a blanket and let her sleep.

A strange buzzing sound started from somewhere in the room.

What the hell is that.

Ruth guessed from its rhythmic pattern it was a mobile phone vibrating somewhere.

Glancing around the room, she saw Sarah's jacket, which had been draped over the back of the armchair. She went over and as she fished out the mobile phone, something small fell to the floor.

Ruth glanced down at the screen of the mobile phone.

It read *International Number calling.* She guessed it was either some scam or a phone company.

Bending down, she retrieved whatever had fallen to the carpet from Sarah's jacket pocket.

It was a return train ticket.

To Doncaster!

You have got to be joking, haven't you?

Ruth sat down on the armchair, took another large gulp of wine, and studied the ticket. Sarah had been to Doncaster to see her mum. Part of her was angry that she had gone without telling her. They were meant to be totally honest with each other after everything that had happened. And breaking the terms of the PPS agreement not to contact family members could have significant repercussions. And if anyone were to discover that Sarah was in the UK and giving evidence to the police, that could put everyone she was close to in serious danger.

However, her mum was incredibly ill. And God knows how long it was going to take for the Homicide and Serious Crime Command and the Met's Murder Investigation Team to gather enough evidence to charge Lord Weaver with murder; and the other men with conspiracy. It could take years, and Sarah didn't know if her mum had years left. What would Ruth have done in the same position? What if it had been her daughter Ella who was ill? She knew she would do anything to see and comfort Ella and sod the consequences.

Ruth slipped the train ticket and mobile phone back into Sarah's jacket pocket, got up and decided that before anything, she needed to have a shower.

As she headed for the door, a sleepy voice said, 'Hey, where are you creeping off to?'

Ruth smiled and looked over at Sarah, who was stirring. 'Hello, sleepyhead.'

Sarah smirked. 'Didn't you used to live here?'

'Very funny,' Ruth snorted. 'Yeah, and if I don't have a shower and lie down, I'm going to pass out.'

For a second, Ruth thought about mentioning the train ticket she had found. And then she thought better of it. She was too tired to get into it now.

'Mind if I join you?' Sarah asked with a sexy grin as she got up from the sofa.

'Cheeky,' Ruth laughed. 'In the shower or in the bed?'

Sarah raised an eyebrow. 'I was thinking both, actually. If you're not too tired, that is.'

Ruth put out her hand and took Sarah's. 'If you insist.'

Chapter 38

S *aturday 30ᵗʰ January*

By the time Ruth and Nick went to interview Bella Freudmann, the duty solicitor had arrived and had been briefed on her arrest. Interview Room 2 was sparse and cold. Bella was now dressed in a regulation grey tracksuit as her clothes had been taken for forensics. She had also been swabbed for her DNA. Ruth leant across the table to start the recording machine. The long electronic beep sounded as Ruth opened her files and gave Nick a quick look of acknowledgement.

'Interview conducted with Bella Freudmann, Saturday 30ᵗʰ January, 9.20 am, Llancastell Police Station. Present are Detective Sergeant Nick Evans, Duty Solicitor Cliff Patrick, and myself, Detective Inspector Ruth Hunter.' Ruth then glanced over at Bella. 'Bella, do you understand you are still under caution?'

Bella was staring down at the table as if she hadn't heard her.

'Bella?' Ruth said.

Bella slowly looked up and met her eyes. She seemed completely confused.

'Bella, do you understand you are still under caution?' Ruth said again slowly.

The duty solicitor leant in and whispered something in her ear.

'Yes,' Bella nodded.

'Okay,' Ruth said as she moved the files, so they were in front of her. 'Bella, did you murder your husband, Mark Freudmann?'

Bella glared across the table at her and sneered, 'No, don't be ridiculous.' She then glanced across at the duty solicitor. 'She's being ridiculous.'

'Can you tell us about what happened at your home on the evening of Thursday 21st January?' Ruth asked.

'No,' Bella said as she looked behind her as if someone had said something in the corner of the room.

'You can't tell us because you can't remember or because you don't want to?' Ruth asked.

Bella leaned across the table, put her finger to her lips, and whispered, 'Because I'm not allowed to.'

'Why aren't you allowed to tell us what happened that night?'

'I've been told not to,' Bella said, sounding like a child.

What the hell is she doing?

Ruth shot a look at Nick. This isn't how she was expecting the interview to go, and Bella's behaviour was becoming increasingly bizarre.

'Who told you not to tell us, Bella?' she asked.

Bella shook her head as if this was a completely ridiculous question. 'Who do you think?'

Ruth shrugged. 'I honestly don't know.'

Bella gestured with her head as if there was someone behind her. 'They've told me not to tell you a thing.'

Please don't tell me that Bella is going to go down the diminished responsibility route? Ruth thought angrily.

'Who told you not to tell us anything?' Nick asked.

Bella narrowed her eyes and then whispered, 'I can't tell you their names, can I? I wouldn't get out of this room alive.' She then turned around in her seat and looked back towards the door.

'Bella, there are only the four of us in this room,' the duty solicitor said.

Ruth wasn't going to be put off by Bella's ridiculous antics. She fished into the folder and brought out a photograph of the master bedroom floor and walls. They had been sprayed with Luminol by the SOCOS to show up blood and were covered in splashes and dots of green. 'For the purposes of the tape, I am showing the suspect item reference 7119. A photograph of the master bedroom. The surfaces of the walls and the floor have been sprayed to indicate the substantial presence of blood in this room. Bella, can you explain why there is blood on the floor and walls in that bedroom?'

Bella was sitting inspecting her nails. 'No comment,' she muttered.

Nick was getting impatient and shifted forward in his seat. 'We have matched the DNA from the blood in that bedroom to the DNA of your husband, Mark. Can you explain why there is a significant amount of your husband's blood in that bedroom and why someone has both washed and cleaned those surfaces in an attempt to get rid of it?'

Sitting bolt upright, Bella then turned again towards

the door; put her finger to her lip. 'Shush. I can't hear what they are asking me if you keep talking all the time.'

Nick glanced across at Ruth and shook his head.

'Bella, did you attack and kill Mark; and then attempt to clear up the blood in that bedroom?' Ruth asked.

Bella stared at her with an expression of utter disgust. 'What did you call me, you bitch?'

'I didn't call you anything, Bella,' Ruth said with a frown. 'I asked you a question. Did you attack and kill your husband Mark and then attempt to clear up the blood in the bedroom where he had been murdered?'

Bella stood up and glared at her. 'I don't have to take this shit from you!'

'Bella, please sit down,' Ruth said gently.

'I know you,' Bella growled. 'I know all about you and those boys.'

The duty solicitor glanced up at her. 'Please, Bella. Sit down.'

Bella launched herself across the table in an attempt to attack Ruth. 'I'm going to kill you, you bitch.'

Nick moved and grabbed Bella, forcing her to the ground, and then cuffed her as she screamed hysterically.

Ruth, who was still startled, looked at him. 'I'm going to get the FME right now.'

Chapter 39

R uth had been sitting in Drake's office for ten minutes.

'I think your suspect needs to be seen by a mental health specialist,' Doctor Ian Jenkins said.

Bollocks!

Ruth feared this is what he was going to suggest.

Jenkins was the local FME – the Forensic Medical Examiner – which meant he was an independent senior doctor who worked for the police force. One of his duties was to assess whether suspects were fit to be detained, interviewed, or charged.

'Come on, Ian,' Ruth snorted. 'She's trying to have us on. There's nothing wrong with her. I've spoken to her at regular times in the last week, and there's been nothing wrong with her.'

'Bella Freudmann is showing all the signs of a personality disorder,' Jenkins protested. 'Paranoid delusions, hearing voices, and impulsive, violent outbursts. I would suggest that she is suffering from schizophrenia and psychosis.'

Ruth looked at Drake and shook her head. 'You've been an FME long enough to know that suspects will do anything to get a diminished responsibility plea. A few years in a mental hospital, and she'll be out.'

'Well, in my opinion, she's exhibiting all the symptoms of the mental disorders that I have described,' Jenkins said firmly.

'Bloody hell,' Ruth moaned. 'You don't have to be a doctor to know what the symptoms of schizophrenia are. Anyone who has watched a few films or cop dramas can tell you what they are.'

Drake gave her a look as if to say, *calm it down*. But Ruth was adamant that Bella Freudmann was faking it. She hadn't exhibited any symptoms of mental illness until she was arrested.

Drake sat forward and looked at Jenkins. 'If she were suffering from a serious mental health issue, she, or someone close to her, would have been in touch with her GP. She would have been put on medication, wouldn't she?'

'Possibly,' Jenkins said. 'The thing is, these conditions can lie dormant for a long time. And something like psychosis is actually a symptom, not an illness. Research suggests that a psychotic episode such as the one that Bella is exhibiting can be caused by extreme stress or trauma. And I can't think of anything more stressful or traumatic than murdering your husband and then trying to hide what you've done.'

Feeling annoyed by what Jenkins was implying, Ruth looked at him with a frown. 'Isn't there a sick irony if that's true? She brutally murders her husband in cold blood, and because she finds the whole thing so stressful and traumatic, she suffers a severe psychotic episode, and so she can't be tried properly for his murder.'

Jenkins shrugged. 'There's no way of telling when the psychosis began. Murdering her husband might have been part of her psychosis.'

Ruth shook her head. 'I've just told you we've spoken to Bella on several occasions since she murdered Mark. She was lucid, calm, and unemotional. There's no way she can get away with claiming that she was suffering from a psychotic episode at the time. That's bullshit.'

Drake looked at them both. 'If I remember correctly, under the Mental Health Act, the suspect can be inter-viewed in the presence of an approved mental health professional. And I think that would be a decent compro-mise. We get to interview Bella again, but the suspect has the protection of having someone medically trained present.'

Ruth nodded. 'Fine by me.'

'Agreed,' Jenkins said. 'However, I do need to warn you that if Bella exhibits the same behaviour as she did previ-ously, she will have to be taken to a psychiatric unit for a full assessment.'

Ruth looked over at Drake – she was not happy.

Untitled

An hour later, Nick and Ruth drove into the *Pig Meadow Farm* site at speed. Georgie and Garrow had arrived earlier to execute the search warrant. As they parked in the customer car park, Ruth noticed Georgie and Garrow's unmarked black Astra was parked beside the SOCO van and two patrol cars.

Getting out of the car, Ruth saw Georgie in conversation with a SOCO in a forensic suit in the distance.

Ruth turned to Nick and said under her breath, 'That whole thing with Georgie calmed down now, has it?'

Nick seemed a little defensive. 'I told you nothing happened between us, boss.'

'Yeah, but it wasn't for the want of trying,' Ruth stated.

'On her part, not mine,' Nick said.

'I know, I know. I'm just checking.'

'You've got nothing to worry about,' Nick reassured her as they made their way across the car park and towards the line of blue and white evidence tape that had been pulled to cordon off the site.

Georgie approached, dressed in a forensic suit and wellies.

'Where's Charlie Collard?' Ruth asked.

Georgie gestured to the portacabin that they had visited previously. 'He's in there. And he's not a happy bunny, especially when I told him he wasn't to leave the site. He was banging on about the fact that his daughter has been wrongly accused of murder and that it's a terrible miscarriage of justice.'

'What did you say to that?' Nick asked.

'I told him to shut up and stay put,' Georgie replied. 'How did it go with the FME?'

'Not good,' Ruth said with a shake of her head. 'His opinion is that Bella Freudmann is suffering some kind of psychotic episode. He thinks it might be a sign that she has something like schizophrenia.'

'What?' Georgie snorted angrily. 'Don't you think someone would have noticed that she had schizophrenia before now? She'd be on heavy medication for it.'

Nick gave a sigh. 'Apparently, episodes like this can lie dormant and then be brought on by trauma and stress.'

'It's bloody frustrating,' Ruth admitted. 'But at the moment, we have to play by the rules. The mental health of suspects is a political hot potato at the moment. We have to tread on eggshells.'

Nick gestured over towards a pigpen, where SOCOs were crouched searching through the muddy ground. 'How's it going?'

'Pretty grim. I always thought that was a myth,' Georgie admitted. 'You know, that pigs eat human flesh.'

'Apparently not,' Nick said. 'If I remember correctly, Robert Pickerton, who was Canada's worst serial killer, murdered fifty women and fed them to his pigs on his farm. Apparently, he put them through a wood chipper to make human mince. Then he fed them that.'

Georgie pulled a face. 'Thanks, Nick. I had a bacon sarnie for breakfast.'

'That's if it was bacon,' Nick joked.

Ruth glanced up to see Tony Amis approaching in his forensic suit.

'I'm beginning to think you two are stalking me,' he boomed with a laugh.

'Morning, Tony. Again,' Ruth said with a withering look. 'Have we found anything yet?'

Amis shook his head. 'No, I'm afraid not.'

'I've just had a thought.' Nick frowned. 'Why did Bella go to all the trouble of dumping Mark's body in Lake Vyrnwy and not just let the pigs eat everything?'

'It's a good question,' Amis admitted. 'However, pigs are quite fussy when it comes to eating thick bone matter. They will eat it eventually, but it can take weeks before they tackle it. And that would mean bones like the femur, tibia, and humerus could be discovered weeks or even months after the human flesh had been eaten.'

'So let the pigs eat the head and hands and dump the rest?' Nick asked.

'What about the skull?' Ruth asked.

'The bone of the skull is relatively thin,' Amis explained. 'They might struggle to chew through the teeth. If you need to get rid of the body fast, that's what I'd do. Dump the body at sea, feed the rest to pigs. Although hydrofluoric acid in a big plastic container would do the job in less than a day.'

'I'll bear that in mind,' Ruth said dryly.

Out of the corner of her eye, Ruth spotted a SOCO approaching, holding a plastic evidence bag.

'Got something for us, Fiona?' Amis asked in a cheerful tone.

'Yes, sir,' Fiona said as she pulled down her mask and held up the bag. 'I think we have four human teeth. And from the looks of them, they haven't been in the ground very long.'

Amis looked at Ruth. 'I think we've got our man, don't you?'

Just as Ruth turned, the Portakabin door opened. Charlie came outside with a perplexed look on his face. 'What's going on?'

Ruth stared at him. 'Charlie Collard, I'm arresting you on suspicion of conspiracy and perverting the course of justice. You do not have to say anything, but it may harm your defence if you do not mention, when questioned, something that you later rely on in court. Anything you do say may be given in evidence. Do you understand?'

Charlie pulled a face. 'What the hell are you talking about?'

Ruth pointed to the evidence bag that Amis was now holding. 'I think you're going to find it hard to explain why there are fresh human teeth in your pigpen.'

She then signalled to two uniformed officers, who went over to Charlie and cuffed him.

Charlie glared at her and sneered, 'Why don't you go and fuck yourself, you sanctimonious bitch!'

Ruth nodded but didn't react. 'Okay. I'll see you back at the station, Charlie.'

The officer pushed Charlie's head down as they shoved him into the back of the car.

Chapter 40

Ruth and Nick came out of the lift and walked purposefully down the corridor towards Interview Room 1, where they were due to question Charlie Collard. Nick was on his phone as Ruth ran through the questions in her head.

Nick ended his call and looked at her. 'The lab said they could compare the DNA from the teeth we found to that of Mark Freudmann by tonight.'

'Good,' Ruth said.

They arrived at Interview Room 1 and entered to see Charlie sitting beside his solicitor, Stephanie Kelly.

Ruth and Nick sat down and pulled their chairs up to the table.

'Charlie, I just need to remind you, you are still under caution and that you have been arrested on suspicion of conspiracy and perverting the course of justice,' Ruth said. 'Do you understand that?'

Charlie nodded, his face devoid of emotion. 'Yes.'

Ruth leant forward, pressed the red button on the

recording equipment, and waited for the long electronic beep to finish.

'Interview with Charlie Collard. Saturday 30th January. Interview Room 1, Llancastell Police Station. Present are his solicitor Stephanie Kelly, Detective Sergeant Nick Evans, and myself, Detective Inspector Ruth Hunter,' Ruth said as she moved the case files, so they were directly in front of her.

Nick leaned forward with his forearms on the table and peered across the table. 'Charlie, could you tell me where you were on the evening of Thursday 21st January?'

Charlie sniffed, rubbed his nose, and glanced back at Nick. 'I was at home.'

'All night?' Nick said to clarify.

'Yes.' Charlie pulled a face as if this was a ridiculous question and then exchanged a look with his solicitor.

Nick nodded slowly. 'Can anyone verify that?'

'My wife,' Charlie replied confidently. 'She can probably tell you what we were watching on the telly.'

Ruth cleared her throat as she shifted on her seat. 'So, just to clarify, Charlie, you didn't go out anywhere on Thursday evening?'

'You believe this?' Charlie gave a wry smile as he shook his head at his solicitor and then said sarcastically, 'I can't have gone anywhere, can I? Cos I've just told you I was in all night.'

Nick reached for the laptop to his right, opened it, and watched as it burst into life. 'For the purposes of the tape, I am showing the suspect item reference 3298, which is CCTV footage of the customer's car park at Pig Meadow Farm.' Nick turned the laptop to face Charlie and gestured. 'You recognise this, Charlie, do you?'

'Of course, I bloody do,' he growled.

Ruth gave him a look. 'Could you read to us what date and time the CCTV was recorded?'

'I can't. I don't have my reading glasses,' Charlie sneered.

Ruth peered at the screen. 'That's okay. I'll do it for you. Shall I? It reads Thursday 21st January and the time stamp 23.28.'

Nick pointed. 'And then you'll notice that this Toyota pickup truck arrives and parks just here. Can you see that, Charlie?'

Charlie didn't respond.

'Do you recognise that pickup truck?' Ruth asked.

'No,' he snapped.

'Really?' Ruth said with a look of disbelief. 'Because we've checked with the DVLA, and that pickup truck is registered to you.'

'Is it?' Charlie asked with a sarcastic sneer.

Nick gestured to the screen again. 'And then someone who looks like you gets out of that vehicle. That is you, isn't it, Charlie?'

'I've no idea,' he muttered. 'I don't have my glasses.'

'Well, let's say for argument's sake, this is you driving into the customer car park at Pig Meadow Farm,' Nick said with an ironic smile. 'Which is strange because you were adamant that you didn't go anywhere on Thursday night and that you watched television with your wife.'

Charlie shrugged. 'That's the thing when you work for yourself and run your own business. I get confused about which day is which.'

Nick ignored him and indicated the CCTV again. 'So, you've parked your truck, got out, and now you're walking across the car park where you meet this figure here. Can you tell us who that is?'

Charlie looked at his solicitor, 'No comment.'

Ruth gave him a withering look. 'Really, Charlie? You're going to give us a 'no comment' interview, now are you?'

'The thing is, we can see that the person you met on Thursday night was your daughter, Bella,' Nick said. 'And she hands you a black bin bag which you take away with you. Can you tell us what was in that black bin bag?'

'No comment.'

'We believe Bella murdered her husband Mark on the evening of Thursday 21st January. With the help of her brother Frank, she dismembered Mark's body and placed the torso and limbs in an old chest freezer. Do you know anything about that, Charlie?'

'No comment.'

'However, we haven't been able to recover Mark's head or his hands,' Ruth said. 'We suspect the bin bag that Bella handed to you in the CCTV footage contained Mark's severed head and hands. Can you tell us anything about that?'

'No comment.'

'Charlie, can you tell us what you then did with Mark's head and hands?'

'No comment.'

Ruth reached for the folder and opened it. 'You see, we strongly suspect that you fed Mark's head and hands to your pigs. I think it's well-documented that pigs will eat virtually anything, including human flesh and bones. Is there anything you can tell us about that?'

'No comment.'

Ruth took out a photograph of an evidence bag. 'For the purposes of the tape, I'm going to show the suspect item reference 8286, which is a photograph of four human teeth that were discovered by our forensic officers today in one of your pigpens.' She fixed him with a stare across the table. 'Can you explain why there might be human teeth in one of your pigpens, Charlie?'

'No comment.'

'Our forensic lab is going to test those human teeth for DNA. Then they are going to match that DNA with Mark's DNA,' Ruth said. 'I'm certain that will prove the teeth we discovered today are Mark's. And I can't see how you're going to explain to a jury how your murdered son-in-law's teeth managed to find their way into your pigpen unless you disposed of his head and hands in there.'

There was silence as Ruth stared across at Charlie, who was starting to fidget nervously.

'No comment.'

'Sergeant, can you tell me what the sentence is for conspiracy and perverting the course of justice in the murder case?' Ruth asked Nick.

Nick blew out his cheeks and shook his head. 'In my experience, judges hand out very long sentences for disposing of dead bodies and lying to the police. I've seen them hand out life sentences for that kind of thing on numerous occasions.'

Ruth stared at Charlie and let the tension grow.

'On the other hand, if a suspect pleads guilty and co-operates with the police, they can be given a reduced sentence, can't they?' Ruth asked, continuing her and Nick's little charade.

'They can,' Nick said with nod. 'A reduction of anywhere between a third and half of the usual sentence.'

'That's a lot of time, isn't it, Charlie.' Ruth stared at him. 'Anything you'd like to tell us now?'

Charlie gave her a look of utter contempt, but he couldn't hide the fact that he was rattled. 'No comment.'

Ruth sighed and sat back for a few seconds.

'Just one more thing before we put you back in the

cell,' Ruth said. 'When Bella was diagnosed as having schizophrenia as a teenager, the doctors must have looked for a family history. But she's adopted, so that must have been difficult.'

'Bella doesn't have schizophrenia.' Charlie looked baffled.

'Well, she has a mental disorder that gives her psychotic episodes,' Ruth said, nodding. 'She must have been on medication for that when she grew up. And that's why she's been to The Priory, isn't it?'

Charlie shook his head. 'I don't know what her medical records say, but she went to The Priory for depression.'

There was a silence as Charlie's comment hung in the air.

'Oh, okay,' Ruth nodded. He'd fallen right into the verbal trap she had set him. Charlie had just confirmed that Bella had no history of any schizophrenia or psychotic episodes in her life. She was faking it for a reduced sentence.

As she looked at him, Charlie began to blink as he started to process why they might be talking about Bella's mental health. And if she was going to plead diminished responsibility, he had just handed the prosecution, the CPS, and the police a reliable piece of testimony that his daughter did not suffer from a complex mental health condition.

Chapter 41

R uth and Nick arrived for a second interview with Bella Freudmann. A clinical psychologist, Dr Peter Andrews, had arrived half an hour earlier and had been briefed by both Ruth and the FME.

Ruth leant across the table to start the recording machine.

'Interview conducted with Bella Freudmann, 30th September, 3.20 pm, Llancastell Police Station. Present are Detective Sergeant Nick Evans, Duty Solicitor Tracey Roberts, Dr Peter Andrews, and myself, Detective Inspector Ruth Hunter.' Ruth then glanced over at Bella, who was looking around the room as if there was a wasp flying around. Bella reached up to swat the imaginary insect away from her face.

Wow. She is doing a very good job of keeping this up, Ruth thought.

'Bella, do you understand that you are still under caution?'

Bella was still staring at an imaginary wasp and following it around the room with her eyes.

'Bella?' Ruth said.

Bella slowly looked down and met her eyes with a cold, chilling stare. 'Oh, it's you again, is it?'

'Bella, do you understand that you are still under caution?' Ruth said again slowly.

'Yes. I'm not bloody stupid, am I?' Bella snorted and then smiled at the duty solicitor as if they were sharing a joke. 'She thinks I'm an idiot, doesn't she?' Bella whispered like a child.

'Bella, I wonder if you can remember what you were doing last Thursday?' Ruth asked. 'That's a week ago.'

Bella shrugged. 'How am I meant to remember that?'

'We believe that you and your husband Mark got into a heated argument,' Ruth said. 'Is that right?'

Bella seemed as if she hadn't heard the question and then turned and glared at Dr Andrews. 'Who the hell is that?'

'That is Dr Andrews, Bella,' the duty solicitor explained. 'He's just sitting in on the interview. You don't need to worry. He's not going to say anything.'

'He works for Susanna, doesn't he?' Bella growled. 'I can tell.'

What the hell is she talking about?'

'Do you mean Susanna, Mark's mother?' Ruth asked to clarify.

Bella turned back and gave Ruth a withering look. 'Yes, of course. That bitch of a mother. She always had it in for me. I was never good enough for her precious son. Jesus.'

'If we can get back to what happened last Thursday, Bella,' Ruth said. 'Can you tell us what happened between you and Mark?'

'You do know this is all Susanna, don't you?' Bella said. 'She did all this to frame me.'

Ruth frowned. 'Susanna murdered her own son to frame you?'

'Yes,' Bella shrugged. 'That's just what she'd like. I don't think that she's actually human.'

Nick gave Ruth a look to indicate that he was going to try a different tack. 'Bella, I'd like you to look at something for me, okay.'

'I suppose so.'

Nick reached for the laptop to his right and opened it. 'For the purposes of the tape, I am showing the suspect item reference 3298, which is CCTV footage of the customer's car park at Pig's Meadow.' Nick turned the laptop to face Bella and gestured. 'You recognise this place, Bella, do you?'

'Yes, of course,' Bella snorted.

Nick played the footage forward as he narrated, 'So, this is the customer car park. And this is your father, Charlie Collard, arriving in his pickup truck. And then he parks, gets out, and he walks over here where he meets this figure.' Nick tapped the screen. 'Any idea who this person with a hood up is?'

Bella laughed. 'It's me, you idiot!'

Nick exchanged an uncertain look with Ruth. 'You're admitting that you drove last Thursday to Pig Meadow Farm just before midnight and met your father in the car park?'

'Yes.' Bella shrugged with a curious frown before turning to the duty solicitor and whispered, 'I don't think that's against the law, is it?'

'And you gave him what appears to be a black bin bag?' Ruth asked, wondering why Bella wasn't trying to hide the fact that they had met.

'Yes. So what?'

'Can you tell us what was in that bag?' Nick said.

'Rubbish,' Bella replied. 'My dad always takes my rubbish and gets rid of it for me.'

Is she being cryptic or just very weird?

Ruth leant forward and stared at her. 'What sort of rubbish did you have in that bag, Bella?'

'What I want to know is why you haven't asked me about Terry yet?' Bella said, sounding lucid.

'Are you talking about Terry Fowles?' Nick asked.

'Of course. Terry and Mark were up to all sorts of things. Mark told me his life was in danger. And Terry came to the house last week?'

Nick frowned. 'Terry Fowles came to your house last week?'

'Yeah,' Bella said. 'And he and Mark got very drunk and had an argument. Well, it was a fight, actually. He killed Mark accidentally.'

What?

Ruth looked at Nick as her eyes widened.

'Why didn't you tell us this before, Bella?' Ruth asked.

'He told me if I told anyone what had really happened, he would kill me and my family. I was scared,' Bella whispered.

Nick leaned forward and frowned at her. 'And you were willing to go to prison for Mark's murder rather than tell us the truth?'

'I was,' Bella said, looking at the floor. She then hummed to herself.

'Did Terry help you get rid of Mark's body and clean up the house?' Ruth asked.

'Yes. He was there until the morning, helping us. Then he went home,' Bella mumbled and then continued to hum.

'Where's the weapon that Terry used to murder Mark?' Nick asked.

Bella didn't answer.

'Bella?' Ruth said. 'Can you answer the question, please?'

Bella didn't respond, but her humming got louder.

Nick couldn't hide his frustration. 'Bella?'

This is total bullshit, Ruth thought. But Bella's allegation that Mark and Terry Fowles had had a fight at the house the previous week and Fowles had murdered him created a tiny seed of doubt in her mind.

RUTH SAT AT THE LARGE OVAL TABLE IN THE CONFERENCE room. Around the table sat Drake, Dr Andrews, and Vicky Goodwin from the CPS.

'What did you think?' Ruth asked as she glanced over at Dr Andrews.

He thought for a few seconds. 'If I'm honest, I just don't know. Some of the symptoms Bella is exhibiting are what I would expect to see in a psychotic episode. Hallucinations, paranoia, and delusions.'

'But they could be faked, couldn't they?' Ruth asked.

Dr Andrews nodded. 'Yes, of course. But you would have to know the exact nature of those symptoms, which is why I became a little suspicious.'

'How do you mean?' Goodwin asked as she wrote in her notepad. Ruth had encountered Vicky Goodwin from the CPS on several occasions. She was humourless but bloody good at her job.

'For example, Bella looked at me and claimed that I worked for her mother-in-law, Susanna. And that kind of delusional paranoia is a typical characteristic of something like schizophrenia. However, she didn't pursue it or refer to it again, which doesn't fit the pattern.'

Drake sat back in his chair and stroked his goatee. 'You mean Bella is showing some elements of psychosis, but not in a way that convinces you that she's not acting?'

Dr Andrews frowned and then thought for a few more seconds. 'Difficult to tell. There are no hard and fast rules when it comes to mental illness.'

'But your instinct is that she was faking the illness?' Ruth said, aware that she was trying to put words into his mouth.

'I couldn't go as far as that, I'm afraid,' he admitted with a shrug.

'I have a suggestion.' Goodwin put down her pen and looked at them all. 'Bella is due at Magistrate's Court tomorrow morning to offer a plea. I think she needs to be taken to have a full psychological evaluation.'

Ruth let out an audible sigh. She was certain that Bella was putting on an act. 'I can't believe we're actually falling for this.'

Goodwin shrugged. 'Ruth, Bella will be a given a thorough psychological examination. It's not something she can fake over a long period of time without being found out. I've seen it happen before. After a day or two, a suspect can't keep up the pretence and lets their guard down.'

Drake looked over at Ruth. 'What about her allegation against Terry Fowles?'

'It's never been mentioned before,' Ruth shrugged. 'But we can certainly talk to Merseyside Police and verify Fowles' whereabouts on the 21st.'

'I think that would be a very good idea,' Drake said.

'Do you have anything other than Bella's testimony

that Terry Fowles was involved in Mark's murder?' Goodwin asked.

Ruth shook her head. 'No. We knew that Fowles was an old friend of Mark Freudmann. But there's been nothing in our investigation so far that implicates Fowles in any way. I think Bella is desperate, and she'll tell us anything.'

Chapter 42

Ruth had asked Georgie to speak to Merseyside Police to see if they could rule out Bella's assertion that Terry Fowles had travelled to Snowdonia on Thursday 21ˢᵗ January and stayed there overnight. They were pretty certain that Bella had murdered Mark and, with the help of Frank and Charlie, disposed of his body. However, Ruth didn't want to leave any stone unturned. The CPS would also insist that every avenue of investigation had been looked at. They didn't want a defence counsel using Terry Fowles as a way of casting doubt on Bella's guilt.

Georgie was sitting in DCI Finnan's side office upstairs at St Ann Street Police Station in the middle of Liverpool. Finnan appeared at the door with two cups of coffee and handed her one.

'Thanks,' Georgie said, making direct eye contact with him.

He is definitely fit, she thought, as she checked out his body as he strode over to his office chair and sat down.

'I assume you're back here to talk about Terry Fowles?' Finnan said as he sipped his coffee and held her gaze.

'Yeah,' she replied with a nod. 'Bella Freudmann claims Terry visited them on the 21st January and that Mark and Terry got drunk and had a violent row.'

'And that's the first time she's mentioned that?' Finnan asked with a frown.

'Yeah, well, there's a slight spanner in the works at our end,' Georgie explained. 'Bella Freudmann appears to be having some kind of mental breakdown. There's a chance that she'll be entering a diminished responsibility plead when she's charged with Mark's murder.'

'And you're sure you've got the right person?' Finnan asked.

'We know that Mark was murdered in the bedroom at their house. And we know that Mark's body was cut up and dumped in Lake Vyrnwy. We also have evidence to suggest that Bella drove to meet her father on the night of the 21st January with a bag containing Mark's head and hands.'

Finnan pulled a face. 'Lovely.'

Georgie snorted. 'And then her father fed the head and hands to his prize-winning pigs.'

'Pretty grim stuff, isn't it?' Finnan said with a raised eyebrow.

'Yeah, it is,' Georgie agreed. 'We also know that Frank Collard impersonated Mark to trick people into thinking that Mark was still alive.'

'So, he's facing a conspiracy charge?' Finnan asked.

'Not any more,' Georgie replied. 'He threw himself off a ferry into the Irish Sea.'

Finnan's eyes narrowed. 'And when did Bella allege that Terry Fowles had visited her home and killed her husband?'

'Earlier today.'

'And she hadn't told you this before?'

'No.' Georgie shook her head. 'She claims that Fowles threatened to kill her and her family if she told anyone what had happened.'

'Why didn't she mention any of this when she was first arrested?'

'She was too scared,' Georgie said.

'What does your SIO think?'

Georgie shrugged. 'DI Hunter thinks that Bella is guilty of murdering her husband and disposing of his body. This whole mental illness and the story about Fowles are just a smokescreen.'

Finnan turned his chair and wheeled six inches so that he was in front of his computer. 'I can look at the surveillance log we have on Fowles. Hopefully, that can clear up where he was on the 21st.'

Georgie smiled at him. 'That would be great.'

As Finnan reached over to begin typing, she noticed he was now wearing a wedding ring.

Eh? He's married, she thought to herself. The last time they were in the office, he wasn't wearing a ring. And the two of them had spent the past couple of days sending flirty texts.

'You're married?' Georgie frowned as she gestured to his finger.

'Yeah,' he said, holding up his left hand where there was a silver ring.

'I'm pretty sure the last time I was in here, you weren't wearing that?' Georgie asked.

What the hell was that about?

'Wasn't I?' Finnan gave her a cheeky grin. 'You notice that kind of thing, do you?'

'If I'm interested,' she replied. Should she be annoyed

that he was married? They hadn't done anything except exchange some flirty texts.

'If you're interested?' Finnan laughed. 'Yeah, no, I wasn't. Not for any sneaky reason. I go swimming and have a sauna a few mornings a week before work. I take off my wedding ring, that's all.'

'Oh.' Georgie was unable to disguise the disappointment in her voice. She gave him a knowing look. 'Does your wife know that you send inappropriate texts to other women?'

'I don't send inappropriate texts to other women,' Finnan said, looking directly at her. 'I only send inappropriate texts to you.'

'Piss off.' Georgie rolled her eyes. She wasn't falling for his bullshit.

Finnan laughed. 'I think that's *piss off, sir,* isn't it?'

'You're pulling rank on me now?' Georgie asked with a flirtatious raise of her eyebrow.

'Tell you what. There's an advanced fingerprinting and DNA course coming up next month in Leeds,' Finnan said. 'Two day course, weekend, nice hotel.'

'Sounds interesting.'

'I'm sure you can persuade DI Hunter to send you on it?' Finnan grinned. 'I get the feeling that you get most things that you want.'

'I do,' Georgie chuckled. 'And what would we do in the evenings? You know when we're not sitting in tedious fingerprinting and DNA workshops.'

'Go for a swim and a sauna,' Finnan said. 'Maybe a massage.'

'Sounds nice,' Georgie said, with her eyes fixed on his. She was going to fuck his brains out and use him to get out of North Wales.

'It does, doesn't it?' Finnan smiled as he went back over

to the computer, tapped away, and read the screen. 'That's weird.'

'What's up?' Georgie asked.

Finnan peered at her. 'Terry Fowles was off our radar from 8 pm to 1 am on the 21st. He was spotted arriving at his club at 1 am but nothing for the rest of the evening.'

'It doesn't match Bella's story. She claims that Mark and Fowles got drunk, they rowed, and Fowles killed him. She said that Fowles stayed the rest of the night while they worked out what to do with the body and how to cover up the murder,' Georgie explained. 'But it does mean technically Fowles did have time to drive to Snowdonia, kill Mark and return to Liverpool.'

Chapter 43

'More wine?' Ruth asked as she came into the living room with a bottle of Pinot Grigio. She was cooking a cottage pie for her and Sarah.

'Yes, thanks.' Sarah held up her glass as Ruth topped her up.

The *Years & Years* album *Communion* was playing.

'God, I played this to death when it first came out,' Ruth said, gesturing to the stereo.

'I wasn't even aware of *Years & Years* before you put this on the other day,' Sarah admitted. 'I love it.'

'I knew you would,' Ruth said with a smile. 'Ella got me into them. Actually, I think it's just one person. Olly Alexander.' Ruth glanced at her watch. It was 7.33 pm and Ella was over half an hour late. 'Where is the little bugger, she's late.'

'I think I've got a whole load of music, films, and television to catch up on,' Sarah said.

'Oh, you have to watch *Mare of Easttown*,' Ruth said enthusiastically. 'Kate Winslet is incredible.'

Sarah laughed. 'Don't tell me. It's a cop show.'

Ruth shrugged. 'Of course.'

'Gritty, dark, with a female detective?'

'God, am I that predictable?'

'Yep,' Sarah chortled. 'You would think you get enough of that crap at work. But the irony is that your perfect idea of a relaxing evening is to sit and watch a fictional representation of your actual job.'

'You say it as though it's a bad thing,' Ruth protested, aware that she hadn't broached the subject of Sarah's secret trip to Doncaster. Maybe now they were both laughing and relaxing with a couple of glasses of wine, it would be a good idea to have *that* conversation.

There were a few seconds of silence. Ruth couldn't hide what she was thinking in the back of her mind.

'You okay?' Sarah asked.

'Yeah.' Ruth was stalling for time.

'Really. Your whole expression has changed.'

Ruth went over, sat down, and then looked at her.

Sarah pulled a mock scared face. 'Oh, dear. You've come and sat down. And now you've got that scary, serious look you get, so this is not going to be good.'

'It's fine,' Ruth said unconvincingly. 'Honestly.'

'Which is about as convincing as the phrase, *It's not you, it's me.*'

Ruth took a breath. 'I know you went to Doncaster on the train. And I'm guessing you went to see your mum.'

'How the bloody hell do you know that?' Sarah asked with an angry frown.

'You were asleep on the sofa,' Ruth explained calmly. 'Your phone went off in your jacket. I got it out, and the train ticket fell out.'

'You were going through my things?'

'No. That's not what I said,' Ruth protested. 'It was a complete accident. And I think you might be missing the point here. You travelled to Yorkshire to see your mum without telling me and broke your signed agreement with the PPS.'

'I don't give a fuck about that,' Sarah said defiantly. 'My mum is dying. I'm not going to sit by, here, with her thinking that I'm still missing. That's just not right.'

'But that's what you agreed to do,' Ruth pointed out.

'No. I didn't,' Sarah growled. 'I was told that I had to go into protective custody. And I was *told* that I couldn't contact any members of my family while I was giving evidence to this Homicide and Serious Crime thing. No one asked me if it was okay.'

'But you're putting people at risk by going to see her,' Ruth said.

'You mean I'm putting you at risk?' Sarah snapped.

Ruth shook her head. 'And possibly Ella. And your family in Yorkshire.'

Sarah narrowed her eyes angrily. 'Well, I was willing to take that risk rather than not seeing my mum before she dies. I wasn't going to let her die, believing that her only child was missing and probably dead. No one can expect me to do that.'

'I just wish you would have told me before you decided to go,' Ruth said. 'Maybe we could have talked about it first. Or I could have put things in place that would have made you travelling to Doncaster safer.'

'You would have tried to talk me out of it,' Sarah said.

Ruth frowned. 'I'm not sure that I would have. You were in an impossible position. I don't blame you at all for going. Honestly.'

There were a few seconds of silence as Sarah calmed down.

'Sorry,' she said.

Ruth gave her a kind smile. 'You don't need to apologise. I love you. And I love your mum. I'm devastated that she's so ill. And if I put myself in your shoes, I would have probably done the same.'

'But you're a serving police officer.'

Ruth went over to Sarah and sat next to her on the sofa. She took her hand. 'Listen, if I need perspective on something, you know what I do?'

'No idea.'

'What am I going to think on my deathbed about a certain situation?' Ruth explained.

'That's very morbid, isn't it?'

'No, it's completely liberating,' Ruth said. 'And my guess is that on your deathbed, your one regret would have been not to have seen your mum and reassured her you were alive and well. And that's true whatever the prognosis is for your mum.'

Sarah blinked as she thought about what Ruth had said. Then she gave Ruth a mock sneer.

'What?' Ruth asked with a half smile.

'Who made you so fucking wise all of a sudden?' Sarah laughed.

'Hey, I'm wise when it comes to other people's problems. It just goes flying out the window when it comes to my own.'

The doorbell rang.

'Saved by the bell,' Sarah quipped.

It had to be Ella.

'About bloody time.'.

'Ruth?' Sarah said quietly.

'What?'

'Thank you.'

Chapter 44

Sunday 31ˢᵗ January

'RIGHT, EVERYONE.' RUTH STRODE TO THE FRONT OF THE CID office to conduct morning briefing. 'Let's get up to speed with this investigation.'

Garrow looked over with a grim expression. 'The coastguard has been in contact to say they've retrieved Frank Collard's body.'

'Thank you, Jim,' Ruth said. 'Okay, so Bella Freudmann was interviewed under caution twice yesterday. In the first interview with myself and Nick, Bella exhibited increasingly strange behaviour and tried to attack me. She was then examined by the FME, who recommended that Bella be seen by a mental health professional.'

There were some disgruntled murmurs from the assembled team. Suspects claiming or faking mental health issues wasn't a new thing. But it was incredibly frustrating for everyone working on an investigation. Detectives wanted to get justice for Mark and his family. They didn't want his killer to get a reduced sentence or end up in a psychiatric ward on a false diminished responsibility plea.

'Okay, guys. I know that's frustrating.' Ruth put up her hand to pacify them.

French looked over. 'Is that what her defence counsel is going to plea, is it?'

'We're not sure yet,' Ruth explained. 'What I think will happen at the Magistrates' Court later is that there will be a recommendation that Bella be given a thorough psychiatric evaluation to determine if her mental health issues are legitimate. So, we have to tread very carefully.'

Georgie shook her head. 'Jim and I spoke to her on several occasions, and there was nothing wrong with her. She was very sharp and lucid. Just a bit unfriendly.'

Ruth nodded. 'That's mine and Nick's opinion too. Her performance so far has been incredibly convincing. So, what we're looking for is anything that would show Mark's murder was premeditated. If her defence claim that she is suffering from a psychotic episode, they can put a violent attack down to that diagnosis. And that allows them a diminished responsibility plea, a reduced sentence, and time in a psychiatric hospital rather than prison. I'm pretty sure that none of us want that?'

There were murmurs of agreement from the CID team.

'What about the ferry tickets, boss?' Garrow asked. 'Frank Collard booked those a month before the murder.'

There were a couple of nods of agreement around the room.

Ruth shook her head. 'I agree with you, Jim. Booking those tickets convinces me that there was something strange going on between Bella and Frank, and they planned to murder him and disappear over to Ireland.'

'But a defence counsel would drive a lorry through that as an argument,' Nick said. 'A brother and sister booking ferry tickets to go away and visit Ireland isn't evidence that Mark's murder was premeditated. It wouldn't stick.'

'Exactly,' Ruth said. 'So, what I need us to do is to scour everything. Computer hard drives, phone, and bank records. Anything that shows Bella demonstrating that the murder was planned.'

'What's happening to Charlie Collard, boss?' French asked.

'I'm talking to the CPS today,' Ruth said. 'As soon as we have DNA confirmation that the teeth we found at *Pig Meadow Farm* belong to Mark Freudmann, he will be charged with conspiracy and perverting the course of justice.'

'I spoke to DCI Finnan late yesterday, boss,' Georgie said.

'What did he have to say?'

'He checked the surveillance log they're running on Terry Fowles,' Georgie explained. 'Fowles' whereabouts between 8 pm and 1 am on the 21st are unaccounted for.'

Ruth frowned. It wasn't good news. 'Where was he at 1 am?'

'He arrived at The Attic nightclub in Liverpool,' Georgie said.

Nick looked at Ruth. 'So, Fowles has five hours to travel to Wales, murder Mark and get back.'

'That's not what Bella told us, though, is it?' Ruth said. 'She claimed they were drinking all night, got into a row, and Fowles attacked Mark. He then stayed to help clean up and dispose of the body. She told us he left in the morning.'

'Fowles' fingerprints and DNA will be on the PNS or HOLMES, won't they?' French suggested.

HOLMES stood for the Home Office Large Major Enquiry System. It was an extensive computer database for police to collate and cross-reference information in major investigations.

'They're bound to be,' Nick said with a nod.

'Why don't we get forensics to run Fowles' prints and DNA against the evidence taken from the crime scene and see if we get a hit,' French said.

'Good idea, Dan. Have a word and see if they can do that today, please.'

'You think Fowles could be involved, boss?' Georgie asked.

'Not really,' Ruth said. 'But I'd like to be able to rule him out. Jim, can you talk to the DVLA and Merseyside OCP? See what vehicles are registered to Fowles or vehicles he has use of. Then talk to traffic and get them to run the plates against ANPR on the major roads out of Liverpool on the night of the 21st.'

'Yes, boss,' Garrow said, writing what she had suggested in his notebook.

That was Jim. Ever meticulous.

'Okay, everyone else, I want you to get cracking on everything we've got on Bella Freudmann. I'm praying that she's made a slip and done something that will allow us to prove Mark's murder was premeditated. Reconvene here at 5 pm please.'

SITTING AT THE BACK OF MOLD MAGISTRATES' COURT, Ruth watched the proceedings. The courtroom had dark blue carpets and chair covers. The walls were painted in an innocuous cream with a large royal coat of arms up high above where the magistrate sat.

As Bella stood in the dock, still dressed in the grey tracksuit, she looked around and drummed her fingers on the brass railing in front of her. She seemed to be muttering something inaudible.

A court official peered over at her and asked, 'Please state your name.'

Bella fixed Ruth with a stare and then looked at the magistrate. 'Why is she staring at me?'

The magistrate frowned. 'Mrs Freudmann, you have been asked to state your name. Could you please do so?'

The defence lawyer stood, gave the magistrate a forced smile, and whispered something into Bella's ear.

Bella laughed at her. 'He knows my name is Bella Freudmann. He just called me Mrs Freudmann!' Bella then looked at the magistrate like a surly teenager. 'My name is Bella Freudmann. Happy? And Bella is short for Isabella, okay?'

'And that's your full name, is it?' the magistrate asked.

'Yes, it bloody is,' Bella said with a smile before looking over at Ruth again. 'That bitch is still staring at me. She works for Susanna, you all know that, don't you?'

The magistrate gave Bella a withering look. 'Mrs Freudmann, could you please refrain from using foul or abusive language in my courtroom?'

'Oh, sorry, your honour,' Bella giggled.

Ruth was studying her carefully. She was doing a hell of a job keeping up the act.

The magistrate peered over her glasses at the defence lawyer. 'I understand that you are requesting a delay in allowing your client to plead? Is that correct?'

'Yes, ma'am,' the defence lawyer responded. 'I would like to ascertain my client's fitness to plea. We have written testimony to confirm that a full psychological evaluation should be carried out on my client before we return for another initial hearing.'

'Very well,' the magistrate said. 'I would like you back here with your client and a psychological evaluation in 48 hours' time.'

Ruth knew that she and the CID team now had two days to come up with something that proved Bella was a cold, calculating murderer who planned to kill her husband. If they didn't, Bella would likely be able to officially enter a diminished responsibility plea. After that, a legal juggernaut revolving around Bella's ability to stand trial would be set in motion – and the chances of her ever going to prison would be severely weakened.

An hour later, Ruth was sitting in her office. The search through Bella's phone, banks, laptop, and anything else they could think of had so far proved fruitless.

Garrow appeared at her door holding a printout. He appeared paler than usual – maybe the pressure of the case was getting to him?

'Jim? Anything useful?' she asked, sitting forward in her chair.

'I hope so,' he said. 'Digital forensics have pulled Bella Freudmann's search history for her MacBook. There's about twenty hits from the past month searching for symptoms of schizophrenia, hearing voices, and other mental health stuff.'

'That's good,' Ruth said hesitantly, but she was already predicting what the defence counsel would argue at trial. 'Is there anything where she looks for the legal implications of having something like schizophrenia? Anything where she's researched how to achieve a diminished responsibility plea?'

Garrow seemed confused. 'No, boss. But surely if Bella was looking up the symptoms of a disease like schizophrenia, that shows she's faking it? It also shows that Mark's murder was premeditated.'

Ruth shook her head. 'Not really. Any decent defence lawyer would argue that in recent weeks Bella had been suffering from a decline in her mental health. She was suffering from delusions or paranoia. She merely went online to check those symptoms and what she might suffer from.' She looked up at Garrow, who seemed a little disappointed that his discovery of Bella's search history wasn't going to be the key to getting her convicted. 'Good work, Jim. Just keep digging away. She will have made a mistake somewhere along the line. They always do.'

'No problem, boss,' Garrow said as he turned and went.

Ruth gave an audible sigh and glanced at her watch. They had a day and a half to find something to prove Mark's murder was premeditated.

Coffee and a ciggie is what I need, she thought, as she got up from her chair, stretched, and clicked her back.

She went out into the CID office and looked at the faces of her team, all working intently at computers or on the phone.

Georgie looked over. 'Boss, I've trawled through the GPS planner on Bella's Porsche. I was really hoping that at some point in the last few months, she would have travelled to Lake Vyrnwy and maybe the actual spot where we found Mark's remains.'

'And?' Ruth asked, already knowing that Georgie hadn't found anything.

'Sorry. Nothing.'

'Okay. It was a good idea.'

French spun around in his chair and pointed to his screen. 'I've got her phone records here. She rings her father about eight times between 6 pm and 11 pm on the 21st.'

Ruth nodded. 'It's definitely useful in terms of evidence.'

'Eight phone calls certainly seems unusual, even erratic,' French pointed out.

'It does,' Ruth agreed. 'But it's very circumstantial. And it's not going to show any premeditation. Bella could have been suffering from a psychotic episode while making the calls. We need to find something that shows she's been cold, calculating, and perfectly sane.'

Nick came striding in through the doors, looking purposeful. 'Just popped down the lab, boss. The teeth from *Pig Meadow Farm* are a DNA match for Mark Freudmann.'

'I'll talk to the CPS,' Ruth said with a half smile. 'Then we can go and charge Charlie Collard.'

It was a result. But what Ruth really wanted to do was to charge Bella with murder.

Chapter 45

C harlie Collard was standing in front of the custody sergeant with his hands handcuffed in front of him by the time Ruth and Nick arrived. As the SIO on the case, it was Ruth's responsibility to transfer Charlie to HMP Rhoswen, where he was to be held on remand; and sign any necessary paperwork. She knew that, given the severity of the offence, he would probably be taken in front of a judge at Mold Crown Court the following morning when a date would be set for his trial.

The custody sergeant looked across at Charlie. 'Charlie Collard, you are charged with conspiracy and seeking to pervert the course of justice in relation to a murder, contrary to common law. Do you have anything to say?'

Charlie appeared broken and no longer had his usual bravado. He just stared at the floor and shook his head.

A uniformed police officer led Charlie out of the back entrance and down some steel steps into the rear car park where a prison transfer van was waiting. The torrential early morning rain had now stopped, but the sky was still a dismal grey.

Ruth and Nick went to the steps and watched as he was bundled into the van by two prison officers. He would be spending the next few months on remand at HMP Rhoswen.

Ruth's phone buzzed. It was Georgie from upstairs.

It must be urgent.

'Georgie?' Ruth said as she answered her phone.

'Boss, we've picked up a signal from Mark Freudmann's mobile phone,' she said.

What?

Ruth remembered it had never been found, but the phone company had confirmed it had remained unused from the 21st January onwards.

'What's the location?' Ruth asked, wondering why Mark's phone would suddenly be on and working.

'Just east of Llancastell,' Georgie explained. 'But it's on the move along the A5, so we assume the phone is in some kind of vehicle.'

'Okay, thanks, Georgie,' Ruth said. 'I'll use the car radio once we get going to get the exact location.'

HALF AN HOUR LATER, RUTH AND NICK PULLED INTO A small car park at a petrol station with a Greggs, Burger King, and Starbucks attached. It was just off the A5, close to Corwen. The GPS signal from Mark Freudmann's phone had stopped at this location for just over ten minutes. They assumed that whoever had the phone had stopped to get some fuel or refreshments.

Getting out of the car, Nick and Ruth surveyed the area. There were only three vehicles. A van with two workmen inside wearing high-vis jackets. They were talking and laughing as they drank tea.

They don't look very likely, Ruth thought.

To the left was an empty people carrier. Wandering over, she could see a baby seat and a seat for an older child in the back. She made the assumption that a family had been travelling and stopped for a break.

That left the car on the far side, which seemed to have two young men inside. At first sight, they definitely looked suspicious. What the hell would they be doing with Mark's phone?

Ruth exchanged a look with Nick, and they walked quietly towards the car.

The young man in the driver's seat seemed to be rolling a cigarette. And then she got a waft of hashish in the air – it wasn't a cigarette.

Looking up, the young man – early 20s, baseball cap, thick silver chain – did a double take and then stopped rolling the spliff.

Shit! I think he's seen us.

The young man spat out the chewing gum he had been chewing as he locked eyes with Ruth and then stared over at Nick.

Before she could react, she heard the roar of a car engine followed by the squeal of tyres as the silver Ford Focus shot out of the car park.

'Shit!' Ruth shouted.

They sprinted towards their car, and Nick clicked his radio. 'Control from Sierra three-six, over.'

'Sierra three-six from Control. Go ahead, over.'

'In pursuit of suspects. Silver Ford Focus, heading west on the A5, three miles west of Corwen, over.'

'Received. Stand by, over.'

They quickly jumped into the car. Nick turned the ignition and hit the accelerator, spinning the wheels as they set off in pursuit.

Once out on the A5, Nick rapidly built up speed as he

worked his way through the gears like a racing driver. They hit 70 mph a few seconds later.

Ruth gripped the dashboard as the car screamed round a bend.

Nick sat forwards a little, peering through the windscreen. 'Where are you, you little bastards?'

The Focus came into view, speeding up a hill about a mile ahead.

'What the hell are little scumbags like that doing with Mark Freudmann's phone?' Nick asked.

'No idea,' Ruth replied. 'I had assumed that Bella or Charlie had got rid of the phone somewhere.'

Ruth felt the Astra's back tyres losing grip and slipping as they cornered another bend.

Nick took a quick look at her. 'Can you see the reg, boss?'

'Not with my eyes,' Ruth admitted as her stomach lurched.

Nick peered as they got closer to the Focus up ahead. He grabbed the radio. 'Control from Sierra three-six, over.'

'Sierra three-six from Control. Go ahead, over.'

'We are continuing our pursuit of suspects. Silver Ford Focus. I now have a registration. Yankee, Foxtrot, one, eight, Yankee, Zebra, Tango. Requesting a PNC check on the vehicle. We are still heading west on the A5.'

'Received. Stand by, over.'

Nick went hammering up the hill and over the crest. The Focus was now only about a quarter of a mile ahead, and they were gaining.

Nick pulled out to overtake a car towing a caravan and shot past it at speed.

'Sierra three-six, this is Control, over.'

Ruth took the radio handset. 'Control, this is Sierra three-six, we are receiving. Go ahead, over.'

'Silver Ford Focus, registration: Yankee, Foxtrot, one, eight, Yankee, Zebra, Tango. Registered owner is a Thomas Matthews, 54 Charles Street, Llancastell, over.'

'Received, out.' Ruth looked at Nick. 'Does the name Thomas or Tom Matthews ring any bells?'

Nick shook his head. 'I'm afraid not.'

A moment later, they screamed through a small village. They were going so fast that Ruth felt the houses and stone walls were only inches from the passenger door.

Just up ahead, a lorry pulled out of a field in front of them. Nick steered the car onto the opposite side of the road, missing it by a few feet.

'For God's sake!' he bellowed.

They careered around another bend, and Ruth shut her eyes. She opened them again as the car flashed past a red sign that read Arafwch Nawr – *Reduce speed now!*

The Focus was now only one hundred yards away. It pulled out to overtake and whizzed past two cars. However, as Nick pulled out to do the same, there was a tractor coming the other way.

Ruth held her breath – there just wasn't enough time or space to get past the second car. Nick dropped down into third gear, and the Astra roared uncomfortably, but the boost in speed bought them a couple of extra seconds, and they made it past with inches to spare.

'Jesus!' Nick yelled.

Suddenly, a small van pulled slowly out of a turning in front of them.

The Focus slammed on the brakes and skidded.

'Bloody hell!' Nick shouted as he hit his own brakes hard.

Ruth glanced ahead. The Focus had clipped the kerb, lost control, and ploughed into a hedgerow.

Ruth felt like everything in her body was contracting as the Astra continued to skid to a halt. She instinctively pulled her knees up and screwed her eyes closed.

After a few more seconds, they came to a stop.

Ruth blinked open her eyes and immediately glanced over at Nick.

'You all right?' she gasped.

'I think so. You?' he said, looking shaken.

Ruth opened the passenger door, got out, and sprinted towards the Focus, which was embedded in the undergrowth. Nick followed.

Her first thought was for the safety of the two young men inside.

As they got to the car, the passenger door opened, and a young man staggered out. He had a gash across his temple, and he looked in a state of shock.

'You okay?' Ruth asked as he sat down on the kerb.

'Yeah,' he mumbled.

A second later, Nick went over and helped the driver out through the passenger door.

'Sit down there, next to your mate,' Nick growled as he pointed to the pavement. 'If either of you try to do a runner, I'm going to really hurt you.'

'You can't do that.' The driver wiped the blood from his nose.

'He can,' Ruth said. 'I've seen him do it.'

'Why were you two driving like a pair of idiots?' Nick asked.

They both shrugged.

Going over to the passenger, Nick started to pat him down. He then pulled out a mobile phone from his jacket pocket. 'Is this your phone?'

The passenger shook his head. 'No.'

'Whose is it then?' Ruth snapped.

'I don't know,' he replied with a sneer.

Ruth fixed him with a stare. 'Yeah, well, you've got a big problem, sunshine. Because that mobile phone belongs to a murder victim, so we need to know where you got it from.'

The colour visibly drained from the passenger's face. 'Someone gave it to me.'

'Who?' Nick barked.

'My brother, Kevin,' the passenger said.

'Where did he get it?'

'He said he'd found it down by Lake Vyrnwy washed up on the bank there,' the passenger explained. 'So, I dried it out for a few days and got it to work. I didn't know it was stolen.'

Ruth looked at Nick. *What a bloody waste of time!*

Chapter 46

By the time Ruth got back to Llancastell, she was feeling deflated. They'd been on a complete wild goose chase across Snowdonia. They had less than 36 hours to find something to prove Bella had premeditated the murder or she was going to plead diminished responsibility.

As they walked along the first-floor corridor, Nick looked at her. 'Don't worry, boss. We'll find something.'

'I hope so,' Ruth said. 'Susanna Freudmann might be a bit of an old battleaxe, but she's totally crushed by Mark's death. And she's given her life to policing and fighting for better conditions for female police officers. I think we owe it to her to get the right sentence for Bella.'

'I agree,' Nick said. 'I don't think there's anything worse than someone trying to play the system like that.'

They walked into the CID office, and several officers looked over. There was something up – she could sense it in the atmosphere of the room.

'What's going on, Georgie?' she asked.

Getting up from her desk, Georgie approached. 'We

think we've got something, boss,' she explained enthusiastically.

'What is it?' Ruth asked expectantly.

Georgie gestured over to Garrow, who glanced up from where he was typing furiously at his computer. 'I think Jim better explain as he found it.'

Spinning round in his chair, Garrow looked at Ruth and Nick. 'I've been trawling through Bella's credit card statements. Six weeks ago, she spent £125 in a B&Q in Llancastell. I decided to ring them to check out what she bought.'

Ruth peered at him as she started to guess what he was about to say. 'Go on,' she said with a mixture of apprehension and anticipation.

Garrow raised an eyebrow. 'She bought five rolls of gaffer tape, plastic sheeting, paint, a chain and padlock, and ten litres of bleach.'

Bingo!

Ruth looked at Nick. It could be the breakthrough they needed.

'That's brilliant, Jim,' Ruth said, trying to work out if the CPS would think this evidence was enough to prove premeditation at trial.

'It gets better,' Jim said. 'She then went into Dragon Sports and bought a serrated edged hunting knife.'

'Which is our murder weapon,' Ruth said.

'I've got their CCTV from that afternoon.' Jim pointed to his screen.

Ruth moved so she could see the screen. Garrow clicked a button, and the CCTV clearly showed Bella at the shop counter buying what looked like a hunting knife.

'If we can show it's the same knife,' Nick said, 'there's no way she can claim murdering Mark wasn't planned.'

Ruth had an idea as she marched over to the nearest phone and dialled the forensic lab downstairs.

'Forensic lab,' said a voice.

'It's DI Hunter. You have a hunting knife with a serrated blade that we retrieved from the chest freezer, and we believe was our murder weapon?'

'Yes, ma'am.'

'Can you get it and read out the serial code that is engraved at the base of the blade, just above the hilt, please?'

'Yes, ma'am,' the technician said and then after a couple of seconds, 'It's two, two, zero, one, eight, seven, four.'

'Thank you.' Ruth put down the phone and scribbled the number on a pad. She looked at Garrow. 'I need the phone number for that shop,' she said urgently.

Typing at the computer, Garrow got the number on his screen, wrote it down on a Post-it, and came over with it. He had also written down the date and time of the purchase – 3rd December 2020.

'Thanks, Jim.' Ruth tapped the number into the phone.

'Hello, Dragon Sports,' said a man's voice with a thick North Wales accent.

'Hi, this is Detective Inspector Hunter of the North Wales Police,' she said. 'I'm making an enquiry about a hunting knife that was purchased from you on the 3rd December. If it was bought on a credit card and I give you the knife's serial number, can you tell me the name of the person who purchased the knife?'

'Yes, of course,' the man said.

'Great.' Her pulse quickened. 'The serial number is two, two, zero, one, eight, seven, four.'

She could hear the man typing into his computer to look at his sales records.

'Okay, I've got that for you,' the man said.

'Great, can you tell me the name you've got there?'

'Yes. It was bought by a Bella Freudmann.'

Thank God!

Ruth looked over at the team with a smile of utter relief. 'Bella Freudmann? Thank you, you've just made my day.'

Chapter 47

Two hours later, Bella had been brought across Llancastell from the secure unit for another interview in light of the new evidence. The clinical psychologist, Dr Peter Andrews, who had been assigned the case, had arrived half an hour later. They were all now sitting in Interview Room 3 of Llancastell nick.

Ruth leant across the table to start the recording machine. The long electronic beep sounded as Ruth opened her files.

'Interview conducted with Bella Freudmann, 31st January, Llancastell Police Station. Present are Detective Sergeant Nick Evans, Duty Solicitor Tracey Roberts, Dr Peter Andrews, and myself, Detective Inspector Ruth Hunter.' Ruth then looked over at Bella, who was glancing around the room like a distracted child.

Time to stop the big act, Bella. We're on to you.

Ruth tried to make eye contact. 'Bella, do you understand you are still under caution?'

Bella slowly met her eyes and seemed baffled. 'What are you doing here?'

'Bella, do you understand that you are still under caution?' Ruth said again slowly.

Bella snorted and then gave a salute. 'Yes, ma'am.'

'Bella, we're interviewing you because there have been some developments in the investigation that we would like to ask you about,' Ruth explained.

Bella shrugged. 'Okay.'

'Can you tell us if you've ever been to a shop in Llancastell called Dragon Sports?' Ruth asked.

Bella frowned and gave a quick shake of her head.

'For the purposes of the tape, the suspect has indicated no,' Ruth said.

Nick took a photo from a folder and turned it around to show her. 'I'm showing the suspect item reference 2923, which is a photograph of a hunting knife with a serrated blade. Have you ever seen this knife before, Bella?'

'No, don't be ridiculous,' Bella replied in a childish voice. 'Why are you asking me that?'

'Bella, we have CCTV footage that shows you entering Dragon Sports on the 3rd December 2020 and purchasing this knife,' Nick said. 'Is there anything you can tell us about that?'

Ruth watched Bella's face for any signs to show that this evidence had rattled her in any way. There was nothing – not even a flicker.

'Bella,' Ruth said. 'The knife that you bought was found in a chest freezer containing the remains of your husband, Mark. We believe it was used to murder him. Can you explain that to us?'

Bella was looking down at her nails and whispering, 'This is Francis. What is Francis doing here? I told her you'd be late. And now look at what she's done, you silly little girl.'

'Bella, the fact that you bought the knife, along with

gaffer tape, plastic sheeting, and other purchases from B&Q, tells us you planned to kill Mark,' Ruth said. 'Is that right?'

Bella clearly didn't hear her, or was pretending not to hear her, as she continued to mutter under her breath.

'So, we believe you knew you were going to murder your husband six weeks before you attacked him in your home,' Ruth said. 'Which means this was not a sudden attack brought on by some kind of psychotic episode, and you will not be able to plead diminished responsibility as a defence for Mark's murder. Do you have anything to say about that?'

Bella continued to talk and then stopped. 'I'd like to go home now. Daddy will be waiting for me.'

Why is she continuing with this when I've explained she won't be able to plead diminished responsibility?

'Bella, I need you to listen to what I'm telling you,' Ruth said, aware that she now sounded like she was speaking to a small child.

Bella stood up and stared at everyone. 'I want to go home now,' she snarled.

'Can you sit down please, Bella?' Ruth asked calmly.

Bella glared at her. 'Make me.'

'Bella, you can stop all this play-acting,' Nick sighed. 'You're going to be charged with murder tomorrow morning. Do you understand that?'

Bella, who was still standing, was looking at her nails again and muttering under her breath.

Ruth sat back and glanced at Nick – they were getting nowhere. She leaned forward and went to click the red button. 'Interview terminated at 3.25 pm.'

Chapter 48

Nick was finishing up some paperwork. If he was honest, he was avoiding going home. In fact, he was planning on going directly from work to an AA meeting where he would meet with his sponsor to talk about what had happened with Fran that week. He needed someone else's perspective on how he had behaved and some pointers about what to do now.

Ruth walked to the front of the room. 'Right everyone, listen up. Unfortunately, Bella Freudmann is still behaving very strangely even though it has been explained to her we now have proof that Mark's murder was premeditated. I have no idea what that's about. It's now up to the CPS, her defence counsel, and the judge to decide how they want to proceed. We've done our job, and I want to thank you for your incredible work. And I will be at the Cross Foxes for the next hour to buy anyone a well-deserved drink who wants to join me.'

There were cheers and whoops from some of the CID team.

As Nick closed down his computer, he saw one of the support staff approaching. He was young and slightly awkward looking with spiky blond hair. 'I'm looking for DS Evans?'

'That's me,' Nick said with a friendly smile.

The young man was holding a newspaper. 'I've just come up from the archives. You requested backdated copies of the *Llancastell Leader*?'

Nick nodded. He had asked them to find any copies from 2019 that referred to Wayne Summers' arson attack or trial. He wanted to see if there was any mention of Fran.

'That's correct,' Nick said as the young man handed him the paper. 'Thanks.'

Putting the newspapers down on his desk, he searched through them. The third newspaper down had a headline on the front – *Neighbour saves children from arson horror.*

Beside the article was a photograph of Fran with the caption – *16-year-old neighbour Francesca Chapel risked her own life to save children from blaze.*

Nick's heart sank.

Shit! You're such a twat, Nick!

Ruth came over with a smile. 'I know you don't drink, but do you fancy coming to the Cross Foxes for an hour?'

Nick looked up at her and grimaced. 'I'd love to, but I've got some serious humble pie to go and eat.' He turned the newspaper so that Ruth could see her. 'That's why I remembered the name, Francesca Chapel.'

Ruth winced. 'Wow, you have got some hefty apologising to do. I don't envy you. I've seen Amanda when she's angry, and it's not pretty.'

'Can I come and live with you?' Nick joked.

'No,' Ruth laughed. 'You have to go and face it like a man.'

Nick nodded as he got up and put on his jacket. 'Wish me luck.'

Ruth raised an eyebrow. 'I think you're going to need more than luck.'

Chapter 49

R uth stood at the custody suite waiting for the custody sergeant to print off the relevant transfer paperwork for Bella Freudmann. As SIO, Ruth needed to sign off the S12 transfer papers that allowed her to be released from Llancastell Police Station and be transferred back to the secure unit on the other side of town.

'If you can scribble on that for me, ma'am?' the sergeant said cheerfully.

'Thanks.' Ruth signed the release and handed it back to him. 'What cell is the suspect in?'

'Number two, ma'am,' the Custody Sergeant replied.

Out of curiosity, Ruth wanted a quick glance at Bella to see if there was any change in her behaviour. Ruth didn't understand why she had continued the pretence of being in the middle of some kind of psychotic breakdown once the new evidence had been presented to her. She had nothing to gain. Maybe she was just too proud to suddenly stop pretending and admit the whole thing had been an act.

Wandering down the custody area, Ruth turned down the corridor where the holding cells were. She got to a dark blue door that had a No. 2 on it. At its centre was a black panel with a metal viewer that could be slid up and down to check on the suspect.

Ruth reached out and gently slid the viewer down so as to make no noise.

Bella was sitting on the blue mattress. She was looking at the wall and having an animated conversation with someone in a whisper.

I don't understand. She doesn't know I'm even watching her, Ruth thought with a growing feeling of unease. *What the hell is going on?*

Ruth continued to watch as Bella continued to chatter and gesture with her hands.

Out of the corner of her eye, Ruth spotted one of the custody officers and went over to him.

'Can I help, ma'am?' the custody officer asked.

'The female suspect in No. 2,' Ruth said. 'She's sitting talking to herself. How long has she been like that?' She knew that officers kept a regular eye on suspects with any mental health issues.

'Yeah, she's been like that for hours,' the custody officer said. 'Whoever she thinks she's talking to must be exhausted because she hasn't stopped.'

'Okay, thank you.' Ruth felt increasingly uncomfortable. She didn't understand.

They knew that Bella and Frank had planned to kill Mark several weeks before the murder took place. It had been a cold, calculated, and ruthless act. It wasn't an explosive attack brought on by some kind of severe mental disorder. However, the woman Ruth had seen today in the interview room and in the holding cell seemed to be suffering from a serious mental illness.

As she went to go, Ruth spotted Dr Andrews coming the other way.

'DI Hunter,' he said as she approached. 'I've just come to check on Bella.'

Dr Andrews went to the door and slid down the viewer. Ruth could see that Bella's behaviour was exactly the same – she was muttering under her breath as if talking to someone.

'I don't understand,' Ruth said, feeling increasingly perplexed. 'Why is Bella acting like that if we suspect she is feigning her illness?'

Dr Andrews gave her a dark look. 'I'm afraid that I now believe that Bella's current mental breakdown is genuine.'

'How can that be?' Ruth asked.

'Up to this point, you've believed that Bella is malingering. That just means she is faking a mental illness to gain an advantage,' Dr Andrew explained. 'It's exhausting for someone who is sane to keep up the appearance of being insane for days on end. It's virtually impossible.'

'Do you think Bella was suffering from this condition when she planned to murder Mark six weeks ago?'

'No,' Dr Andrews said as he gestured to the cell. 'Far from it. There is no way she could have been as methodical and calculating if she were like this.'

'So, what's happened?'

Dr Andrews looked at her. 'I've got a horrible feeling that Bella is suffering from what we call Ganser Syndrome. And her history of depression and self-harm makes her mentally fragile and therefore all the more likely to suffer from it.'

'Sorry,' Ruth frowned. 'I'm not familiar with Ganser Syndrome.'

'Essentially, the pressure and stress of mimicking the

symptoms of schizophrenia for a prolonged period means that Bella is now suffering from a psychotic episode.'

What? Ruth thought in shock. *Are you joking?*

'In layman's terms, are you saying that by pretending to be insane, Bella has actually driven herself insane?' Ruth asked in utter astonishment.

'Yes, that's exactly what I'm saying.'

'And how long can that last?' Ruth asked.

Dr Andrews pulled a face. 'Most cases I've seen have been permanent. She has severely altered the neural pathways in her brain, and often there's no coming back from that.'

Ruth shook her head. She didn't feel any sympathy for Bella, but she didn't get any joy in knowing that she might now spend the rest of her life in a psychiatric hospital instead of prison.

'I guess it's darkly ironic,' Dr Andrews said.

Ruth sighed. 'Yes. And I suppose some might even see it as a form of justice.'

It was dark by the time Nick arrived at the address in Welshpool where Fran lived with her adopted parents. Their house was at the far end of a neat cul-de-sac. It looked like a lovely place to live. It was over-looked by an old church, and there were neat lawns and flower beds outside every house.

Nick had spent the journey trying to rehearse what he was going to say. He had put himself in Fran's shoes and realised that it must have taken a lot to track down Amanda and get in touch. His behaviour had been terrible, and he was scared that nothing he did would heal the rift. What if she decided not to see Amanda because of the way he had acted?

He had spoken to his AA sponsor, Bill, on the journey. That was how recovery worked. Bill had put him straight and, without mincing his words, had told him he had acted like *a bit of a prick*. Bill reminded him of an AA principle taken from The Big Book. Alcoholics needed to avoid a tendency for *contempt prior to investigation*. That was spot on. Nick had trusted his gut instinct and jumped to a hasty conclusion. If he had waited for the newspapers to arrive, all the damage could have been avoided.

Getting out of the car, Nick put his collar up against the icy wind. He walked up the garden path, knocked on the door, and prepared himself.

The door opened, and Fran looked out. She was surprised to see him.

'What do you want?' she asked with a frown.

'Look, you've got every reason to hate me,' Nick said. 'But I came here to apologise. I know that I've made a big mistake. A huge mistake. And I'm so, so sorry. I've acted like an idiot, and I don't expect you to forgive me. But I just wanted to come and apologise.'

Fran thought about what he had said for a few seconds. 'Is that it?' she asked with a withering look.

'I don't know what else to say,' Nick said gently.

Fran gave a shrug. 'Okay. And now what?'

Nick looked at her. 'I don't know.'

'I remembered who Wayne Summers was,' Fran said.

Her comment hung in the air for a moment.

'Yes,' Nick nodded. 'And I know what you did that night.'

'You do now,' Fran said. 'But before that, you thought I was trying to steal off you.'

'Yes. That says a lot about me, unfortunately,' Nick admitted.

'Do you know what it took to get in contact with Amanda?' Fran snapped.

'I can't imagine. But I know it can't have been easy. So, I'm sorry. I really am.'

A middle-aged man appeared at the door. Nick assumed he was Paul Chapel, her adoptive father.

'You must be Nick,' he said very calmly.

'Yes. And I'm guessing you're Paul?'

Paul nodded. 'I can't pretend that I'm pleased to see you, but I've heard most of what you've said to my daughter. Why don't you come in for a minute and let's see if we can draw a line under all this?'

'Okay. Thank you.'

NICK WENT UP TO HIS FRONT DOOR AND KNOCKED. The night air was chilly, and the wind blew and whipped around the front garden.

Amanda opened the door and looked at him. 'What are you knocking for?' She sounded annoyed, and he didn't blame her.

'I didn't know if I was welcome home.'

'You're not,' Amanda said coldly.

'Can I come in?'

'If you must.' She held the door open.

'Oh, I've got something for you,' Nick said with a half-smile.

Amanda narrowed her eyes. 'Look, if you've brought me flowers, you can put them in the bin because that's not really going to cut it.'

Nick frowned. 'I'm hoping it's better than flowers.'

'What the hell are you talking about, Nick?' she growled. 'I haven't got the time or the inclination for you being cryptic.'

Reaching out with his right hand, he motioned, and Fran stepped from where she had been standing.

Amanda's face lit up. 'Fran! Erm, what are you doing here?'

Nick and Fran looked at each other.

'You go first,' Nick said.

'Nick came to see me to apologise. He sat down with

my parents, and I think we've managed to sort it out,' Fran explained.

There was a look of intense relief on Amanda's face. 'Do you know how happy that has made me to hear that.'

'Shall we go in? It's a bit cold out here,' Nick said, ushering Fran inside.

Amanda, who now had a tear in her eye, hugged Fran. 'I was scared that I'd never see you again.'

'No way. I love spending time with you,' Fran said with a smile.

Nick looked at Amanda. 'I'm really sorry.'

Amanda rolled her eyes. 'You're still a total bell-end.'

'I really am,' Nick agreed.

'Yeah, you really are,' Fran joked.

Megan toddled out of the kitchen wearing a bib that was covered in food stains.

Crouching down, Amanda took Megan in her arms and lifted her up.

'Megan, this is Fran,' Amanda said. 'She's your big sister.'

Chapter 51

Wrapping the blanket tightly around her shoulders, Ruth put the newly lit cigarette to her mouth, took a deep drag, and blew a long plume of smoke up into the cold night air. Steamy breath and smoke entwined and formed a white haze.

Ruth pondered all that had happened in the past ten days and the surprising conclusion to the investigation. She had been a copper for nearly thirty years, but she had never come across Ganser Syndrome.

As she gazed up, the moon had now turned out in all its glorious fullness. A great silver-white sphere. The last of the day's light had faded, and the sky glimmered with what looked like an array of stars over her head. In the distance, the church spire rose into the sky, gently illuminated by the moonlight.

'What the bloody hell are you doing out here?' came a voice.

It was her daughter, Ella.

'Smoking,' Ruth replied drolly.

Ella appeared. She was holding a glass of wine in one

hand and a bottle in the other. 'See, you've got your regulation granny blanket wrapped around you again.'

'I love this blanket,' Ruth protested, taking another drag of her cigarette.

Ella rolled her eyes. 'I bought you one of those fleecy blankets with armholes for Christmas, for God's sake.'

Sarah came out and laughed. 'She loves that bloody old thing. She won't even let me wash it.'

Ruth shook her head. 'Can you two get off my case, please?'

Sarah looked at her. 'Are you coming inside any time soon?'

'No,' Ruth said. 'I'm happy out here looking up at the sky.'

Sarah disappeared inside.

'Hippy,' Ella joked as she poured more wine into Ruth's glass. 'If you stare at the moon for too long, doesn't it make you go mad?'

Ruth frowned. 'I don't know. Isn't it a full moon that makes everyone go mad?'

Sarah arrived holding a bundle of blankets. 'If you're not coming in, then we're coming out.'

'What if *I want to be alone*,' Ruth joked in her best Greta Garbo impression.

'Don't be so bloody miserable, Mum.' Ella put the bottle of wine down on the table and dragged some chairs noisily across the patio.

Sarah put her phone on the table, plonked herself down, and placed a thick blanket over her knees. 'By the way, the theory goes if a full moon can affect the tides on Earth, it can also affect the liquid in our brains. Which is why we have all those legends around full moon.'

'And hence we have lunacy from lunar, right?' Ella said, taking a glug of wine.

Ruth raised an eyebrow. 'I've had enough dealings with the nature of lunacy this week to last me a lifetime.'

'Didn't Hamlet fake his madness?' Sarah asked.

'Don't ask me,' Ruth moaned. 'I was terrible at Shakespeare at school.'

'That's right. Hamlet pretends to be mad so he can murder Polonius,' Ella said.

Sarah's phone buzzed noisily on the table, but she was sitting too far away to pick it up.

Ruth looked over at her.

'Can you pick it up for me?' Sarah asked. 'Actually, just put it on speaker. It'll be some twat trying to sell me something, no doubt.'

Ruth held up the phone, pressed *answer*, and then *speaker*.

'Hello?' Sarah said in a sing song voice.

'Sarah?' said the voice of an elderly woman.

'Mum?' Sarah's eyes widened as she jumped up from the chair and went to take the phone from Ruth. 'Are you okay?'

'There's a man here who says he knows you,' Doreen said. 'He says his name is Vitali. He says to say hello.'

Enjoy this book?
Get the next book in the series
'The Chirk Castle Killings' #Book 12
on pre-order on Amazon
Publication date June 2022

My Book
My Book

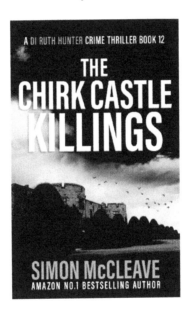

The Chirk Castle Killings
A Ruth Hunter Crime Thriller #Book 12

Your FREE book is waiting for you now

Get your FREE copy of the prequel to
the DI Ruth Hunter Series NOW
http://www.simonmccleave.com/vip-email-club
and join my VIP Email Club

London, 1997. A series of baffling murders. A web of political corruption. DC Ruth Hunter thinks she has the brutal killer in her sights, but there's one problem. He's a Serbian War criminal who died five years earlier and lies buried in Bosnia.

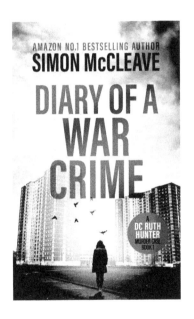

My Book
My Book

AUTHOR'S NOTE

Although this book is very much a work of fiction, it is located in Snowdonia, a spectacular area of North Wales. It is steeped in history and folklore that spans over two thousand years. It is worth mentioning that Llancastell is a fictional town on the eastern edges of Snowdonia. I have made liberal use of artistic licence, names and places have been changed to enhance the pace and substance of the story.

Acknowledgments

I will always be indebted to the people who have made this novel possible.

My mum, Pam, and my stronger half, Nicola, whose initial reaction, ideas and notes on my work I trust implicitly. And Dad, for his overwhelming enthusiasm.

My excellent publicists, Emma Draude and Emma Dowson at EDPR. My designer Stuart Bache for yet another incredible cover design. My superb agent, Millie Hoskins at United Agents, and Dave Gaughran and Nick Erick for invaluable support and advice.

Made in the USA
Middletown, DE
15 October 2023

40810491R00179